Last Day in Limbo

Last Day in Limbo

Peter O'Donnell

The Mysterious Press
New York

Library of Congress Catalogue Number: 84-062906
ISBN: 0-89296-103-1 Trade Edition
ISBN: 0-89296-104-X Limited Edtion

First American Edition

Cover photograph by Marvin E. Newman
Cover type by Larry Ottino
Cover design by Michael Stetson

\

One

FOR TWO days now they had seen no sign of human life, except for the incongruous helicopter which had clattered along the river line as they were beaching the canoes on the sandy strip which hemmed the small creek. The pilot had circled once, perhaps to take a look at the unlikely travellers below, then continued down-river for a short distance before turning to slide up the great forested slope and pass out of sight beyond the crest. It had looked like a huge dragonfly, skimming the tops of the Douglas firs and ponderosa pines.

The slower-moving water in the creek was a few degrees warmer than in midstream, but still breathtakingly cold to the human body. Modesty Blaise swam underwater, peering at the pebbled bottom, enjoying the tingling bite of the river on her skin after the long hot morning. They had battled through seven stretches of rapids since sun-up.

She surfaced, gasping. Standing thigh-deep in the water, she bent to wring out her black hair. As she straightened up she saw John Dall ten paces away on the tiny beach, a ciné-camera held to his eye. Sunlight glistened from her wet naked body as she waded towards him. 'You've got a nice centre-spread for the *Baptist Times* there.'

'Nobody sees this, honey. It's a souvenir for my old age.'

She grinned, threw back her hair, set her arms akimbo and struck a hipshot pose, head poised with the seductive tilt of the pin-up model.

'Hold it while I zoom in. Fine.' He lowered the camera and watched her emerge from the shallows to stand facing him, wondering if he would ever again enjoy himself quite so much as he had enjoyed these past three weeks with her. She kissed him wetly, picked up her towel from where it hung on the bow of the two seater canoe, and began to scrub herself dry. When she saw that he stood quietly watching her she said, 'You know, you're practising to be a dirty old man, Johnny.'

'That's a long way off. When we started this trip I was forty, now I'm thirty-five.' His usually impassive brown face creased in a smile as he spoke. With the slate-grey eyes, thick black hair and high cheekbones, it could have been the face of an Indian. To see him now, in a worn buckskin shirt and water-stained denim trousers turned up at the cuffs, it would have surprised few to learn that his grandmother's name had been Tall Owl In The Tree. More surprising was the fact that he controlled a huge industrial empire and was a millionaire many times over.

Modesty said, 'How's the food coming? I'm starving.'

He jerked his head towards the belt of tall bushes which lay between the small creek and the clearing where they had made their mid-day camp. 'Charlie's fixing the trout now, and there's some cold squirrel left from last night.' Charlie Long Arrow was their guide, sixty years old, made of leather, and pure Shoshone. He had at first referred to Modesty as 'Lady'. Now it was 'Tall-Leg Lady'.

Modesty said, 'Go and watch him, Johnny. I know he's the best cook for thirty miles, but that's not saying much when there's no competition. He cooks everything flambé.'

'A little bit well-done is all. You're just a greenhorn dude.' Dall turned to cross the strip of beach and make his way through the bushes, amused at the absurdity of what he had said. She could start eating where a coyote would leave off, and this was a heritage of the childhood years when she had lived like a creature of the wild.

As he came into the clearing his muscles locked in mid-stride, mind frozen with unbelief. The cooking fire between two small rocks glowed red and almost smokeless. Beside

8

it Charlie Long Arrow lay face-down, very still. There was something horribly wrong with the back of his head. An area as big as a man's palm was concave and blood oozed slowly amid the dark hair.

A tall gangling man with shaggy fair hair, wearing new jeans and a check shirt, stood watching Dall. Held casually in his hands was a side-by-side shotgun, pointing at Dall's stomach. His long chin moved regularly as he chewed gum.

Slowly Dall completed his stride, and slowly raised his hands. He drew breath to speak, loudly enough for Modesty to hear and take warning, but the gangling man shook his head, flicked his eyes to Dall's right, and said softly, 'Keep it buttoned, friend.' Sweat broke on Dall's brow with the huge inward struggle to throw off the paralysis of shock that gripped his mind. He turned his head and saw a second man standing close to the bushes, a stocky man with a dark jowl, wearing a wide-brimmed hat. He was looking through the bushes towards the river, a gun held loosely to his shoulder. There was a revolver at his hip, in an open holster tied down by a thong round his thigh.

Anger, frustration and fear replaced shock. Behind an impassive face Dall juggled madly with the options. Charlie Long Arrow must be dead, or as good as dead with his head caved in like that. If the two men were out to kill them all, then a shouted warning might give Modesty the ghost of a chance to get away. If she took it. And if the stocky man hadn't already got her lined up.

But if it wasn't a mindless killing, then what? Did they want Modesty because she was a woman, or Dall because he was John Dall? Long seconds passed. Nobody moved or spoke. Dall found himself deciding that this was no senseless slaughter, the men were too quiet and purposeful. With the decision he relaxed by a tiny degree, and very slowly lowered his hands to his sides, keeping them well in view. Nothing happened.

9

Dall had built his empire by making sound judgments, and above all by picking capable men and women, the right talent for the right job. What he faced now was something quite outside his experience. He did not have the know-how to cope with it, and was aware that whatever he might try to do would probably be wrong. Not so for Modesty. He had never seen her in action, and she rarely spoke of past exploits, but there had been one or two interesting occasions when Dall had sat up late with Willie Garvin, that remarkable Cockney who had shared many years of her life and who knew her as no other man would ever know her. You could get Willie to talk a little, if you didn't try to drag the whole story out of him, but quietly prodded him to reminiscence of those moments which in retrospect he found amusing.

Yes . . . this was her kind of business. Dall looked from the gangling man to the other, and his heart sank a little. Two professionals. Two shotguns. One revolver. He could not begin to imagine how she might cope. Focusing his eyes between the two men, he called upon the stoic patience he had inherited with his Indian blood, and stood waiting.

Beside the canoe Modesty zipped up her jeans, pulled on the loose denim shirt and slipped her feet into the moccasins, then stood combing the tangles from her hair, gazing down-river. Ahead it bent sharply between canyon walls, and she could hear the warning sound of rapids. According to Charlie these would be the last, and the rest of the journey would be comparatively easy, bringing them to the little one-street town of Harmony Falls.

The river they were travelling was a tributary of the Salmon, and for two weeks now they had been weaving an arduous way through the great Idaho Primitive Area in their Canadian canoes, Modesty and Dall in the seventeen-foot two seater, Charlie in his fourteen-foot single. It had been a good trip, she thought, inspecting a broken nail. Willie Garvin would have enjoyed it. He and John got on well together. It was a pity he had already promised to spend this month instructing at the big house in Sussex which purported to be a Statistical Records Establishment. She piled damp hair on top of her head, tied it with a piece of weather-bleached ribbon, spread her towel over the baggage piled in the canoe, then turned and made her way through the bushes. She was looking down, adjusting the ribbon, as she entered the clearing. 'I think we ought to repack the canoe for balance, Johnny. Those rapids sound pretty hairy—' She lifted her head, and instantly the process of appraisal wiped everything else from her mind.

Charlie Long Arrow, surely dying if not dead. John, standing unhurt. Tall man with a Marlin 12-gauge goose gun, which would throw a three-inch Magnum. A glint of drying blood on the butt. Short, muscular man covering her from six paces with a side-by-side 12-gauge Parker held at waist level, a Colt .45 holstered at his hip. Both men relaxed, experienced.

No chance.

Dall had watched the stocky man back away from the bushes, and knew she was coming ten seconds before she entered the clearing. His throat had ached to cry out to her. She came into view, thoughtful, fiddling with her hair, saying something he could not take in. He saw her lift her head, then stand still, face suddenly expressionless. For perhaps two seconds her eyes roamed blankly over the scene, then she seemed to shrink, shoulders hunching in shock, mouth falling open, chin trembling. Slowly she lowered her hands from her hair, then clapped them suddenly over her mouth, eyes darting wildly.

The tall gangling man said, 'Don't git started yelling, lady. You got work to do.'

She took her hands from her mouth, her breathing noisy, then with a wordless sound ran towards John Dall, arms outstretched. The Marlin shotgun followed her. She clung to him, quavering shrilly, 'Johnny, what is it? Who are they?'

And then, a whispered breath in his ear: 'I'll play it. Not soon. Hit me when I cry.'

She began to sob with rising hysteria. He held her away and slapped her sharply across the face. 'Get hold of yourself, for Christ's sake! How the hell do I know who or what?' He looked towards the tall man. 'Maybe you can tell me.'

The man spat out his gum and grinned. His teeth were very white. 'Good you stopped her yellin', mister. Can't stand yellin' women. Can't stand nosy fellers, neither. Now you jes' lissen, huh? You an' her act nice an' do what I tell you, then nobody gits ripped in little bits, see?' He patted the gun.

Modesty made a whimpering sound. Dall shrugged and said dourly, 'So?'

'So in a while we're all gon' take a walk right up this 'ol hill.' The man jerked his head towards the forest slope rising steeply behind him. 'But first you're gon' pack all up in them canoes, along with this dead feller, too.' Another nod of his head indicated Charlie Long Arrow. The gun did not move as he spoke. 'Now while you're a-doing that, I'm gon' stand by to shoot you right through your gut if you don't act nice, an' my friend there, he's gon' do the same for your woman. I makin' sense to you, mister?'

Dall said, 'Let's both make sense. If you're getting paid for this, I'll pay double.'

The stocky man giggled. The tall man said reflectively, 'That's close to not acting nice, mister. You an' her better start packin' up, like I said.'

Modesty clutched at Dall's arm, her voice high and shaking. 'Please, Johnny! Please don't argue!'

The tall man said, 'Like she says, friend.'

It took only three or four minutes to kill the fire, gather up the cooking and eating utensils and take them to the canoes. Dall was appalled at the ease with which the two men kept them covered throughout the operation, giving

12

no glimmer of an opening. Carrying Charlie was a nightmare, for Modesty was snivelling and stumbling, and twice she dropped his feet. Dall knew the act was necessary, knew it was to plant the image of a harmless and terrified woman in the minds of their enemies. But he also knew now that Charlie was dead, and this had kindled a bitter and growing fury within him. When she dropped his legs for the second time, causing Dall to lose his grip under the limp arms so that the body thumped down horribly on the pebbly shore, he almost hated her for laying such indignity on the old Shoshone.

As they heaved Charlie Long Arrow into the smaller canoe, the tall man said, 'Only two life-jackets. Guess a stoopid Injun wouldn't wear one. Take 'em out, mister.'

Dall obeyed. Modesty stood gazing blankly, arms hanging limp, as if she had passed from terror into numbed shock.

'Right. Now git them canoes in the water.' The gun bore steadily on Modesty. Slowly she moved to face Dall across the stern of the two-seater, and together they eased it into the quietly moving water of the creek. The tall man said, 'Git her movin'.' Dall hesitated, then gave the canoe a push which sent it sliding out into the edge of the current. The water's grip strengthened on the drifting craft, and it began to spin slowly round, rocking a little as it gathered speed.

'Now the Injun.'

Thirty seconds later the smaller canoe, bearing Charlie Long Arrow's body, was on its way down-river.

'Them rapids gon' take care of 'em,' said the tall man. 'Pick up them life-jackets an' let's go.' He moved his rifle to point up the forested slope. Modesty stood gazing vacantly down-stream as if she had not heard. Dall picked up the two life-jackets, took her arm and began to guide her towards the bushes. He was startled to note that his hand was shaking, and hoped that the cause was anger rather than fear. Soberly he tried to look within himself, and knew that for the first time in many years he was deeply afraid.

13

Quickly he drew his mind away from this and put it to better use. Uncontrolled, the canoes would surely capsize at the next rapids. They might be smashed to pieces, they might float on down-river. Charlie's body might be found—or not. If so, the picture would be that they had spilled at the rapids, and Charlie Long Arrow's head had been stove in by a rock. The other two bodies would never be found.

Dall gave a little shake of his head. It didn't make sense. Whatever the motive, if he and Modesty were to be killed it could have been done already. If the men knew who he was, and this was a snatch for ransom, then there was no point in giving the impression that he was dead. And why take Modesty? If they knew who *she* was—but no, that was out. He had seen the amused contempt in their faces at her terror. They could not know her name, or what it meant.

So . . . ? He could find no answer to the puzzle. And where the hell were they heading for, anyway? There wasn't even a dirt road or old lumber track for ten miles. For that matter, where had these two come from?

They were moving uphill now. Beside him Modesty trudged slowly, like a zombie, withdrawn into herself. The two men moved six paces behind, guns held loosely in front of them. He could hear their heavy breathing above the sound of his own, for the slope was steep. From the river the forest had looked dense, but it was different on the ground, for the trees gave each other space to breathe and the undergrowth was light. The carpet of pine needles was a curse, slithering underfoot with each upward step. Already his thigh muscles were beginning to ache.

After a little while Dall half-turned his head and panted, 'Just tell me one thing. Where are we heading? Where *is* there to go?'

The tall man was chewing gum again. He said, 'Keep goin', mister. Not far now.'

14

Two minutes later Modesty began to stagger, the breath rasping in her throat. She sank to her knees. 'I can't . . . I can't . . .' She looked up at Dall, her face loose with exhaustion.

The two men had halted. Dall looked back at them and said, 'She's beat. It's tough going.'

The tall man wiped his brow with a shirt-sleeve, glanced at his companion and said, 'We'll take a couple minutes, Jake.'

Dall held out one of the life-jackets. 'Here, honey, sit on this.' She looked at him balefully, snatched it from his hand, then got laboriously to her feet and trudged with slithering steps to a low hummock of rock which broke the surface beside some dried scrub. Her legs folded, and she collapsed in a half sprawled half sitting position, head hanging on her chest.

The tall man said, 'Looks like she figures it's your fault, mister. Tha's a woman, every time.'

Jake giggled. The tall man gestured and they both moved up the slope a little way, then turned and squatted on their haunches, a few paces apart, watching Dall and Modesty. Dall fought against the beginnings of despair. No chance. They had given no flicker of a chance so far, and they weren't going to give one. His mouth was dry, his stomach clenched, and the sense of utter helplessness ate into him like acid.

Modesty was bowed forward, hugging her knees, her face hidden. He wondered if she wanted him to talk to the men, and said, 'Are you two working for somebody?'

He might not have spoken. The tall man chewed slowly. Jake stared speculatively at Modesty. Two minutes passed and the tall man stood up. 'Git going.'

Dall looked across at Modesty. She lifted her head as if with an effort, stared at him with blank rejection for a long moment, then began to get slowly to her feet. Dall rose, his legs aching. She did not want him near her, that was the message, if he had not imagined it. He saw her stumble, then recover. In the same instant a small breathy cry broke from her lips and she froze, staring down. Her right foot was hidden by the scrub. She stepped back a pace and said in a quiet, shocked voice, 'Snake . . . it bit me.'

For one wild moment Dall thought it was a trick, but then he saw the colour of her face. Beneath the tan it was chalk-white. She sat down heavily, pulling at the cuff of her jeans. Dall started towards her, and saw the twin trickles of blood running from the punctures low down on her shin.

The tall man said, 'Stay where y'are, mister.'

Jake moved past Dall, and spoke for the first time. 'Warn't a rattler. Didn't hear it. Copperhead most like.' He glanced to see that Dall was covered, then laid down his gun and moved to Modesty.

The tall man said, 'Goddam. Still, ain't much meat on the bone there, so likely she ain't took much poison. Cut an' suck, Jake. Git a strap round her knee first.'

She sat awkwardly, her back to the river below, the bare leg drawn up. Jake started to squat, reaching for her ankle, and as he did so Dall saw it happen. Her moccasined foot flicked out in a kick to the crotch, then instantly hooked between his legs to jerk him forward as he squealed with the shock. Even as he was falling upon her she reached out, her left hand twisting to snatch the Colt from its holster, her right clamping about his windpipe. From the corner of his eye Dall glimpsed the barrel of the tall man's rifle swinging towards her, saw that the whole of her trunk and half her head were shielded by the stocky man's body, and then heard the roar of the Colt as she fired.

A great red flower appeared high up on the tall man's chest, and Dall heard the gasping grunt as the nervous system was paralysed by the shock of the heavy bullet. The quid of chewing gum shot from the open mouth, and in the same instant the shotgun bellowed under the in-

16

voluntary contraction of the trigger-finger. At a range too close for the shot to spread, the mass of lead hit Jake squarely in the middle of the back. The thickset figure jerked and juddered beneath the hammerblow, then rolled on its back as Modesty thrust the torn body away. She was coming to her feet when the tall man fell forward down the slope, slithered a few feet on his face, then lay still.

Dall realised that his muscles were only just beginning to tense for action. The whole thing had begun and ended in less than two seconds. He let out a long shaky breath and said dazedly, 'The snake? Was it . . . ?'

'No.' She was picking up the Parker shotgun, the Colt still held in her left hand. 'Get that Marlin, Johnny. Come on, quickly now.' She began to move up the slope, bearing to the right. Dall dragged a hand across the back of his sweat-soaked neck, bent to pick up the fallen shotgun, then followed her up the hill. She halted where the ground flattened behind two pines with some low scrub between them, looked about her, then lay down on her stomach and signalled him to get down beside her.

Before Dall could speak she said softly, 'Keep your voice low, Johnny. Maybe they'll come and maybe not, but we're nicely placed if they do.' She was propped on her elbows, scanning the slope, glancing down towards where the two dead men lay, the Colt close to her right hand, the Parker held loosely before her, resting on a protruding root.

Dall said in a hoarse whisper, 'Maybe *who* might come?'

'Whoever else was in the helicopter.'

He closed his eyes and rested his head on a damp fore-arm. Of course. The helicopter. That was the answer to the puzzle. Somebody wanted John Dall and/or Modesty Blaise in a big way, big enough to lay on an expensive operation. The canoes had been spotted, the mid-day camp had been marked. The helicopter had landed in a clearing somewhere on the crest or just beyond. The tall man and Jake had come down through the woods, killed Charlie Long

Arrow, made the snatch, and started back up the long hill with their prisoners.

He lifted his head and whispered. 'How many would it carry?'

'A Bell Long Ranger takes seven. But they had to leave room for us, so it wasn't carrying more than five. The pilot, those two . . .' she nodded down the slope. 'Two more at the most, but maybe not. We'll just have to wait.'

'Not go up and get the bastards?'

He saw a little smile pull at her lips. 'Too dicey. We don't know their fire-power, and we've had our share of luck for today.'

'Luck?'

She nodded. 'That tall one was fast. I thought I could drop him well before he could get that gun round to bear. Just as well I was using Jake as cover. Lucky the blast didn't go right through him, anyway.'

Dall found that his whole body was trembling with re-action. He said, 'Jesus, I'm shaking like a leaf.'

She put a hand over his. 'I know. I'd be the same if I hadn't been too busy thinking what to do. It's been rotten for you, Johnny, just waiting. Breathe deep and talk, it'll soon pass.'

He turned on his back and rested a forearm across his eyes. If they came, she would see to it. He examined him-self for a spark of injured male pride, found none, and grinned to himself. She was better at this than he was, and so what? It was just as goddam well. The grin faded as he remembered Charlie Long Arrow. *So long, Charlie. They killed you dirty, but Tall-Leg Lady sure as hell didn't give them long to enjoy it.*

After a little while he said, 'You even had me fooled. I thought a copperhead had got you.'

'I made a couple of little punctures with a thorn.'

He lifted himself on an elbow. She was still gazing quietly up the slope. He said, 'Wait a minute, your face was *grey*.'

18

'I know. You sit down and you breathe very deeply for a couple of minutes or so. Hyperventilation, they call it. Then you hold your breath, tense your muscles, and stand up. All the blood drains from your head. You can pass out if you're not careful, but I sat down again quick.'

He looked at the Colt. 'It didn't spoil your aim.'

'No. That's heavy for me, especially left-handed, but I knew it was a good gun.'

'Knew? How?'

'The way he wore it, the condition of the butt and as much of the breech as I could see in that cut-away holster. The fact that it's been fitted with an adjustable rear sight, and the hammer's been de-horned, and the barrel shortened. It had to be a good gun. He was a shooting man.'

'He met a shooting lady.' Dall touched her arm gently. 'You're an education, honey.'

She frowned a little. 'I'd like to have winged him, so we could ask questions, but it was too tricky with an unfamiliar gun, lying down and left-handed. I was four inches out with that shot, anyway.'

'I'm glad you didn't just wing him. The bastard killed Charlie.'

'Yes.' She was thoughtful for a moment. 'I'd guess it was you they wanted, but in that case why take me as well?'

'I've been trying to figure that myself.' Dall looked up the slope through the trees and sighed. 'Jesus, I only wish Willie was here. You'd go up and sort them out with him alongside.'

'That's different, Johnny.'

'I know it's different. I'm not beefing, honey, I'm just honest-to-God wishing.'

She turned her head and gave him a smile of warm affection. 'You're not so bad for a half-breed billionaire. I've got time for you.'

'Best paleface squaw I ever had.' A huge yawn came suddenly upon him. He found that his nerves were quiet now, but that an immense sleepiness possessed him. She must have understood, for she said, 'Go on, take five, Johnny. It's safe enough.'

There was no doubt of that, he thought. All the same, it was absurd to go to sleep under such circumstances. He closed his eyes for a second to rest them, and was roused ten minutes later by the sound of the helicopter. It was moving slowly, a hundred feet above the tree-tops and a little to one side of the spot where Modesty and Dall lay. He had to lift his voice to be heard above the clatter of the rotor. 'Reckon they can see those dead guys from up there?'

She shrugged, not looking up, still watching the wooded slope of the hill. 'Foliage is pretty thick, but maybe. Don't talk for a while, Johnny.'

After three or four minutes of slow cruising, the helicopter suddenly lifted and soared away over the crest. The noise dwindled and died. Dall looked at Modesty and kept quiet. Yes, it would be a neat trick to leave a couple of men at the landing spot, and fly away. You wouldn't be ready for anyone making a silent stalk down through the woods then. Except that Modesty was ready.

For a full hour he lay watching her, fascinated. Her patience seemed infinite. But for the slow breathing and the tiny movement of head and eyes, she might have been carved of wood. The bleached scrap of ribbon holding her piled-up hair was an absurd touch, but she did not look absurd. At last she laid the gun down carefully, turned on her back and put her hands behind her head. 'They must have gone. Probably there was only the pilot left anyway.'

'Maybe. But don't start wishing we'd gone after him. We were ahead, and it's never wrong to take a profit.'

She gazed up at the tree-top greenery. 'I've never been a big wisher. The thing is, now what?'

He sat up, brushing pine needles from his shirt. 'I guess we go home. The river's out, with no canoe, and I don't know how we keep our direction or what we do for food and shelter, but I figured on leaving all that to my smart-arse paleface girl.'

'Getting home's no problem. I meant after. Will you go to the police?'

Dall rubbed his chin. The two men were dead, and she had killed one of them. Justifiable homicide, of course, but he didn't want her name and picture spread over all the papers. Neither did she. Supposing it to be a kidnap attempt on him, a police investigation would get nowhere, for there was nothing to go on. But it could well put Modesty in a bad spot if whoever was behind the kidnapping felt vengeful. He said, 'Can we cover it?'

'If you want to. But they might try again, Johnny.'

He shrugged. 'Police protection's not a lot of use, they can't keep it up for long. Better to hire a private bodyguard if I want protection.'

She looked up at him uncertainly. 'You're innately law-abiding, so don't cover it for my sake.'

'I'm innately crazy about you, and I don't want the papers having a three-month ball with this. Jesus, can you imagine the headlines? *Dall's Fast-Draw Squaw Blasts Snatch-Fiends*.' He took out a handkerchief and wiped his face. 'Let's play it quiet. What do we do with those two?' He nodded down the slope.

She got up and moved off towards the place where the dead men lay, saying, 'Bring that Marlin, and wipe it clean, Johnny.'

Two minutes later the Marlin lay beside the tall man, with his prints on it. The Colt .45 lay close to the stocky man's gun hand. She studied the scene for a moment. 'There won't be much left of them after a few days, and it's long odds they'll never be found, but if they are you could figure they shot each other.' She turned to Dall. 'Now I want to see about Charlie Long Arrow.'

'Charlie? He's God knows how far down-river by now. Or maybe trapped between rocks in the rapids.'

21

She shook her head. 'I don't think so. I was having a good look at the river just before it all happened, and thinking we'd have to be careful on that next bend. The river swings hard there, and we could have grounded on the outside of the curve. Without our weight, the big canoe is almost certain to have ended up half-beached under some bushes, and with any luck we'll find Charlie there as well. If our canoe's not holed, that's a plus. It's the quickest way home.'

He was about to ask her why she wanted to find Charlie, but decided to wait and see. It seemed he was always asking questions. She said, 'Bring the life-jackets along, Johnny,' and started down the slope at an angle which would take them down-river, the Parker cradled under her arm.

Thirty minutes later, half swimming half wading, clinging to tree roots and undergrowth, they found both canoes in the thick bushes hemming the outer curve of the river, just before the forested slope gave way to steep canyon walls. Charlie's was gashed, and half full of water, the other was intact. Chest heaving, Dall looked down at the body of Charlie Long Arrow. He was shrunken in death, and looked very small.

Modesty said, 'He hasn't any family left. He told me.'

'A loner,' Dall nodded, and stood waiting.

She rummaged among the equipment and said, 'If we get a rope on the canoe we can haul it back to that tree right on the edge of the bank, then we lift Charlie out.'

'Out,' Dall repeated. 'Right.'

Together they carried him two hundred yards up the slope, lurching and staggering, resting often, but this time she did not let him fall. An hour after she had found the place she wanted, Dall stood with machete in hand, muscles aching, looking up to where Modesty crouched twenty feet above on a platform made of cut saplings. Two pines growing close together on a small plateau supported the saplings. Charlie Long Arrow lay on the platform, his hunting bow beside him, unseeing eyes staring up through a tracery of twig and leaf to the clear blue sky beyond. Modesty was making a last check of the lashings which held the main supports of the platform before following Dall down. They were both sweating, grimed with countless crumbs of bark.

She hung from the edge of the platform, then dropped down beside Dall and said, 'That's fine, Johnny, just fine.'

He sucked a broken blister on his palm. 'Until we got started I figured you were setting a cover-up scene, like that other one.'

She shook her head. 'I'm sorry, I should have explained. You've been very patient.'

'My middle name.' He looked up at the platform. 'Is that how his people do it, when it's time for the Happy Hunting Ground?'

'Some of them. Some are buried by rivers, other in rock-slides. We were talking about it a few days ago, not just about dying, but the old Indian ways in general. He had twenty dollars saved, and he'd got someone to write on a paper that he wanted to go this way.'

'How the hell did you get him talking? I never got more than two syllables out of him at a time.'

She fingered a speck of bark from the corner of an eye. 'It was after we went hunting together that day, when you were making camp. I borrowed his bow and got a blue grouse. That was a big coup for a squaw.'

Dall looked up at the platform again, then down at Modesty's dirt-smeared face. 'But why, honey?' he said gently.

'He wanted it, and I liked him. It was the only thing left we could do for him.'

Dall pushed a lock of hair away from her eye. 'But . . . Charlie's gone. Or do you reckon he knows?'

She gave a neutral shrug. 'No idea, Johnny, and it doesn't matter anyway. He was an old Indian who'd had the best of his life and I'm not going to grieve over him, but I liked him and I've done the best I could. Now it's finished, so

23

let's go home.' She bent to pick up what remained of the coil of rope.

Dall said, 'My God, you're a romantic.'

She straightened up, looking at him indignantly. 'Of course I'm a romantic, dum-dum! And proud of it. There's not enough of it about these days.'

They made camp that night five miles down-river and well before dusk, so that they needed to use no lights. Their camp was a little way inland, and the canoe was well-hidden. In the morning, when they woke in the small tent, Dall drew her to him and they made quiet, unhurried love. It was very good, as good as all the other different times and moods and ways. Afterwards, as Dall lay with her head cradled on his shoulder, he felt her warm body shake as she gave a smothered laugh.

He said, 'You'd better smile while you explain that, lady.'

'I was just remembering your headlines.' Her body pressed against his. 'You're a bit of a snatch-fiend yourself, mister.'

But later, as they paddled easily along a quiet stretch of the river, she turned a sober face to look over her shoulder at him and said, 'You'll be careful, won't you, Johnny?'

'Sure.'

'Would you like me to cancel my flight? I could get Willie over and we could snoop around a little.'

'No, leave things the way they are. There's no lead to follow, unless they try again.'

'So be careful. And call me right away if they do. Promise?'

'I promise.'

He watched the easy swing of her back, the smooth movement of her shoulders under the thin shirt, and thought with longing how much he wished she would cancel her flight for good. But that was not the way she wanted it, and perhaps she was right.

Two

DAMION READ through the transcript of the cable he had decoded, and picked up the year-old magazine clipping which showed a colour photograph of John Dall and the woman he now knew was called Modesty Blaise. The caption spoke only of John Dall and companion, and they had not posed for the picture, probably had not even known that it was being taken. They were coming off Dall's yacht, and the picture was one of a dozen in the magazine article, a travel piece on Mexico.

Still holding the transcript and the picture, Damion wandered to the window and stood looking out at the dancing sparkle of morning sunlight upon Lake Thun. He was a tall man, very fit, with a rather incongruous cherub-face, round and smooth and innocent, haloed by bright fair hair. His father and mother had been Czechs who co-operated enthusiastically with Heydrich during his reign of butchery in the war years, and who had escaped to South America a year before Damion was born. They were dead now, but he had inherited their tastes. Damion had killed his first man before he was twenty, and not a few since. He was a happy man, serving a unique master who provided sufficient opportunities for Damion's talents.

A touch of excitement bubbled through him as he looked at the picture again. Quite a woman. Hard to handle, no doubt, but you could always find a way. Perhaps, with the failure of the kidnapping, the story was ended now, and the moment of opportunity had passed. Even his master, Paxero, would have to accept that it would be madness to try again.

Damion shook his head and gave an admiring chuckle. The whole gigantic game was crazy anyway, particularly when you remembered that Paxero didn't play it for himself. Still, a man as rich as he was could afford to satisfy almost any obsession, providing it was known only to those who were in no position to talk. It was a pity the Dall-Blaise snatch had failed. Those two were ideal types for Limbo.

Damion gazed thoughtfully out over the lake. He had a powerful feeling that the Modesty Blaise link was not yet ended, for there was an extraordinary connection that Paxero did not know of, and one that Damion had no intention of revealing. It was the kind of coincidence that occurred in everyday life so much more often than the laws of chance could possibly justify, the kind that in fanciful mood one might see as a thread of destiny.

He put a hand to the special pocket inside his crisp fawn jacket and drew out the slim gold watch. It was a beautiful instrument, a quarter-repeater by Breguet, with a white *guioché* dial, Roman numerals and blue-steel moon hands. Made a hundred and seventy years ago, it was as elegant as any modern watch. Damion had had it valued at three thousand pounds. Inside the back, engraved in cursive script, were four words : *To Danny from Modesty.*

Paxero had never seen that inscription. It might not have mattered if he had, for it would have meant nothing, but Damion was glad now that he had not shown the inscription to his master when, three years ago, he had pretended to have bought the watch from a receiver in New York who thought it too hot to handle.

To Danny from Modesty. Damion knew well enough who 'Danny' was. Danny Chavasse, the Frenchman who looked uncannily like Maurice Chevalier at thirty, but with curly hair. And Modesty . . .? It was an uncommon name, and an uncommon woman who could make a gift that cost several thousand pounds. Modesty Blaise came into that

26

bracket, though. Damion smiled. It was very intriguing. He slipped the watch back into the pocket, flicked the zip across the top, then turned and went out of the room. It was time to give his master the story. But not the whole story.

*   *   *

Paxero was having one of the ugly dreams. He was not a small boy, as he had been at the time, but Tia Benita beside him was young again, crouching in the bushes with him, holding a hand over his mouth to prevent him screaming with terror as the men in shabby uniforms who had come on horses did strange and horrible things to the women, tearing their clothes away, writhing on top of them. His father, uncles and brothers were already dead. The men on horses had made a game of that, chasing them, riding them down, slashing with the long swords.

He knew, because it was a familiar dream, that in the end three young girls would be taken away and the rest would be killed. And then, when it was all finished, Tia Benita would look at the rosary clutched in one hand, and fling it way from her. Then she would tear the cheap little cross from where it hung at her neck, and stamp it into the earth, not saying anything, not weeping, but with her bony face set in a mask of iron.

The dream was not exactly as it had been in reality, for now it seemed that the dead men were alive again, buried in the ground with only their heads showing, and the horsemen were about to begin the trampling. This came not from his own memories but from Tia Benita's, who had seen it in childhood and told him the story so many times that it was a part of him.

He woke at Damion's touch on his shoulder and sat up quickly, the fear and hatred fading with the dream. It did not happen so often these days, and he had long since learned to throw off the effects within a few seconds of waking. Damion had moved away and was raising the blinds, letting sunlight into the large, elegantly furnished bedroom. He said, 'Good morning, Pax. Would you like breakfast here or shall I tell the girl to set it on the terrace?'

Paxero yawned. 'Later. I'll swim first.' He got out of bed and pulled on a white Thai-silk dressing gown. An inch or two shorter than Damion, he was thicker in the body, heavier, but without fat. His face was square, his jaws dark even when freshly shaven, and his hair thick and straight. He felt a touch of amusement as he went to the bedroom fridge to pour himself an orange juice. Damion, he knew, would have swum, showered, shaved, dressed and breakfasted an hour ago. Now, dressed in his beautiful fawn suit, he would have that little sense of superiority felt by the well-groomed early riser for the man in the dressing gown just out of bed. This did not trouble Paxero, who felt no corresponding sense of inferiority. Their morning habits were different, that was all. After sundown their tastes in relaxation were remarkably alike.

Damion said, 'I'm afraid there's bad news.' He fluttered the decoded cable. 'Martinez says Dall and the woman got away.' He smiled. 'I said you should let me handle it.'

Paxero finished pouring the orange juice, his face without expression, then said, 'No chance the police can backtrack?'

Damion shook his head. 'None. A dead cut-off.'

'What happened?'

'He put two Specials on the job. Country boys, the ones they call the Hillbillies. Jason was flying the helicopter. He spotted the subjects, and set the two men down fairly close. They went down through the woods to make the pick-up. Some time later Jason heard two shots. He waited. Nothing happened, so he assumed it had gone wrong and got out fast. Martinez came back with him next day to take a look. Both men dead.'

28

'Did Dall go to the police?'

'Not that we know of.'

Paxero drew in a slow breath and let it sigh out again, moving his head from side to side. Damion grinned and said, 'I know. You sold a lot of Dall Enterprises stock short. It was bound to go down when he went missing.'

Paxero shrugged. 'I can always use a loss.' He sat down in an armchair by the open window, frowning. 'Hell,' he said quietly. 'Aunt Benita really wanted those two.'

'She aimed high with Dall.'

Paxero's head came round and his dark eyes were very cold. 'That's what it's about.'

Damion lifted a hand. 'I know, I know, Pax. But the whole thing's a pretty—' he was about to say 'crazy business', but the word crazy would make Paxero really angry. Damion corrected himself smoothly, 'a pretty bizarre business. I like it, you know that. But there are limits, and to try for Dall again goes beyond the limit. Aunt Benita can't have everything she wants. Or everyone.'

Paxero put down his empty glass. 'She can have anything and anyone she wants, any time,' he said quietly, 'provided I can get it for her without blowing the whole thing wide open. Trying again for Dall comes into that category.'

Damion nodded, relaxing a little. Paxero was very sane. Of course, there was an area where he was not sane, but that was true of everybody to some degree, himself included no doubt. If you had Paxero's cold nerve and financial muscle you could indulge your aberration. If it was a harmless one, you were simply regarded as eccentric. If not, it had to be kept secret. The great thing was that whenever you went out collecting people chosen by Aunt Benita you had to set things up so that it looked like an accident, not a snatch. Death by misadventure, and no bodies recovered. Dall's trip to the Idaho Primitive Area with the girl had offered a perfect opportunity, unlikely to be repeated.

29

Damion held out the magazine clipping to Paxero and said, 'As a matter of curiosity I've been checking on the girl. It rather looks as if she might be the one who put the Hillbillies down.'

Paxero's eyebrows lifted. 'The girl?'

'Yes. Her name's Modesty Blaise.'

'It rings a faint bell.' Paxero frowned, trying to remember. 'Yes, Sarmiento, that top man from Salamander Four, the industrial espionage group. He said she'd given them a bad time on two occasions. She and a man called Garvin, I think.'

'More than likely.' Damion took out a lighter and began to burn the transcript of the cable in an ashtray. 'I don't quite know where she came from, but it seems she's well known in the underworld. By the time she was twenty she'd taken over a small gang operating from Tangier and built it up into a big organisation called *The Network*. Garvin was her ramrod.'

'And nobody ever put her away?'

'I don't think Interpol tried too hard. They rather liked her. She passed a lot of useful information on the flesh mobs and drug mobs. Wiped out a few herself, and picked up a lot of cash loot doing it.'

Paxero was studying the picture with new interest. He said, 'What is she in now?'

'They made a packet and retired. But the word is that she and Garvin occasionally involve themselves in an operation for some British Intelligence department. The heavy stuff. Some say they're blackmailed into it, others that the top man is a friend of theirs.' Damion shrugged and let the last fragment fall into the ashtray. 'Either way seems unlikely, but they were definitely involved in preventing that Kuwait take-over a while back. It only got a few oblique whispers in the papers, but I've talked with a mercenary who was in on the operation, and it was certainly a big job.'

Paxero looked at the girl in the picture. She wore dark blue shorts and a yellow shirt. Her black hair was tied carelessly back in a pony-tail, a small duffle-bag swung from one hand, and her head was turned as if she were speaking to John Dall as he followed her from the yacht's gangway. It was just another picture of another attractive girl, yet there was something more than the splendid legs, the admirable figure, the long and beautiful neck. The camera had caught her in movement, and even though it was frozen here on paper, it added an extra dimension to her, an exciting dimension.

Paxero looked up, and now his dark eyes were half-hooded, a touch of heaviness in them as he looked sideways at Damion, almost slyly, and ran his tongue across his lower lip. 'She'd provide us with a few enchanting nights, Damion. Marvellous to play with, I should think.'

Damion rolled his eyes upwards and gave a soft whistle, then shrugged ruefully and said, 'Tremendous. But not the willing type I'm afraid, Pax. And you couldn't buy her, she's already loaded.'

Paxero nodded reluctant agreement. 'Pity about that. It's always better to buy. There's a slight sense of disappointment when they turn out to be the willing type.'

Damion grinned. 'That blonde girl wasn't,' he said reminiscently. 'Maude really hated us. I thought she'd quit days before she finally did.'

'Yes. I was beginning to wonder if that one was up to something,' Paxero said thoughtfully. He stood up and handed Damion the clipping. 'But she was just a woman. Most of them will do any amount of pretending for a nice big chunk of money.'

'I'm sorry we didn't get this one for Limbo,' Damion said. 'Being loaded wouldn't have made any difference then. Incidentally, are you going to send Aunt Benita a message at the plantation?'

'No.' Paxero gave a curt shake of his head. 'She'd rather

31

set her heart on those two, so I'd like to see her and do a little gentle explaining.'

Damion sometimes wondered if Paxero was actually afraid of Aunt Benita. He said, 'When do you want us to go, Pax? You've got bits of business in Geneva right up to the end of the month.'

'We'll finish that first, there's no hurry. Aunt Benita's waited six months for Dall and the girl anyway. She knows these things take time.' He stood up, stripped off his robe and pyjamas, and moved to the wardrobe to take out a pair of swim-trunks. 'Tell Charlotte I'll have breakfast on the terrace in half an hour, will you?'

*   *   *

The blonde girl stood with her back to the door of the big empty room. As he moved silently up behind her, Willie Garvin could see the faint outline of her bra-strap showing through the thin green shirt she wore tucked into brown denim slacks. He lifted the Colt .38, glanced down at it with distaste, then put the muzzle against her spine and said, 'Stick 'em up.'

The girl froze, then raised her hands. Without pause or warning she spun to her right, short curls bobbing with the movement, right hand slicing down and across to catch the outer side of the forearm and sweep the gun-hand clear of her body. But she met no resistance, for the forearm was not there, and next second the hammer of the gun pointed at her middle fell with a metallic click.

'You're dead, Maude,' said Willie Garvin.

She glared up at him. Her eyes, like his, were blue, but round and babyish, which was usefully deceptive in her profession. 'That was a clever-dick trick, holding the gun in your left hand.'

'There's no law against villains being left-handed, Maude. Come on, try it again.'

32

Tight-lipped, she turned. Willie said, 'And don't sulk. It's not like you.'

She made no answer, but stood waiting. Willie frowned. He had never seen Maude Tiller like this before, and it troubled him. Something must have happened, and he wondered what it might be. He knew she had returned from an assignment just over a week ago, but she was still alive, unhurt, and doing a week's refresher course at the big house in Sussex, so it hardly seemed likely that the job had been a tough one for her.

He lifted the gun again and put it against her back. 'All right, stick 'em up.'

Maude obeyed and said, 'Which hand are you holding the gun in?'

'Jesus, I'm a KGB agent and you ask me which 'and? You're just being awkward, Maude.'

'All right, you're supposed to be teaching me, so tell me what I do now. There's nothing about left-hand right-hand in the instruction book.'

'With all respect to your chief instructor, that's not all that's wrong with it. I'm teaching you to use your 'ead, Maude, that's what counts.'

'Are you criticising the works of the Mighty Jacoby?'

'Don't stir it up. Jacoby's good at practice, but *you* 'ave to work in the field, and it's different there.'

'He hates your guts.'

'Just so long as you still love me, Maude. Now turn your 'ead, not quick, just nice and steady, till you can glimpse one of my shoulders.'

Maude turned her head barely into quarter profile. 'Yes. I see what you mean. It's in your right hand.'

'Good. And if the bloke didn't shoot on sight he's not going to do it on a little turn of the 'ead. So now you spin right.'

She whirled, swept his gun-hand out of line, and pivoted to bring herself behind him, an arm whipping across his throat. Next moment Willie's right hand had twisted behind his back to thrust the muzzle against her ribs. He said, 'Not that way, Maude. Not while I've still got the gun.'

'That's what the book says.' She disengaged.

'I'm going to 'ave a word with Sir Gerald Tarrant about that book.' He faced her and held out the gun, moving his hand as he continued. 'Look, once the gun's out of line, there, you've got a split second to do something, and there's only one thing to do. Disable 'im fast. So you step forward outside 'im with the left, and give him your right knee 'ard in the goolies.'

'I like it. Can we try that now?'

Willie stepped back and grinned. 'When you're feeling less 'ostile, Maude.' He moved away to put the gun in the rack. 'It's mostly a waste of time anyway, except as a bit of practice for your reflexes. People don't stick a gun in your back. They're more likely to stand about six feet away and point it at your middle.'

'So what do you do then?'

'Ah, that's the important question. What you do then is use your tongue.'

A deep voice said, 'We're not training bloody lizards here, Garvin.' Willie turned. The door stood open and Jacoby was moving into the room, his feet in light gymnastic shoes making no sound on the tatami mats which covered the floor. Like Willie, he wore a T-shirt and black stretch slacks. A man in his middle thirties, Jacoby was beautifully muscled and moved like a tiger. His hair was black, sleeked back above a broad face with cold grey eyes, and he stood two inches taller than Willie Garvin.

'You're a caution, you are, Mr Jacoby,' Willie said amiably. 'I didn't expect Maude to use 'er tongue like a lizard. I meant she should use 'er brain to think with and 'er tongue to talk with.'

Maude moved to stand against the wall, watching the two men. She had the feeling that Jacoby was on the prod

34

for trouble. He said contemptuously, 'And what does Maude say to the man with the gun?'

Willie shrugged. 'That depends on the situation, Mr Jacoby. There's no script, you 'ave to play it by ear.'

Jacoby rubbed a blue, smooth-shaven chin and said quietly, 'I'm glad your month's up today. I'm buggered if I know what Tarrant thought he was doing, sending you here.'

'I don't think it was anything special,' Willie said vaguely. 'He just asked if I'd come down 'ere to the Training Establishment for a spell on the unarmed combat bit. Said 'e thought a fresh mind on it might be useful.'

'And do you think your fresh mind's been useful?'

Willie Garvin picked up his sweater from the top of a locker. 'Well, there are one or two things I'd like to 'ave a chat about.'

'You can stuff your chat, Garvin.' Jacoby's voice was ugly. 'You're a bloody anarchist. In two weeks you've undermined my teaching with every trainee you've handled.'

Willie shook his head. 'I 'aven't knocked you with any of 'em. Just offered a few extra ideas, maybe.'

'Ah. The gospel according to Modesty Blaise.' Jacoby half-chanted the words with heavy scorn.

Willie smiled. 'I don't know a better way of 'elping people like Maude stay alive, and that's what it's all about, isn't it?'

The soft answers were fuelling Jacoby's temper. He said, 'She's a dike, isn't she, Modesty Blaise?' He expected a response, anything from anger to action. What he did not expect was the immediate burst of genuine laughter from both Willie Garvin and the girl.

'You're a proper card, you are, Mr Jacoby.' Willie pulled the sweater over his head.

Jacoby chewed his lip savagely for a moment. 'I notice you've been giving Maude special attention. Hoping to make it with her?'

Maude stepped away from the wall and said a little tiredly, 'Willie made it with me a long time ago, if it's of any interest, Mr Jacoby.' Two years ago now, she recalled, when Tarrant had put her in to handle communications for a request job that Modesty and Willie were doing for him. But that was none of Jacoby's business.

She watched him rest his hands on his buttocks and switch his gaze to Willie as he said, 'Nice work. I didn't know Maude was an easy screw.'

Willie yawned, but Maude saw a tiny furrow appear in the middle of his brow. She moved towards the door, saying, 'I'll take a shower. See you in the canteen, Willie.'

Jacoby said, 'I'll tell you what. How about you and me having a workout, Garvin? Like right now?'

Maude stopped and turned. In a genuine fight she would have had no anxiety for Willie, but an alleged workout was something else. If Willie used practice techniques, scaling down his moves, Jacoby could cripple him by seeming accident; and he was a hard, dangerous man who would not scruple to do just that. She tried to catch Willie's eye, to signal a warning, but he was gazing at Jacoby in surprise.

'A workout? What's the point, Mr Jacoby?'

'Then you could show me what it's all about.'

'I don't want to prove anything, thanks.'

Jacoby gave a short laugh, and the tension in him slackened. It was a pity to be denied sending the renowned Willie Garvin home with a broken arm, but to have made him chicken out was good enough. He said, 'I get what you mean about using your tongue to stay out of trouble.'

'I labour for peace,' Willie said gravely. 'Psalm 'undred and twenty, verse six.'

Jacoby shrugged. 'Christ knows how you ever got your rep,' he said, and turned away. He had moved only two paces towards the door when he gave a sudden yell: '*Watch it, Maude!*' In the same moment he pivoted towards her, moving very fast, perfectly balanced. She tried to counter as his hand hooked about her neck and he spun on the ball of one foot, tried to die on him and kill the throw by becoming a deadweight, but he was too strong, and she could not relax fast enough. Her body flew over his bent back, somersaulting. It was a high throw and a cruel one, for even with the breakfall and the straw-packed tatami mats she came down on her back with an impact that shook the floor and drove the breath from her body.

Jacoby straightened, bouncing springily, and shot Willie Garvin a hard grin as he snapped, 'Slow, Maude, slow! God, you don't expect a villain to send you a postcard, do you?' Maude rolled over, sick and dizzy, then came slowly to her hands and knees, lifting her head with an effort, eyes kept studiously blank to hide the salt fury within her.

Willie Garvin was smiling, but the tiny furrow in his brow was perhaps deeper now. Jacoby looked at him, lifted an eyebrow and said, 'Any comment?'

Willie shook his head and felt in the pocket of his slacks. 'Never seen it done better. What I always say is they've got to learn the 'ard way.' He withdrew his hand from the pocket and held it cupped, crossing towards Maude as she got shakily to her feet. 'Swallow a couple of these, love, they'll steady you up a bit.'

Jacoby said sharply, 'Hang on! What are they?'

'Never seen these before?' Willie turned and moved towards him, straightening the curled fingers. Jacoby stared down. The palm was empty. Then it blurred as Willie's fingers stiffened and the whole forearm stabbed forward like a piston. It had only twelve inches to travel, and like a broad blunt spearhead the hand drove home into Jacoby's solar plexus with utter precision. The beginning of a sound from Jacoby's throat was sharply cut off, the ruddy complexion faded to whey, and he folded to the floor like a stringless puppet, tumbling on to his side with knees drawn up, mouth wide in the vain effort to overcome the paralysis of his diaphragm and drag air into his lungs.

37

Willie said soberly, 'That's the sort of thing it's really all about, Mr Jacoby.' He moved to the girl and gently took her arm. 'Come on, Maude. School's over.'

As they moved along a corridor of the big house Maude said thoughtfully. 'That was quite a lesson, Willie.'

'Nothing clever about it. But I 'ope Jacoby takes it to 'eart.'

'Oh. I thought perhaps you'd killed him.'

'No. Even if 'e passes out, the breathing'll start again. Right as rain in ten minutes. A bit pensive, maybe.' They halted outside the Reception Office. 'Go and get your case, Maude. I'll sign you out on the completion form, then we'll go and 'ave a nice lunch somewhere.'

She looked away. 'No, I think I'll go straight home, Willie. But thanks. Thanks for everything.'

'All right, I'll drive you 'ome.'

She hesitated, then gave a tired shrug and turned to move up the broad, uncarpeted stairs. Willie watched her go. There was definitely something troubling Maude, he decided.

Rokesby came out of the office, a sheaf of papers in his hand, glasses perched on the high bald head which had earned him the nick-name of Grock. He gave a wide-mouthed grin and said, 'Hallo, Willie mate.'

'Hallo, Grock cock. Do me a TF14, will you? It's me last day, so I'm finishing early. So's Maude Tiller.'

'Better let the Mighty Jacoby know. He was looking for you about ten minutes ago. Had a nasty glint in his eye if I'm not mistaken.'

'That's all right, Jacoby knows. We just 'ad a chat.'

Three

IT WAS a pleasant, roomy flat at the top of a three-storey conversion, which allowed the sun to bring light and cheer. The furnishing and appointments were tasteful and not cheap. There were several good originals by artists almost unknown to anybody, and quite a collection of silver. Maude's parents farmed five hundred acres in Worcestershire and had set up a trust for her as a child which now produced a useful private income. They believed her to be a small cog in the Civil Service, which in fact she was, though it would have shaken and frightened them to know the kind of work she was sometimes engaged in.

Willie knew Maude Tiller as a cheerful companion, easy to be with, happy in bed, and given to amiable clowning which tended to hide a considerable efficiency. He had never asked how she came to be an agent of Tarrant's department in the Foreign Office. He surmised that she had probably transferred from an admin section for a particular job, and then stayed on. That was the haphazard way London tended to do things. It was a miracle the intelligence machine worked so well.

She had showered and changed into a cotton roll-neck shirt, then made a simple meal of soup and cold meat for them both. She had not invited Willie to take a shower, which he found a little strange. It seemed to him that since arriving at the flat she had kept a distance between them, perhaps without being aware of it. At the moment she sat in a black hide armchair, legs curled up, stirring her coffee and looking down at it, concentrating on the small act as if it were important.

It was the first time he had found Maude Tiller hard going, Willie thought, puzzled. Throughout lunch he had carried the burden of the conversation with small response from her. Now he settled back in the corner of the settee and let the silence grow. Almost two minutes passed before she became aware of it, then she looked up, gave him a smile and said, 'How's Modesty?'

'Fine. I talked to 'er on the phone last night. She's just back from Idaho.'

'Anything special?'

Willie was sure that something special had arisen, but she had not wanted to speak of it on the phone. He said, 'Just a vacation. With John Dall—d'you know 'im?'

'Of him. I wouldn't have thought a multi-million tycoon was Modesty's type.'

'That sounded a bit bitter, love. What's Modesty done?'

She looked surprised. 'Modesty? Nothing.'

That left only multi-million tycoons, but Willie did not press the point. He said, 'No, they're not 'er type as a rule, but John's all right. I told 'er I'd run into you down at *Three Meadows*. She said to give you 'er love.'

'Same from me when you see her.'

The beginnings of a theory were forming in Willie's head. To test it he said casually, 'How's your back after the Jacoby treatment?'

'Oh . . . a bit achy.' She grimaced. 'For about two seconds I could have cheerfully killed the bastard.'

'Like me to ease it with a massage?'

She knew there was more than skill in his hands, an element of magic that dissolved the soreness of muscle and ache of bruised flesh; but she stiffened at his words and said quickly, too quickly, 'No, it's all right. Not worth bothering about.'

Willie put down his coffee cup and said gently, 'Maude, are you worried that any minute now I'll make a move to take you to bed?'

'No. Well . . . oh, I don't know.' She rubbed one eye and looked confused, then gave an awkward laugh. 'Maybe.'

'That's a bit silly, isn't it? When was I ever pushing?'

She sighed and shook her head. 'You're not, Willie. I'm sorry. But it would be sort of natural for us to go to bed, and I . . . I just don't feel like it.' She looked at him miserably.

Willie grinned. 'Cheer up, love. It 'appens to everyone. Might even 'appen to me one day. But just relax and stop worrying, eh?'

'All right.' He could see relief in her as she got to her feet. 'More coffee?'

'Yes, please. What was Switzerland like?'

'Pretty Swiss. How did you know I'd been there?'

'I was in Grock's office ten days ago when 'e was on the scrambler to London. From what 'e said, I gathered you'd be coming down to the SRE as soon as you'd been de-briefed on return from Lake Thun.'

'Grock needs a shaking up from Security.'

'It was only me,' Willie said mildly. 'Grock knows I'm on our side. What 'appened at Lake Thun, Maude?'

Her face looked pinched as she handed him the cup of coffee. 'You know I can't talk about that. For God's sake let's stop talking about me anyway. How's life at *The Treadmill* these days?' This was Willie's pub, on the Thames near Maidenhead.

'Nice and gossipy. Thanks.' He took the cup from her. 'All right in short bursts, but a bit like a television soap opera sometimes. I might be popping off to Guatemala soon.'

She put down the coffee-pot very slowly and stared at him from narrowed blue eyes. 'What the hell do you know, Willie?' she said softly.

He blinked in astonishment. 'About what?'

'Guatemala.'

'Well, it's a country of Central America with a population of about five million. Monetary unit is the quetzal—'

'Oh, don't be bloody silly.'

Willie sighed. 'Maude, a couple of our friends are over there just now, friends of mine and the Princess. Name of Collier. Steve and Dinah Collier. Maybe you've 'eard of them.'

She said uncertainly, 'Isn't she the blind girl who was caught up in that Sahara job? The treasure thing?'

'That's right. So was Collier. And before that we ran into 'im on the Lucifer caper. We sort of brought them together, I suppose. Collier's a mathematician, statistician and psychic investigator. He's over in Tenazabal doing a study of the Mayan calendar in relation to the stars, or something. All very complicated. Anyway, we thought we might go and see 'em, that's all.'

Maude had relaxed. She smiled apologetically and said, 'Sorry. I just thought . . .' She let the sentence fade away, then turned to pick up a box of cigarettes and said, 'Why does he want to know about the Mayan calendar?'

'I don't think 'e does particularly. It's a paid job for the Cultural Institute of Guatemala. Some bloke called Paxero's sponsoring it.'

She froze for a moment, hands gripping the ebony box, then carefully opened the lid and took out a cigarette. Forcing a smile she said, 'There are some funny professions around.'

'Sure. Like yours, love.' Willie stood up to light her cigarette. 'Look, you've gone off multi-million tycoons, off Guatemala, or maybe a Guatemalan, and off Lake Thun. The name Paxero doesn't make you laugh much, either. With that lot for starters I bet I can twist the rest out of Tarrant.'

She sat down, closed her eyes for a moment, inhaled on the cigarette, then looked up at him a little wearily. 'All right, what happened doesn't matter much, so I'll tell you. But if you want to know *why* I was put on to Paxero you'll have to get it from Tarrant.'

'Go on then.'

42

Her hand shook a little as she lowered the cigarette from her lips. 'It was a very general brief. I was instructed to get close to Paxero and find out anything I could about any undercover operations of his.'

'Financial? Criminal? What sort?'

'Not specified. A listening job.' She looked at Willie directly. 'Getting close means going to bed. That's when men talk. It wasn't my first time, you understand.'

He nodded. It was part of the job, if you were a woman. Sometimes if you were a man. Sex was a useful weapon. He had used it himself, so had Modesty. Personally, and because there was a curiously old-fashioned streak in him, he disliked the idea for women. They were different, more complex emotionally, more finely tuned. It could be very unpleasant for a woman. He shrugged mentally. In Maude's job, if the worst that happened to you was unpleasant, you were lucky.

She said, 'If we're going to start counting, it was the second time I've popped my cork for the department. You can sort of separate it from yourself, shut it off in some way.' A grimace. 'Like whores do, I suppose. Only it wasn't like that this time. Paxero has a . . . I don't know, friend, companion, personal bodyguard maybe. A man called Damion.' She stubbed out the half-smoked cigarette and said in a rough voice, 'They like to take their girlie pleasures together. A threesome. And the name of the game is Humiliation.'

Willie studied the wall beyond her. 'I'm sorry. Did they 'urt you a lot, Maude?'

She sat huddled forward, her hands pressed between her knees, and shook her head. 'Not much. That's not their kick. I wish it had been, I could have taken it better. No . . . they make you act out fantasies with them. Childish, ridiculous mostly. Sometimes not. Sometimes very much not. Always degrading.' She looked at him. 'Stupid, isn't it? I'm not exactly a novice in bed, and anyone in my job shouldn't

make a fuss about a few days of sexual degradation. What
the hell? I should be able to laugh about it.' Her body began
to tremble. 'But it gets to you, Willie. After a while it . . .
it leaves your self-respect in ashes. I feel so shrivelled, so
shamed. And I'm ashamed of feeling this way, but I can't
help it. Something's dead in me, that important woman-bit
. . . and I'm mourning.'

He wanted to go to her, but held still, knowing she would
cringe. After a moment she went on, 'They pay big money.'
A shaky laugh. 'I did well out of it. The worst part was
pretending to be a girl who hated it but was pretending to
enjoy it. For the money.' Her face crumpled. 'And at the
end of it all I came back with nothing.' She began to cry
with hardly a sound.

Willie went to the trolley and poured her a double
brandy. He put it down on the coffee table and said, 'Drink
up, Maude.' He was cold with anger, towards Tarrant, towards Paxero and Damion, towards kinky men everywhere,
and even towards Maude in some measure. She sipped the
brandy slowly, gained control of her breathing, dried her
eyes, and looked at him with a twisted smile. 'So now you
know. I'm just making a big production out of a cheap
script.'

'Does Tarrant know?'

She looked away. 'In technicolour. A full report. Useful
material for any time we want to get at Paxero. Oh, he was
sympathetic, assured me that when it came back from the
psychology unit it would go on file unread until needed. But
writing it was like being crucified. Then he sent me down to
Three Meadows. I think he imagined a week's hard training
would take my mind off things.'

It could have been more subtle than that, Willie thought.
Perhaps Tarrant had envisaged a little helpful therapy from
Willie Garvin. He said, 'Look, Maude. Take a few weeks'
leave. I'll fix it with Tarrant. Come away with me, anywhere you like. No sleeping together, you don't want any-

one near you till you've got over this. Best if we do something a bit tough. Look, suppose we flew out to El Golea. Seven days camel ride, and I'll show you where I buried the treasure of Mus, near Fort Kerim. Make a nice trip, that would.'

She managed a genuine half-smile. 'Just good friends? Like you and Modesty?'

'It works, Maude. Honest.'

She shook her head. 'Thanks, Willie, you're very sweet. I just want to be left alone.'

'It's the worst thing you can do, love. Look, I'm 'aving dinner with the Princess at the pent'ouse tonight. You come along. It'll take you out of yourself.'

'Uninvited?'

He waved a hand at the phone. 'No problem.'

'I . . . just don't feel like it, Willie.'

'All right. Come out with me somewhere this evening. Dinner, bowling alley, theatre, anything.'

'And you stand Modesty up?'

Willie sighed and rested his hands on his hips. 'We don't have that sort of problem, Maude,' he said gently. 'If I cry off, she'll know it's something important.'

She locked her hands together and said doggedly, 'No. You don't understand.'

'I know. I'm not pretending to, just wanting to 'elp. I'll tell you what, though. Talk to the Princess, she'll understand. She's been through it more than once, every which way, and as bad as you could 'ave it.'

'No. I can't talk about it any more. And don't tell her, please Willie. Don't tell *anyone*.' Her voice rose a little.

'All right, love, all right. I promise.' He stood feeling helpless, defeated, wishing he could reach her, wishing that by some magic he could turn tragedy to comedy and hear her laugh. That would be the beginning of healing for her.

She said quietly, 'Maybe I'll take some leave and go home for a while. It's good on the farm.'

'You do that. Can I come and see you?'

'When I get back, Willie. In about a month, maybe.' She stood up. 'I'm grateful, and I'm very fond of you, but I'd like you to go now.'

'Sure.' He picked up his jacket. 'Just don't let 'em get you down, Maude.'

'I won't. Can I take a raincheck on that camel idea?' Her smile was no longer entirely forced, and he felt that talking had at least done her a little good.

'Any time,' he said. Some interesting thoughts were beginning to seed in his mind. At the door he turned and looked back at her with a grin. 'See you in a month, then. And I might 'ave a couple of funny stories to tell you.'

Before she could frame a question he had gone.

*   *   *

The evening had not yet grown cool, and it was pleasant on the penthouse terrace looking out over Hyde Park. Shuffling the cards, Willie Garvin said, 'I once knew a girl called Rosita. Little Spanish girl she was, very passionate. Used to wear those big ornamental combs in 'er 'air. Did I ever tell you about 'er, Princess?'

'Was she the trapeze artist?'

'No, that was Francesca, from Cadiz. Rosita came from Seville.'

Modesty put out her cigarette, watching his hands. She was almost sure he was holding out a ten-card stack in his palm, but not quite sure enough to make a challenge. His hands were larger than hers, of course, which gave him an advantage.

'Used to wear these combs in bed,' Willie went on. 'But in what you might call the throes, she'd fling 'er 'ead about a lot, and they'd come loose.' He put the pack down for her to cut. She eyed it, felt it carefully as she cut, and decided that it was intact now, the ten-card hold-out stacked on top ready for the deal. Willie picked up the upper half of the cut pack, and said as he slapped the lower half on top of it, 'Dangerous, it was. I nearly got stabbed in the throat once. Still got the scar.' He tilted his head, pointing under his chin.

Involuntarily she glanced up, then immediately down again. The pack lay on his palm as before, but she knew that during the moment of misdirection he had made a one-handed shift to restore the cut. She laughed and said, 'Damn. Never mind the deal. What do I get?'

'Three Queens. I get a full 'ouse.'

'I'm not sure you weren't cheating with that Rosita story.'

'No, it's true, Princess. I kept one of 'er combs for a souvenir.' He slipped a hand in his pocket and took out a curved, silver-plated comb. 'Came across it the other day when I was tidying up.'

She sighed. 'I ought to know better than to disbelieve your girl stories. You don't need to make them up.'

'I did change this one a bit. The scar wasn't on me chin.' He put the deck of cards on the table. 'Your turn, Princess.' He leaned back, watching her hands carefully as the long fingers separated the deck and riffled it together again in a waterfall shuffle. She squared it, then her eyes narrowed. 'You've got a hold-out. Four cards, maybe five.'

He lifted his hands in a gesture of surrender, then reached into his pocket. 'You got me. I stashed the aces when I took the comb out.' He drew four cards from his pocket and tossed them on the table. 'Wish I could judge a short pack like that.'

'You'll get by, Willie.' She looked at her watch. 'Let's go in and listen to some music.'

'Sure.' He was on his feet, drawing back her chair for her as she rose. Weng, her houseboy, had put on two wall-lights and a standard lamp in the big living-room with its golden cedar-strip walls and tiled floor scattered with splendid rugs from Isfahan and Bukhara.

Willie put a Sidney Bechet tape on the hi-fi, volume turned low, then took one of the big armchairs. Modesty sat curled in the corner of the chesterfield. She wore a long green hostess dress. Her hair, newly coiffed, was piled in a chignon. Willie wore a light grey suit with a pale yellow shirt and dull gold tie. He had his own key to the penthouse, his own room and wardrobe there. Sometimes, if he stayed unexpectedly in town overnight, she might find him about the place in the morning. But when she asked him to dinner, as tonight, he put on a suit and tie and brought her flowers.

She had told him about the incident in Idaho over dinner. They had discussed it, speculating with professional economy on what might lie behind the attempted snatch, then dropped the subject for lack of sufficient information. They had played two games of bezique, spent half an hour on their own peculiar game of card jugglery, and were content now to talk or not to talk, as the mood took them.

Willie sat with eyes half-closed, looking at Modesty, not studying her, simply enjoying her as he might enjoy a painting or a piece of music that gave him pleasure, letting it happen to him. She looked very beautiful now, but at many times and in many places he had seen her otherwise; hard, fierce, dangerous, dirty, sweating, wounded. He had known her in all conditions, and understanding between them was total. He had long considered himself the most fortunate of men.

She looked across at him and said, 'What little thing's bothering you Willie?'

He half laughed. 'Does it show?'

'It does to me.'

'Sorry.' He made a gesture of apology. 'I'm a bit worried about a friend who's 'ad a bad time. Can't tell you about it, though. I promised.'

Maude, she thought. He was with Maude today. She said, 'Just let me know if there's any way I can help. Is it going to hold you up for the trip to Tenazabal?'

48

'I'm not sure.' He rubbed his chin. 'How long are Steve and Dinah going to be there?'

'Quite a while. I had a letter from Dinah today. Steve's been laid low for a bit with tummy trouble.' She smiled. 'Apparently he calls it The Guatemalan Quickstep, and says he's discovered he could have been a champion sprinter.'

Willie chuckled. 'That sounds like Steve.'

They were very close to the Colliers, in fact had brought them together in grim and brutal circumstances, at a time when Steve had been Modesty's bed-fellow and Willie had been Dinah's. The close friendship had continued quite undisturbed by the Colliers' marriage.

Modesty said, 'I thought I'd go out in about two weeks' time. You could follow on if you're not clear by then.'

'Sure. I'll see 'ow it goes. Any other news?'

'Yes. Dinah's pregnant and very happy about it.'

'That's nice. And Steve?'

'According to Dinah he's very glad it took, because he says he wouldn't want to go through all that disgusting business again.'

Willie leaned back and laughed.

*   *   *

Two days later, at ten in the evening, Sir Gerald Tarrant sat in the passenger seat of a Jensen as it cruised quietly along the M4 towards London. It had not been particularly convenient for Tarrant to accept Willie's invitation to dine at a little place out-of-town, but he had several reasons for doing so. For one thing he liked Willie's company, for another he had hoped Modesty would be with them, though he had been disappointed in this. Then there was the matter of his debt to them both. He owed them one life. His own.

'Yes,' he was saying now, 'I thought you'd wring something out of Maude Tiller. In fact I rather hoped you might —er—help the girl over this rough patch. Take her away somewhere, perhaps?'

'She wouldn't go.' Willie moved in to give way to a small van which clattered past with engine hammering furiously. 'A rough patch? You're a right bastard, Sir G.'

'I know that, Willie. I have to be,' Tarrant said mildly. 'Sometimes my people get killed or tortured or both. What do you want me to do? Stop?'

'You didn't 'ave to send Maude out on a sex job, did you?'

'No, not specifically. But do bear in mind that she's not the only woman agent I have, and that I delegate a certain amount of work.'

'Meaning what?'

'It's quite a large organisation. I have a man who, among other things, is responsible for providing women for various jobs. Some of them are tarts and don't know who they're working for—a photography and blackmail job, say. Sometimes we need a trained agent. Nobody's arm gets twisted. I wanted a girl for Paxero, I specified the requirements, and the girl sent up to me for briefing turned out to be Maude Tiller. I happen to like Maude, but I can't play favourites.'

'She might quit the job after that lot.'

Tarrant looked out of the window. 'She'll think about it. I don't believe she'll go beyond that.'

'Christ knows why she does it anyway, or any girl for that matter.'

Tarrant nodded. 'It's an interesting question. After all, there's no glory or glamour in the work. Our psychologists have various theories, mostly conflicting, but I happen to know the reason in Maude's case. That's why I don't think she'll quit.'

They were on the Cromwell Road extension now, and Willie slowed to a halt at traffic lights, turning to look at Tarrant. 'Go on.'

'I hesitate, Willie. It's quite bizarre, these days. I only discovered it quite by chance, a few unguarded words.'

'Try me.'

Tarrant sighed. 'Maude's a patriot,' he said apologetically.

'Without being a flag-waver, she actually has a great regard for her country and its ways. In fact, feels she owes it something. I imagine she'd be horrified to realise I'm aware of her quaintness.'

Willie drove in silence for a while, thinking of Maude Tiller, thinking about her clowning and about the slightly dumb-blonde persona she projected. At last he said, 'Why Paxero?'

'Classified, Willie.'

'Oh, balls. D'you think I couldn't find out?'

'It was a request from our American friends. You know, I once toured the CIA Buildings, some of them anyway. It's an astonishing place. You can press a button for virtually any information you want about anyone or anything.'

'So?'

'Somebody became intrigued by the fact that over the past five years or so an above-average number of above-average well-to-do people have met with death by accident but with no bodies to show for it. Drowned, burnt, missing aircraft, buried under an avalanche in one case. All kinds of odd things. I believe a computer spat it out in the first instance.'

Willie said thoughtfully, 'Like somebody might go for a trip in the wilds somewhere and not come back?'

'That would do nicely. Well, they sorted out all data on all these disappearers, and gave it to some computer to play with, and guess what came out?'

'Nothing?'

'Almost nothing. Except that Ramon Paxero might, perhaps, just possibly, point something percent, be a common factor. His own yacht went down with thirty people in the Bermuda Triangle. Or disappeared, like many another. I believe the theory is that all the ships and aircraft which vanished from that area in the past fifty years are now in a museum on Aldebaran or some such planet, trophies of little green men.'

'Aldebaran's a sun, but never mind. Why wasn't Paxero on 'is own yacht when it 'appened?'

'I don't know. He's a businessman, so there could be a dozen reasons. Another odd thing is that once or twice Paxero has sold stock short just before some key industrialist went missing believed dead. Not often enough to make it more than a coincidence, though.' Tarrant shrugged. 'Our American friends may know more than they told me. We're not interested here, but I owe them a considerable favour, so when the request came through to have a close look at Paxero I complied.'

'And Maude found nothing?'

'Not a significant shred.'

'Just came back with a few memories.'

Tarrant frowned. 'You're being tiresome, Willie. It's happened, and I can't change it. Why the hell don't you do something to cheer the girl up and make her forget it?'

'I've got that in mind.'

'Good.'

After a little silence Tarrant said, 'I've had a complaint about you from Jacoby, of course. Should I get rid of him?'

'No. He's a nasty bugger, but that's not a bad thing. You're training agents, not trying to make the world go round with love.'

'I thought you disliked his methods.'

'Jacoby teaches set forms of combat as well as anyone you can get. But 'e doesn't teach 'em to think, so get somebody else in to do that.'

'Suggestions?'

'Not me, for a start. What about Jack Fraser?'

'I can't spare him from the office, and it wouldn't fit the image he's created of a bumbling civil servant.'

'Well, just get anyone good who's been in the field and up the sharp end. They don't 'ave to be combat champions, just smart.'

'I'll think about it.' Tarrant peered through the windscreen. 'Aren't you going to drop me at my flat?' They were moving through Belgravia, turning into Melton Square.

Willie said, 'Just made a detour to show you something.' He brought the car to a halt and opened the door. 'Come in for 'alf-an-hour and 'ave a drink.' Without waiting for an answer he got out, closed the door, and walked up the short path to the front door of a house in a Georgian terrace. By the time Tarrant had gathered up hat and brolly and followed him, the door stood open.

'No gentleman should be without a bachelor pad in London,' said Willie, and waved a hand. 'Welcome to Garvin Towers.'

'*Yours?*' Tarrant moved into the dark hall and heard the door close behind him. 'God, it must have cost you a fortune!'

'It's only money.' Willie switched on the lights. Deep pile carpet. An elegant staircase. Panelled walls. Not very good pictures in very fine frames. An atmosphere of quiet opulence.

'Come on up, Sir G.'

The living-room was lofty with an open fireplace, leather armchairs and settee, and a well-filled dark oak book-case along one wall. The heavy curtains were drawn. Tarrant gazed about him, still surprised. 'Did you take it furnished?'

'Not much choice. It was all on impulse. Sit yourself down and 'ave a brandy.' Willie moved to the sideboard. 'That's if I've got any. There 'asn't been much time to check the inventory. Ah, 'ere we are.' He poured two glasses.

'Well . . . here's to your new pad, Willie.' Tarrant drank, then gazed round appreciatively. 'It's not exactly you, but I like it. I like it very much.'

'Good. D'you mind if I leave you for a minute?' Willie looked at his watch. 'I just remembered I've got a call to make.'

'Take your time and leave the brandy.' Tarrant reached for his cigar case and leaned back in the deep armchair. He felt pleasantly relaxed, pleasantly stimulated, and a little envious. This place would have suited him very well, if he could have afforded it. He couldn't quite see Willie Garvin in residence here, and thought it had probably been a mistaken impulse. He wondered what Modesty thought, or if she had been here yet.

The minutes passed. He smoked in a quiet reverie. After ten minutes he looked at his watch, carefully knocked the ash from his cigar, then went out into the carpeted passage and called, 'Willie?'

'Along 'ere, Sir G.' The voice was low and came from the end of the passage where a door stood open. 'Don't shout the place down.'

Curious, and with growing unease, Tarrant moved along the passage and turned into the open doorway. On the far side of the bedroom a picture had been removed from the wall to reveal a safe. The door of the safe stood open. Willie Garvin held a cluster of glittering jewellery in one fist, and with the other hand was holding up a three-strand pearl necklace. He shot a look of pure mischief at Tarrant and said, 'Makes you think, eh? My 'unch was right, he's crooked as a corkscrew.'

'What?' Tarrant said blankly.

'Blakeson. The bloke who lives 'ere.' Willie put the jewellery in his jacket pocket. 'What's a bachelor stockbroker doing with this in 'is safe? If it's not loot, I'm the Queen of Bulgaria.' He closed the safe, spun the combination, and hung the picture in its place. Tarrant registered dazedly that he was wearing surgical gloves. Willie patted his bulging pocket. 'You could retire on this lot, my old darling. On the pearls alone, for that matter. Tell you what, you can 'ave the pearls. Come on, let's wipe those glasses and tidy up.'

He moved briskly past Tarrant and out of the room. Tarrant had the clear physical sensation that his brain had suddenly twisted round on its stalk and was facing the other way. He blundered out into the passage at a tottering run, on legs that seemed not to belong to him.

'Willie!' he croaked in a desperate whisper. 'For Christ's sake, are you drunk or mad?'

'I'm fine, Sir G. First time I cracked a safe for profit since I don't know when.' He swept into the living-room and began to wipe the brandy bottle and glasses on his handkerchief. 'Look, don't drop any ash, and don't leave that cigar be'ind.'

'Put it back! Put that bloody stuff back!' Tarrant said in a cracked voice. He was a man used to keeping a cool head in emergency, but this one had engulfed him totally and without warning.

'Don't worry.' Willie looked at his watch. 'I've been casing this place for a couple of weeks, and Blakeson won't be 'ome till well after midnight tonight. Never is on a Wednesday.' He put the bottle and glasses away, moving with crisp precision, took the cigar from Tarrant's numbed hand, crushed it out in the ashtray, flicked the handkerchief from Tarrant's top pocket, spread it on the table, tipped ash and cigar-stub into the centre, wiped the ashtray clean with one corner, then bundled the whole lot together and thrust it in Tarrant's jacket pocket.

'Right, get your 'at and brolly and we'll pop along.'

With a huge effort Tarrant called up the ability to speak. *'Willie . . . ! If you don't put that stuff back now, I'll . . . I'll . . .'* He stopped, lost, unable to think of any threat he could make.

'Shhh!' Willie stood with head cocked, listening. Next moment he was at the door, snapping off the light. In the faint glow of light from the passage Tarrant saw him move to the window and part the heavy curtains slightly. At the same moment there came the sound of a car door slamming.

'The bastard's back early!' Willie whispered. 'Move!'

To the extent that Tarrant was capable of conceiving any

55

coherent notion, he wished fervently to be dead. His arm was grabbed, and he was hustled along the passage. It was dark now. Willie must have switched off the light. There was a narrow-beam flash-light in Willie's hand. Through a door. A bedroom. Not the one with the safe. A wardrobe. Willie opening the door, pushing clothes aside.

'In 'ere, quick! No time to get down and out the back.'

Tarrant found he had obeyed, was sinking down on his haunches with his back to the side of the wardrobe. Hat and brolly were thrust into his hands. Downstairs, the front door slammed. The flashlight beam shone on Tarrant's face. From behind it Willie's voice whispered. 'Keep quiet and don't move. I'm going under the bed. We'll scarper when it's safe. Might be quite a while, but just sit tight.'

The door closed. Tarrant squatted in the womb-like blackness, still unable to think, able only to feel, and the turmoil of emotions that racked him made sweat spring out on his forehead. If he were discovered . . . if he were found here, like this, what in God's name could he say?

Something was bruising his thigh a little, something in his pocket. It couldn't be the bundle of ash and cigar-stub. Very cautiously he felt through the cloth. Little round objects. A string of them. Oh, Jesus Christ Almighty, the pearls! Willie must have slipped them in his pocket . . . *'you can 'ave the pearls.'*

A vast hatred rose within Tarrant and a string of vile curses flowed through his mind. Moving warily, he wiped his clammy brow. Distantly, from the living room perhaps, came the sound of music. He could just recognise the overture to Verdi's *La Forza Del Destino*.

Some time later he was listening dully to Preziosilla singing the Rataplan Chorus. Act Three of four. It seemed that —who was it? Blakey? Blakeson? It seemed he was an opera fan. Tarrant prayed that the swine would go to bed after this act. He was getting stiff, getting sleepy with the poor ventilation, but the first impact of shock had passed

56

now. He eased one cramped knee slowly, then the other, and settled down to wait with fiercely conflicting emotions. On the one hand he could have relished taking an axe to Willie Garvin at this moment; on the other hand it was an enormous relief to know that Willie was close by, with his wide experience of such matters, and would surely get them both safely away.

Much later he roused from a nightmarish doze to the faint rattle of the wardrobe door. His head came up with a jerk as the door swung open. The light in the bedroom was on, and at first his vision blurred. Then, as his pupils adjusted, he saw that the man looking down at him was not Willie Garvin. His heart sank in final resignation. He looked at his watch. Almost two am.

The man wore pyjamas and a dressing gown. He was in his middle forties, with a lean dark face and a large beak of a nose. There was a hint of accent in his voice as he said pleasantly, 'I hope you are not dangerous?'

'I can assure you of that,' Tarrant said stoically, and tried to rise, but found his stiffened muscles were unwilling. 'I'd be obliged if you'd help me to stand up.'

It took almost half a minute to get Tarrant out of the wardrobe. He was careful not to glance towards the bed as he said without much hope, 'My presence here is quite innocent, but difficult to explain.'

The man said, 'Come and have a drink.'

Tarrant followed him limpingly along the passage to the living-room, a faint hope burgeoning within him. If Blakey, Blakewell or Blakeson was a villain, as Willie had said, there was just a faint chance . . .

He took the pearls from his pocket and said, 'I'd like to return this portion of your property, and to guarantee the return of the rest if you could see your way to taking no action.'

Opening the sideboard cupboard, the man glanced round and said, 'Property? Oh, those pearls aren't mine, neither is the rest of it.' He nodded towards the table, and Tarrant gazed with stunned incomprehension at the little heap of glittering jewellery there. The man said, 'It's all Willie's, and you could get the lot for a fiver, I believe.'

Tarrant lifted the pearls and stared closely at them. They were rubbish. Not even good paste. He moved to an armchair and sat down quickly, his legs collapsing under him, then leaned back and closed his eyes. Thirty seconds later he opened them again. 'You're a friend of Willie Garvin's?'

'Yes.' The man smiled. 'From quite a while back. I specialise in International Law, and I used to act for Modesty Blaise.'

'I see.' Tarrant picked up the glass of brandy waiting for him. 'And Willie asked if he could borrow your place here for a few hours tonight, and asked you to return at a particular time?'

'Yes.'

'And told you to open that wardrobe door after a few hours?'

'You're very quick,' said the man. 'Let me say at once that I've no idea what this is about, or who you are. I might guess, but I won't.'

'Thank you. I've yet to find out myself what this is all about,' Tarrant said grimly. The relief which had flooded him only a few moments ago had now been swept aside by a cold and growing fury. A joke, was it? A bloody idiotic joke? He thought of the utter misery and humiliation he had suffered in the wardrobe, and though he was not a vain man his sense of outrage was hard to contain.

The man in the dressing gown said, 'He left a cryptic message for you which might indicate what it was all about.'

'A message?'

The man indicated a sheet of paper lying on the table. Tarrant picked it up. There were two lines in Willie's large but surprisingly neat hand: *I thought this might cheer Maude up a bit.*

58

Tarrant put the note in his pocket. 'Thank you,' he said politely, 'that's very amusing.' He put down his glass and stood up painfully. Then without warning the wild humour of it came over him like a great wave, sweeping away his mountainous indignation as if it had never existed. He began to chuckle, then to laugh helplessly, finding huge relief after the strain of the past hours.

Oh, rare Willie. Himself, Sir Gerald Tarrant no less, master of a Secret Service department, huddled in that wardrobe with his bloody bowler and brolly, sweating cobs, visualising ghastly consequences. Oh, the impudent Cockney bastard.

He sobered at last, and said, 'Do you happen to know where he is now?'

The man looked at his watch. 'Airborne. He was flying out from White Waltham at about one-thirty, I believe.'

'If he phones you to—er—see how it went, will you give him a message for me, please?'

'Of course.'

'Just say I'd be glad if he'd let me tell Maude myself. I think I can do it in a way to cheer her up even more.'

'I'll pass that on. Would you care for another drink?'

'Thank you, but I think I'll go home now.'

'I rang for a cab just before I disturbed you.' The man moved to the window and parted the curtains. 'Yes, it's waiting.'

'You're very kind. I hope I haven't kept you up late.'

'Not at all. It's always a pleasure to be able to do Willie or Modesty a favour. I'm somewhat in their debt.'

'I know how you feel.'

The man accompanied him downstairs to the front door, shook hands and said, 'I'll wish you goodnight.'

'Thank you, I wish you the same. Oh, just one thing. Do you happen to know where Willie's gone?'

'I believe he mentioned Zurich.'

'Thank you.' Tarrant got into the cab, gave his address, and sank back wearily.

It wasn't difficult to guess why Willie had gone to Switzerland. That was where the other half of the job he had set himself was located. For Tarrant he had devised an impudent practical joke, not as revenge for Maude but as a shot in the arm for her. It would appeal to her zany sense of humour, and if she could begin to laugh it would be a first step on the way to restoring her bruised spirit.

But what in God's name had Willie got in store for Paxero and Damion? Tarrant whistled soundlessly to himself. That would be something different; which was all very fine and intriguing, but also highly dangerous. Paxero was a big man, and even Willie might be biting off more than he could chew.

Winding down the window he looked across Hyde Park to the tower block surmounted by the penthouse where Modesty lived, and thought it might be a good idea to talk to her as soon as possible. Tomorrow, in fact. He looked at his watch. No, later today.

Four

It was Danny Chavasse's one-thousandth day on the plantation called Limbo. Others had been here longer. There were no big new intakes now. Mostly the new slaves came in ones and twos, though there had been a group of five a few months ago, three bucks and two women.

They had gone through the usual stages; incredulity, stubborn rebelliousness, attempts to stir up mass revolt, attempts to set up an Escape Committee, and finally the descent into inertia, acceptance and obedience. There were sixty-four of them now, two-thirds being bucks. One buck and one woman had died in the last year, but it was much longer than that since Miss Benita had had anyone beaten to death. Nobody ever spoke of it. Nobody ever forgot it.

The work was hard and gruelling, but everybody was used to it now. As long as you did your job and broke no rules, the mistress wouldn't have you whipped. There was always a little current of fear, of course, but you became used to that too. If you thought about The Outside too much, you went mad. That had happened to the red-haired girl, Miriam, and to the withdrawn older woman, Pauline. Dr. Kim Crozier had done all he could to prevent them being put down, but it was hopeless. He was as much a slave as any of them.

Danny straightened up and moved to the next shrub with his hoe. The coffee cherries were ripening to red-purple and it would soon be time for picking. He looked along the line of grey-barked shrubs with their glassy paired leaves, and saw the white-shirted figures of the other slaves working this section. There was Bissau, who had owned a chain of garages in France, and beyond him Hart, the Texan. Somewhere Outside they were probably still trying to settle Hart's huge oil-based estate. Farther along the line, Teresa was on low steps using the sprayer against leaf-rust, Selim standing beside her with the container on his shoulder. Beyond them, Giulio, Chard, Bridget, Stein, and a dozen more, hoeing, weeding, spraying.

Danny Chavasse took off his canvas slipper and looked at the cut on his foot. It was still suppurating a little. He moved along to where Mr Sam, one of the overseers, lounged in the saddle, hand-gun on his hip, carbine in a saddle holster, whip looped over the pommel. A bush-hat shaded his broad black face. It was the overseers you feared most, because they had been hand-picked for quick reaction and low intelligence, and exercised the unthinking harsh-ness of many of their white counterparts in the Deep South long ago.

Danny Chavasse stopped a few paces from the horse and said, 'Got a bad foot, Mr Sam. Can I go to Dr Crozier?'

The overseer pushed back his hat and shook his head. 'Keep it till noon break, boy.'

Danny nodded and turned away, tensing a little. A flick of the whip across his back was quite likely. It did not come, and he relaxed. Mr Sam was in a good mood today. On the way back to his place he passed Dawn. At thirty-five there were streaks of grey in the dark hair drawn tightly back. They had not been there a year ago.

He said, 'Hallo, Dawn.'

'Hi, Danny.' She leaned on the hoe, eyes weary in her thin face. 'Come and sleep with me tonight. Help me over a bad patch.'

'I've got Martha for the rest of this month, sweetheart. We don't want any trouble.'

'Mistress won't care, neither will they.' She jerked her head towards Mr Sam.

'Martha will. Let's see if we can get each other next time.'
He moved on.

The slaves had evolved their own sex arrangements, though there was always difficulty at first with any new intake. The system was based on survival. About a third of the men and a few of the women were not interested. Sometimes a woman wasn't interested at first but became so later, when she had settled in. The men were usually interested at first, but sometimes lost it. A loosely organised committee fixed a monthly roster. If you were single, you weren't allowed to have a permanent partner. That had been tried and proved a failure, provoking infidelities, jealousies, squabbles, fights, and on one occasion a killing. Miss Benita had hanged the man who did that.

If you wanted to be in, then you went with the rules, otherwise you could stay out. An exception was made if you were husband and wife on intake. There had been several such couples over the years, but only one pair now remained together. By decree of the Mistress, every woman had to be available for the overseers at regular intervals, and this was a big factor in breaking up married couples.

Miss Benita didn't allow breeding, thank God. Dr Crozier was responsible for ensuring that there were no pregnancies. He had been on the plantation since the days when the early intakes were clearing, planting and building, and he was still the sanest of any man or woman among the slaves. Danny Chavasse dreaded to think what life in Limbo would be like without him.

When the noon break came, Danny limped down the dirt path towards the prefabricated hut where Dr Crozier lived, a hundred yards from the slave quarters and close to the small wooden church. On Sundays and twice during the week you crowded in there and sang spirituals—if you were wise. Miss Benita liked her slaves old-fashioned, even though she had never set foot in the church herself.

The reaction of Limbo's prisoners to slavery would have

63

interested a psychologist, Danny thought, glancing up at the small spire. Almost a third of the slaves were fervent worshippers now, singing with passion about green pastures, and sweet chariots coming for to carry them home.

He halted in front of the church and looked north along the valley. To his right, two hundred yards away, the river formed the eastern boundary of Limbo. On the far side the land sloped steeply up from the bank, a few scattered trees rising above the thick undergrowth. Where the ground levelled into a plateau, the solid jungle of the Petén resumed the march broken by the river and the plantation.

The main road through the middle of Limbo rose at a gentle slope to the northern edge of the plantation, where the irrigation pipe ran, then fell slightly across open ground to the big house. From where Danny stood he could see only the roof of the Colonial Georgian house where Miss Benita lived with her servants. They were all women, mainly older women, poor mestizos taken from a grinding life of slash-and-burn farming in the Petén. For them the plantation was luxury.

To the right of the big house was the barrack-like building where the Specials were quartered, twenty mercenaries. There were kennels a little way from the building. The mercenaries did patrol duty with their dogs, handled roll-calls, hunted any runaway, carried out punishments, and were ready to deal with any revolt. Regular supplies of magazines, books, tapes, films, and mestizo girls were brought in by helicopter for their entertainment. They could hunt, fish, and ride, for the horses and mares which had been brought in as foals during the early days had bred well. Sometimes two or three of the men would be ferried out, to return a week or a month later with new slaves.

But nothing could prevent their lives here being claustrophobic, Danny Chavasse reflected. However much they were paid, they could hardly contemplate remaining here till they died. Yet neither could Paxero contemplate sending

64

a man back Outside, except for a supervised slave-hunt. At least, not until the whole thing was over. This was a thought which gave Danny Chavasse uneasy nights.

Slowly he scanned the valley, as if seeing it anew. There were the two long rectangles of coffee-trees, standing rank upon rank, with the road running between. On the western boundary-road were the big sheds and the patio areas where the coffee cherries would be spread, raked and turned for drying. Two of the sheds were for storage, one was the laundry, and two more were simply wall-less shelters with long benches set beneath. Here, when the time came, the slaves would sit hulling the dried fruit by hand, for hour after hour, to free the beans within. And some time later the big supply helicopter would come to take the crop away.

A toy, Danny thought. The whole thing was a toy for a mad old woman to play with.

He went on down the dirt path to the surgery. As he entered, Valdez came out from behind the partition, buttoning his white cotton trousers. He had once been a plump man who owned an immense estate in Paraguay and would think nothing of losing more in one night at a casino than ten of his peons could earn in a lifetime. He was no longer plump. Surprisingly, he was one of the very small handful who had managed to resist falling into the grey inertia of the slave mentality.

He rubbed his buttock, nodded at Danny, and said, 'I hope you do not want a shot of penicillin. Kim's needle is very blunt.'

Dr Kimberly Crozier came from behind the partition. He was in his middle thirties, as black as any of the overseers, and the most respected slave on the plantation. He said, 'I used a new needle, Valdez. You just have a tough arse.'

'It is not from sitting around.' Valdez looked at Danny. 'We are on laundry tonight, yes?'

'That's right. With Lois and Julie.' The men wore cotton

shirts and trousers, the women shirts and calf-length skirts. Miss Benita liked her slaves clean, very clean, and there were always four at work in the laundry shed every night, using big wooden dollies in barrels of hot soapy water well-laced with disinfectant. Valdez wrinkled his nose and put a hand tenderly to his ear. 'Try to stop Lois complaining for three hours without stopping, Danny. I have an ear infection.'

'I'll try.'

Valdez went out. Crozier said, 'What's the trouble, Danny?'

'Just a sore foot. I cut it a day or two ago and it doesn't want to heal.'

'Sit down and let's take a look.' The black hands were firm and gentle. 'I'll clean it out and put a dressing on, but come and see me again tomorrow.'

Danny glanced out of the open door of the surgery and said softly, 'There's a rumour that Paxero's making another visit.'

'Yes. One of the mestizo girls told me yesterday when I was giving them their weekly check-up.'

'New intake?'

Kim shrugged. 'I hope not. It unsettles everyone for a few weeks. We may not like Limbo much, but we're all scared of closedown.'

That was true. The danger was that somebody in a new intake might try to escape. It was impossible of course, but by some million-to-one chance it might succeed. Nobody doubted what would happen then. Miss Benita's plantation would vanish from the face of the earth. Paxero would certainly have contingency arrangements for that. One witness tottering out of the jungle with an impossible story would have small credibility as long as there was nothing else and nobody else to back it up.

'How do you think they'd work it?' Danny said.

Kim finished strapping on the dressing. He knew his people well, and there were six with sufficient fibre to be

66

trusted completely. Danny Chavasse was one, Valdez another. Then there was the bald-headed Schultz and his wife, New Yorkers past middle-age who had been among the first intake, and were the only couple who had not split up; Teresa, the Italian actress who had once done so much for the world's gossip-columnists; and Marker, the South African diamond man who had earned himself three floggings in his first six weeks on the plantation.

Kim said very quietly, 'When the day comes, I think they'll burn everything in the valley. They're ready to blast half the hillside into the river a little way down. It's fast water. Enough to flood the valley six feet deep in a week and thirty in a month. I guess it would take longer than that for anyone to come and investigate, especially as Paxero's a big wheel in Guatemala.' He straightened up. 'Cigarette?'

'You're not supposed to share your privileges, Kim. Is it safe?'

'I'll watch from the door.' Crozier broke open a pack of cigarettes, gave one to Danny and lit it. 'If I was back in Los Angeles I'd be telling you to give it up.' He moved to the door. 'Hell, if I was back in Los Angeles I'd spend most of my time prescribing tranquillisers and sleeping tablets.'

'Did you come in with the very first intake?'

'Before. I had to be set up and ready.'

Jesus, Danny thought. That must be six years ago. He said, 'How did they pick on you? I mean, you're not white and I guess you weren't rich.'

'Good guessing.' Kim glanced over his shoulder and smiled briefly. 'Maybe Miss Benita figured some of the females would just hate to have nigger hands on them, but I think it was mainly because I had no ties or family.'

'How did they get you?'

'Easy. Paxero had just started his New Santiago project, to open up the country inland.' He gestured vaguely towards the west.

Danny nodded. 'I saw pictures in a magazine once, when I was Outside. A fifteen-year development job, they said. I suppose that's his cover for this place.'

'It accounts for a lot of to-and-fro around a big hole in the jungle called New Santiago. I answered an advertisement for a resident doctor on the site. They checked me out, took me on, flew me up there. Then I died of snake-bite. I'm one of the few guys who knows where he's buried.' Kim drew on his cigarette. 'You came in with the big intake, didn't you?'

'Yes. A happy gathering of the wealthy elite on Paxero's yacht. Wealthy elite doesn't include me. I wasn't exactly on the breadline, but they could have bought me up with loose change.'

'How come you were aboard?'

'I'd been idle for quite a while, just playing around. A friend offered me big money to write an inside piece on the cruise for a Sunday newspaper. I didn't need the money, but I fancied the cruise, so I checked the passenger list and decided I'd become Julie Boscombe's boyfriend. I had about two weeks to do it.'

'Just like that?'

Danny smiled reminiscently. 'It's my speciality. I seem to have some sort of knack.' He inhaled. 'There was a time when I did it professionally.'

'You? A gigolo?' Kim turned his head to stare.

'No. I was on salary. Can we skip that bit?'

'Sure. But you've still got the knack. Did you know I sometimes prescribe *you* when one of the women gets shaky?'

'I had an idea the draw was rigged now and then.'

'What happened on the yacht?'

'It was simple. Four of the stewards were Specials. They just took over the ship one night, backed by sub-machine guns. That fair-haired bastard Damion was in charge. A cargo boat came alongside and took us off. Then they pulled the

68

plug out of the yacht, or whatever you do with ships you don't want any more, and down it went. Heavily insured, no doubt.'

'What about the crew?'

Danny lifted his hands and mimed a chattering machine-gun. 'Fifteen of them. Damion loved it.'

'Oh, Christ.'

'I don't think people are real to men like Damion and Paxero. Except Miss Benita, she's real to them.'

Kim threw his cigarette away. 'For God's sake don't put it around, Danny, but we may be coming to the crunch.' He nodded along the valley and tapped his chest. 'That old woman could go any time. Heart. I was called up there last week. She could last for two or three years or she could go tomorrow.'

Danny Chavasse felt sweat prickle on his brow, and wiped it with the sleeve of his shirt. His first thought was that all the slaves must be alerted, ready to put up a desperate battle for survival when the moment came. Perhaps they could seize guns from the overseers, perhaps . . .

His imagination failed. You might rally half a dozen. Desperation might bring in a few more. But for the most part they were cattle now, passive, without the will to defend themselves, let alone attack. He said, 'Any ideas, Kim?'

'If there were any ideas to have, I'd have come up with them sometime during the last six years.' For a moment bitterness and anger touched the ebony face. At one time Kim had hoped some of the mestizo girls would talk when they went back Outside. They were not prevented from leaving Limbo, and over the years he had known at least twenty who had grown weary of the life and asked to be taken out. Kim Crozier was now quite certain that not one of them had lived to reach New Santiago. As Danny Chavasse had said, people weren't real to Paxero. He took the small stub of Danny's cigarette and threw it out of the doorway. 'The only thing I can do is keep that old woman alive as long as possible.'

'And hope for what?'

'God knows. Is there anyone among the slaves who has the remotest hope that someone, somewhere, might be suspicious, might be . . . investigating?'

Danny shook his head. The almost infinitesimal hope that he had kept within himself for the last three years was too small to be spoken of.

Kim Crozier sighed. 'Well . . . do your best to keep everything cool, Danny. You're good with the women. I don't want Miss Benita to have any more shocks or excitement.'

'Any more?'

'She had a disappointment. A couple she'd seen in a magazine and picked out as ideal slaves for Limbo. That's how she does it, these days. The man was Dall, John Dall, I don't know about the girl.'

Danny looked up, a feather of some almost forgotten emotion tickling his spine for a brief second. 'Dall Enterprises. I've read about him. I used to know somebody who knows him.'

Kim gave him a mocking smile and said, 'Big deal.' The smile faded. 'Anyway, they didn't get John Dall. Paxero snatched and missed.'

'How do you know?'

'Jesus, I'm the doctor, Danny. I check the mestizo girls every week and they chatter like monkeys. Not a sparrow falls in Uncle Tomsville without I get to hear.'

'That could be useful if it comes to the crunch. What happened with Dall and the girl?'

'Paxero had a three-man team flown out for the job. Martinez and the two Hillbillies—'

'The who? I don't mix with the Country Club set up there, Kim.'

'Two ex-cons from Kentucky. Mean bastards.' He grinned suddenly. 'But only Martinez came back.'

'What happened?'

'That's what Paxero would like to know. It was off the Salmon River somewhere. Dall and this girl were on some back-to-nature kick, can you imagine? So the Hillbillies picked them up nice and easy, but somewhere between the pick-up and the helicopter, Dall ups and shoots them with their own guns. *Pow!* How about that?'

Danny Chavasse sat very still. He knew the calibre of the Specials. Paxero hand-picked them. Dall might be a very tough character, but he wasn't good enough to take men like the Hillbillies once they had the drop. That called for something very special. His mind reached back eight years, and he was twenty-eight again, sitting in the big sunlit room she used as an office in the white villa that looked out over Tangier. Perhaps she was twenty then, but nobody in *The Network* gave thought to her age or sex, not any longer.

It was three years since she had taken over the Louche gang and started to build a new organisation. Now it was big-time, and she was 'Mam'selle', who ran it, a freak whose age and sex were of no moment.

Danny Chavasse was a little afraid of her. His work was strictly non-combatant and he had never seen her in action, but he had heard enough stories from the frontline men. Some were no doubt exaggerated, but he knew she had gone up against some frightening and powerful people. Garcia, her aging lieutenant, had once told him how she destroyed the Salamut mob, and Garcia did not exaggerate.

In her office that day she had said to Danny Chavasse in her usual cool manner, 'You've done a good job with Willie Garvin. I thought you'd need six months to groom him.'

'He learns very fast, Mam'selle. A natural. You will find him relaxed and at ease in any company and under any circumstances now.' Danny permitted himself a polite smile. 'To see him deal with a headwaiter is an experience.'

'Good.' She rose from her chair and moved to stand gazing out of the window. Danny had started to get up, but without turning she said, 'Sit down. And don't speak of this to anybody. Garcia wants to retire at the end of the year. He's more than earned it. I'm going to need somebody good to replace him. I know it's not long since I took Garvin into the organisation, but I think he might just fill the bill. What's your view?'

'I don't know his capacity for heavier work, Mam'selle. It is said he is very good with a throwing-knife.'

'Don't worry about that side of it. He doesn't like or use handguns, but outside that he's the best you'll ever see in your life. I'm concerned with personality now, so do you think he can handle Garcia's job?'

Danny thought it over. 'Yes, Mam'selle. I believe he has enormous potential.'

'Good. So does Garcia. I'll start Willie running in tandem with him from now on.'

There was a long silence. She did not turn from the window. To his surprise, Danny saw that her hands were gripped tightly behind her back, interlaced fingers moving slightly as if some measure of tension had come upon her. He waited, then said politely, 'Is that all, Mam'selle?'

'I'll tell you when to go.' She turned to face him and crossed her arms, hands holding elbows. 'I've got a job for you, Danny.'

'Yes, Mam'selle.'

'It's back to the old routine. Information.'

'From a woman?'

'Of course.'

Danny Chavasse specialised in women. Young or old, they found him irresistible when he switched on the magnetism that was his peculiar gift, a gift as much a mystery to him as to those who wondered how he did it. Danny had known failure, but very rarely. Perhaps his success lay in the fact that he never had to pretend, but always genuinely and ardently desired to make the woman happy. Or perhaps his gift was that he could always detect the nature of her need.

72

A woman talked when she was happy, whether she was an industrialist's wife, a lady's maid, a banker's daughter or a diplomat's mistress. Danny had gleaned information from all these and many more, information most useful to *The Network*.

He said, 'How long shall I have from the time of making contact, Mam'selle?'

'A month.' She moved to the desk, relaxing. 'She's staying at the El Greco on Lanzarote, and her name's Jeanne Fournier. I've booked you in for four weeks as from Tuesday.'

'She is alone? No escort?'

'That's right. An easy one for you, Danny, except I understand she's a spinsterish type.'

'The type does not matter, Mam'selle,' he said without vanity. 'On what matter am I to seek information?'

She lit a cigarette, her eyes thoughtful. 'I'm hoping I'll be able to tell you that soon after you've made contact. This is a long-shot operation and a little hazy at the moment. Just do your usual stuff to start with, Danny. I'll be in touch with you at the El Greco as soon as I've something definite for you.'

'Very well, Mam'selle.'

'All right. That's all.'

As he rose there was a tap on the door and Garcia came in. He acknowledged Danny with a nod of his greying head and said, 'Osmani brings his cargo into Sahgafa Bay tonight, Mam'selle.'

She stared. 'You're certain?'

'Garvin got a radio tap on the line from Osmani's house last night. It's certain.'

'Good. I'll lead the boat party myself. Let Garvin handle the beach party, but keep an eye on things, especially when he briefs his men, that's when it counts.'

Danny Chavasse felt a little cold. He would not have enjoyed the notion of tangling with Osmani . . .

As if from a distance he heard Kim Crozier's voice saying, 'Let me know when you get back, Danny.'

He blinked, and looked about the little surgery. Kim stood eyeing him with puzzled amusement. Danny rubbed his face and said, 'Sorry, Kim. I was a good few years and a good few thousand miles away. You were saying the Hillbillies got shot with their own guns. I like it.'

He had no doubt whatsoever of the girl's identity now, the girl who had been with John Dall. Excitement stirred deep within him. If she followed it up, if she had any sort of lead, if she fingered Paxero and Damion, if she ever caught a glimpse of the Breguet watch . . . if, if. The infinitesimal hope grew a little larger. Odds down from a million-to-one to . . . a hundred-to-one, maybe?

Kim was saying soberly, 'It didn't do much for the old woman's heart, though. She thought the snatch had been pulled off, then she heard Dall's name in some newscast, about him being appointed to some Government advisory council, and that he'd just returned from a vacation. She had Paxero called on the scrambler radio to find out what happened, then the heart started up.' He shrugged. 'Still, there's two real mean bastards less, so let's have a drink to this guy Dall next time I get some liquor.'

Danny Chavasse stood up. He was not full of hope, but he had more than a crumb to nourish now. He said, 'It wasn't Dall who put them down, it was his girl.'

'His *girl* did it? Ah, come on, Danny, I knew those guys. They were killers.'

'I knew the girl, Kim. I once worked for her. She's been up against killers before, up against opposition to make your flesh creep.'

Kim Crozier was silent for a little while. He was thinking that Danny was a contained man, a realist whose tongue never ran away with him. At last he said softly, 'Could this help?'

Danny moved to the door and stood gazing across the

74

valley, seeing nothing, remembering. 'It just might,' he said. 'I mean, if she ever had reason to believe I'm not dead, she'd find me. You can bank on that, Kim. She'd come for me.'

'Look . . . don't start pipe-dreaming, Danny.'

'I won't. I'm not. I said "if".'

'Even then. How would she find you?'

'I don't know. But somehow.'

'You must be pretty important to her.'

'No. But that wouldn't make any difference.' Danny glanced at the sun. 'I've only got about fifteen minutes left to eat. I just hope Martha's kept some for me. Thanks for the foot, Kim.'

'You're welcome.' Crozier patted him on the back. A little pipe-dreaming in moderation wouldn't hurt Danny Chavasse, he decided. It might even help with the long day's work. He smiled and said, 'Introduce me to this dame when she comes for you. She sounds unusual.'

Danny nodded. 'You could say that.' He set off towards the slave-quarters.

Five

LAKE THUN was quiet under the late afternoon sun. The man on the small motor cruiser fixed his rod in position with a twist of wire and sat down in the cockpit. He was a big man with dark hair and a sallow face, wearing a long-sleeved grey shirt and faded slacks. A neutral sort of man.

Shading his eyes, he watched the little boat with the outboard motor come closer in fits and starts as the engine wavered, picking up for a few seconds then fading again. Puzzled, he watched the girl in headscarf and dark glasses give the outboard a kick with her heel. It stopped. She gave it a long look, then sat down, set two short oars in the rowlocks and began to pull towards him. At a little distance she rested on her oars, turned and called, '*Je suis en panne, m'sieu. Pouvez vous m'aider?*'

He stood up and beckoned. '*On peut toujours essayer, mam'selle.*'

'*Merci infiniment.*'

As she came alongside the man drew the two boats together and took a turn round a cleat with the painter of the small boat. He said, 'It's all right, Princess. I'm on me own.'

'I didn't want to mess anything up.'

'Come aboard. I'll fetch the outboard over, just for the look of it.'

Two minutes later they were in the cabin. Modesty said, 'I've been scouring the hotels looking for you, then I thought of the lake.' She took off her dark glasses. 'And even at a distance I know that coffee-brown persona of yours.' She leaned forward and rested a hand on his. 'Willie love, I

76

know all about what happened to Maude. Tarrant told me, after you'd twisted his tail.'

'Ah.' Willie relaxed and his puzzlement vanished. Now he understood, and was glad. 'She didn't want me to tell you, Princess. You can understand.'

'Yes. But she's a silly girl. You could have helped.'

'She wouldn't let me try. So then I thought I'd, you know, try an' give the whole thing a bit of a comic twist.'

Modesty giggled. 'You made a good start with Tarrant. He promised me he'd milk it for all it was worth when he tells Maude.'

'That's good.'

She put her head a little on one side, inquiringly. 'Don't feel bound, but could you use a hand, Willie?'

An enormous contentment expanded within him. He had worked solo and on his own initiative often enough, but always as part of an operation in which she was involved. Being on this Paxero caper without her had somehow taken the spice out of it. He grinned at her, not needing to reply, and she said, 'All right, I'm in. But it's your caper. Have you got it worked out? I've been trying to think what the hell you might get up to, but I haven't even made a guess so far.'

'I got the theme worked out,' he said, 'but the execution's a bit tricky. We can cut a few corners with the two of us on it, though.' He lifted field-glasses from the seat beside him and pointed through the window to the northern shore of the lake, a quarter of a mile away. 'That's Paxero's villa, Princess. No staff living in. A man and two girls come every morning. Damion's a blond Mr Universe type, he's first out for a swim in the morning. Paxero looks useful stripped, too. He swims later. A few people come and go, mostly men on business by the look of 'em. They keep one car 'ere and another parked at the marina in Thun. Dine out every evening, taking their cruiser across to Thun and going on from there by car.'

She was looking through the glasses. 'They keep the cruiser in that boat-house under the villa, below the terrace?'

'That's right. No steady girls, at least I 'aven't seen any the four days I've been 'ere. I expect they save it up till they find a girl they can take to Kinksville like they did Maude.'

Modesty said, 'Maude's report went to Tarrant's head-shrinker. He said the degradation bit probably stemmed from the fact that Paxero was a peasant boy in Guatemala, no doubt treated like dirt by the hidalgos. So for sex he likes to pick the high-class free-loading type of female and make a circus of humiliating her.' She put down the glasses. 'There's no shortage. You can see them haunting the bars in all the best hotels.'

'The shrink's probably right about Paxero, not that it makes any difference. This one's for Maude.'

'You've got a long way in a short time, Willie. Where are you based?'

He pointed a thumb over his shoulder. 'I've got a little chalet on the south side. I'm on the Maurice Dupont from Algeria passport.'

She smiled. 'Mind one of those brown contact lenses doesn't fall out. What's the theme?'

It was hot in the small cabin. Sweat was trickling on their bodies and beading their upper lips, but they were both impervious to discomfort when prudence called for it. In all likelihood nobody had remarked their meeting, but the less they were on view together the better.

Willie said, 'I thought I'd snatch 'em, Princess. Paxero and Damion.' Her eyes widened a little. 'Not for ransom. I'd like to get 'em right off the scene for a few months. It shouldn't be too 'ard to fix so their boat catches fire and sinks when they're coming back across the lake one night. Then it'll look like they've drowned.' He stared. 'Something wrong?'

'No, not exactly.' She swivelled to extend her long bare legs along the seat, frowning a little. 'It's ambitious, but

78

that's all right, it only needs careful planning.' She looked at him. 'Sorry, I had a funny sense of *déjà vu* just now. Maybe if I forget it I can pin it down. Where would you plan to take Paxero and Damion?'

'Take 'em out by air. I'll 'ave Dave Craythorpe standing by with a Cessna at Bern a week from today onwards. He comes in with two coffins, the remains of a departed couple being flown back to Istanbul or somewhere for burial. But they're empty, and we pop Paxero and Damion in. It'll be at night, of course, and they'll be well doped. The Swiss aren't bothered about what goes out, only about what comes in.'

'Tricky making the switch at an airfield, Willie. Might be better to take them down through the lakes by boat and get them across into France. Dave could land at one of the old wartime strips there and pick them up.'

He nodded. 'Better. I've got all the maps we need at the chalet.'

'Getting Paxero and Damion out is just an admin. thing. Where does the comic bit start, Willie?'

He smiled. 'I thought I'd take 'em to Malaurak.'

She sat with a finger to her lips, mind darting as she tried to solve the puzzle from his clue. Malaurak was a patch of sand, a tiny sheikdom in the Arabian peninsular ruled by Abu-Tahir. Twenty years ago, during her lone childhood wanderings, she had spent almost a year with his tribe as a goat-herd. Much later, in *The Network* days, oil had been found in the sheikdom, and at once came an attempt to overthrow Abu-Tahir. Since the population of Malaurak numbered only between three and four thousand, and the protagonists only a few dozen, it had been a very miniature affair. Modesty had paid the debt of bread and salt by flying in with Willie Garvin and a highly efficient team of twenty men. The attempted coup had been smashed in a week.

Malaurak was now very wealthy, and benevolently feudal. It had roads, schools, cars, and an irrigation programme,

79

but was still essentially tribal. Abu-Tahir's tent had become a palace covering four acres, but the way of life within had changed little. He was an old man now, and when he died Malaurak would vanish, would be absorbed by its neighbours. But until that time came it would remain a small echo of the past. To go there was to step back a hundred years.

Modesty said, 'Dammit, Willie, I still can't see the pay-off. Abu-Tahir could put them to herding goats or digging ditches for a few months, but there's not a lot of sparkle to that.'

'Aversion therapy, Princess. The harem.'

She caught her breath, then leaned back and laughed with delight. She and Willie had had the rare privilege of visiting the harem. She remembered walking through the sumptuous halls with old Abu-Tahir, his arm linked through hers.

'Sixty-two of them, Modestee. Aiee, if only it could have been so when I was young! But now I am old and sleep alone. All women weary me, but you. The harem is for my people's pride, no more. Look at them now. They are like she-camels on heat. See how they regard Willee?' He chuckled bawdily. 'If we lock him in here for a week, he will be as a husk when they finish. Ho, Willee, you wish to try?'

She remembered Willie's genuinely uneasy look, remembered the almost palpable atmosphere of predatory hunger in the harem as he said, 'No thanks, Your 'ighness. I got a few years left yet, and I'd rather pace meself.'

Abu-Tahir had grinned through his beard. 'I have a punishment for any bad man of my people who breaks the laws made by Allah for men and women. I put them in prison.' He waved an arm about him. 'Here. In a week they beg to be flogged, to dig ditches, anything to be taken from my she-cats with their hot and greedy thighs.'

In the little cabin Modesty wiped the sweat from her face and said, 'Now there's sparkle! That's my Willie.'

'I thought they could just wake up and find themselves there, Princess. Leave 'em a couple of months, then dope 'em again and bring 'em back. They'd never know where they'd been. A sort of lost weekend, times thirty. Except they wouldn't forget it in a hurry.'

'God, Willie, they'll go up with the blind by then. I can see those women now. And Abu-Tahir will play, he'll love it. Have you been in touch?'

'I was waiting till I'd got firm plans. He's like King Hussein, a radio ham, so I can call 'im any time. Talk in Arabic and ask if 'e can look after two guests for a bit.'

She nodded. 'That's no problem. Even the snatch shouldn't be too difficult. The real nitty-gritty is transport from here to Malaurak, but we can work on that while we're doing the reconnaissance.' She reached across and ruffled his hair. 'It's a little gem, Willie love. I can't wait for us to tell Maude.' She glanced out of the window. 'Have you been inside the house yet?'

'Not so far. Just the boat-'ouse.'

'But you plan to?'

'I think it's necessary, Princess. We might be able to snatch 'em on the lake at night, but it's probably a lot easier to take care of 'em in the villa, get 'em doped and across to the chalet ready for transport, then run their boat out an' blow it up in the middle of the lake. That way we could be ten miles away before anyone's got around to looking for wreckage.' He paused, thinking. 'Where you based, Princess?'

'The Métropole. It's a little hotel off the main road east of the lake. I'm not under my own name, and I don't spend much time there. They think I'm doing two-day and three-day tours, sightseeing, so I can come and go without any raised eyebrows.'

He rested his foot on the outboard which lay on the cabin floor. 'I reckon the best bet is to assume I can't fix this for you, so I take you in tow back to where you hired the boat, then I ask you back to the chalet for a drink, and we've struck up an acquaintance.'

'Fine.' She plucked at her damp shirt. 'I can do with a shower as well as a drink.'

'Me too.' He bent to pick up the outboard, looking mildly surprised. 'You know, it's 'ot in 'ere, Princess.'

*   *   *

Two days later, in the early hours, and a full ninety minutes after the last gleam of light had vanished from the curtained windows of the villa, Willie Garvin perched on a first floor sill easing a flexible metal strip into the closure of the casement. He wore a thin roll-neck sweater, slacks, plimsolls and gloves, all black. After five minutes he had worked the catch down so that it no longer gripped the metal frame. Warily he eased the window open.

No bells sounded, and he let out a silent sigh of satisfaction as he climbed in. The villa might well be wired for alarms; but by night, and when the house was occupied, it was more likely that only the ground floor alarms would be switched on. The room he had chosen to enter was on the front of the villa, facing over the lake, and no light had shown from it during the six days of his surveillance.

He drew the curtains slowly, quietly, then flashed a thin beam of light round the room from the pencil-torch in his gloved hand. It might have been part of a film studio's prop department. Costumes. Racks of female clothing, some period, some modern, but all bizarre on closer inspection, with omissions, additions, and cutaway parts. Obscenely bizarre. There was headwear, too, and grotesque masks, long plumes, a pink top-hat, a small rocking-horse, a crinoline frame, a striped orange and black bentwood chair with a hole in the seat, a tangle of soft-leather straps which might have been a human bridle.

So this was the property department. Poor Maude.

82

He switched off the torch and eased the door open carefully. Still no bells, which almost certainly meant that the upper floor was clear of alarms. His purpose was to make himself thoroughly familiar with the house, and he set about it methodically now. Within half an hour he could have drawn a scale-plan of the upper floor with the general layout of furniture. Most of that time had been spent in the bedrooms where the two men were sleeping and in the attached dressing-rooms. He had not used the torch again, to avoid spoiling his night vision.

Very warily now he descended the stairs. If all the downstairs doors were shut he could assume that the ground floor was wired for alarms. Opening a door would trigger the bells, or treading on a contact pad under a rug. Protection might be more sophisticated than a simple contact-breaking system. There could be movement detectors, infra-red rays, a microwave Doppler device. He hoped not, and thought it unlikely, for this was a rented villa and not a place where Paxero was likely to keep valuable treasures.

Two of the doors leading off the hall stood open. A good sign. He moved through one of the doorways into the big living-room. Still no bells. Down here it would be safe to use the torch, and he could move more quickly. In particular he wanted to know if there was an integral way from the villa into the boathouse. He found the kitchen. There was one half-glazed door leading out on to a sideway which connected with the front drive. The door was bolted, and he did not open it.

Softly he padded back along the passage. He was halfway across the big living-room, the torch throwing an oval glow on the floor ahead of him, when the lights clicked on.

Willie froze. Paxero stood in the doorway immediately ahead of him, bare to the waist, wearing slacks and rope-soled sandals, an automatic pointed at Willie's middle. A voice from behind said, '*Haut les mains.*' Willie lifted his

83

hands. So he had guessed wrong. There was an alarm system in operation, and somewhere he had triggered a muted signal in one of the bedrooms. He turned slowly. Damion, in red shorts, a T-shirt and beach shoes, stood in the doorway through which Willie had passed only moments ago. Damion also held an automatic. Willie spread his fingers wide, the little torch clipped in the fork of his thumb, showing that he carried no weapon, and said, '*Je ne vais rien faire, messieurs.*' His French was fluent, with a Marseilles accent.

Paxero motioned with the gun and said in French, 'Over against the wall. Face it. Lean forward, hands flat on the wall.' Willie obeyed. Damion came forward to one side of him, keeping the gun well away, and ran a hand over his body and down each leg in turn. He took the torch, tossed it aside, then moved away and said, 'He's clean, Pax.'

From a few paces behind, Paxero said, 'Good. Now turn round, pig, and keep your hands high.' Again Willie obeyed. Both guns were very steady on him from front and side. He thought briefly that it was just as well Maude Tiller, during a training session, had never asked him how to cope with this precise situation, because there was no answer. Not yet anyway.

Paxero said to Damion, 'Do we know him?'

'No. He's a professional thief, I suppose.'

Willie said wearily, 'Not professional, m'sieu. A thief by intent, I admit, but even there I have failed.'

Damion smiled. 'Ah, this is your first attempt? And you were driven to it because your wife and children are starving?'

'No, m'sieu.' Willie looked at him with dull, hopeless eyes. 'I have a young wife, very beautiful, very expensive. I am in debt.' He shrugged. 'I would steal to keep her. I make no excuse.'

Paxero moved a little closer, his eyes ugly with sudden fury. 'You would steal, eh? You would steal from me? Take

84

what is *mine?*' Without moving his eyes from Willie he spoke to Damion. 'Shoot him if he resists.'

His foot lashed out suddenly in a kick to the stomach. Willie rode it, went back against the wall, then dropped to the floor, knees drawn up, arms crossed over his head, rolling, jerking, blocking, as the rope-soled sandal drove at him again and again, taking most of the kicks on his arms and shoulders, riding them, diverting them, using all his hard-won skill without letting it be apparent. And never attempting to counter. He was quite certain that Damion would shoot at the first hint of reaction.

Paxero's spasm of fury lasted well over a minute, and at the end of it Willie Garvin lay huddled in a corner of the room, gasping, groaning, a trickle of blood running from the corner of his mouth.

Damion said, 'Steady, Pax. If you've given him a punctured lung the police will have to ask questions.'

'*Qu'ils aillent se faire foutre!*' Paxero growled, but he turned away from his victim. 'Get them on the phone and have them collect him, Damion.'

Damion moved to the phone, listened, then shook his head. 'It's dead. He must have cut the wires.'

Paxero opened a silver box and lit a cigarette. 'Go along the road to the Magdalena, you can phone from there. They have a night porter.'

The hotel Paxero had named was a hundred yards along the road and on the other side. Willie Garvin gave a wavering groan, and felt a little happier. A few seconds later he heard the front door slam. Through half-closed eyes he saw Paxero pull an armchair round and sit down. He was six paces away, one hand holding the gun and resting on the arm of the chair, the cigarette in his other hand.

Willie moved a shaking hand to wipe the blood from his chin, and Paxero said, 'Don't move, pig.' Willie let his hand fall, and waited.

Paxero's anger had passed now, and he drew on the

cigarette reflectively. What had the pig said about a young and beautiful wife? But no, there was small chance of opportunity there. If she adored her fool of a husband and would do anything to save him, that might have provided good entertainment. But it wasn't so. The pig was stealing to hold her, if what he said was true—

Paxero's thoughts ceased abruptly, and he would have toppled forward from the chair if a hand had not caught him by the hair and drawn him back to lie slumped. Willie opened his eyes when he heard the soft impact of the blow, and saw Modesty standing behind the chair. In her right fist was the kongo, the little sandalwood dumb-bell that she used with such precision, striking to the nerve-centres to stun or paralyse. She was dressed in black, as he was, her hair tucked into a beret. He saw that she still wore the ear-plug, with the wire running up under the edge of the beret to the tiny receiver.

He got briskly to his feet, wiped the blood from his chin and said, 'Thanks, Princess. Damion outside?'

'Yes, I took him as he came out of the front door. He didn't see me.'

'I'll go an' fetch 'im in.'

'You're all right?'

'Sure. I bit me lip to show some blood. He was going pretty strong, and I reckoned it might make 'im think.' Willie went out of the room. Modesty picked up the pencil torch, half of which consisted of a miniature radio-transmitter, and put it in the thigh pocket of her slacks. She had heard Paxero going pretty strong, as Willie had put it. Outside in the black canoe moored against the boat-house she had heard everything, from the moment when Damion's voice had said, '*Haut les mains . . .*'

Willie came in carrying Damion over one shoulder, and dropped him on the big settee. 'I suppose we might as well make the most of it, Princess?'

'Yes.' She was opening a small flat box, taking out a hypo-
86

dermic. 'It's a pity we're not all geared up for the snatch, but I don't fancy keeping these two under wraps for a few days while we fix it.'

Willie stood with one hand on his sore ribs, watching her as she injected the two men. Three grains of phenobarbitone would give them several hours of undisturbed sleep, and meanwhile a thorough and unhindered inspection of the villa could be made. You never knew what you might learn, and you could never know too much about your subjects.

Modesty put the hypodermic away. 'Did he hurt you much, Willie? I'll see to you when we get back, but are you all right for half an hour or so?'

'No sweat. I've been done over with boots, Princess.'

'All right. I'll take upstairs, you look around down here.' She thought for a moment. 'Concentrate on the alarm system, Willie, we need to get round that when we come in for the snatch.' She glanced at the two unconscious men. 'Tonight doesn't change anything. They'll know you had somebody covering you, but they won't imagine we'll be coming back again.'

Ten minutes later Willie had found two electronic devices, one in the living-room and one in the passage. He had also found the control box in the kitchen, and the key for it in Paxero's trouser pocket. He was taking an impression of the key on a piece of soap when Modesty appeared in the doorway.

She said, 'Leave it, Willie.'

He looked up. There was an extraordinary expression on her face, a blend of shock, doubt, unbelief. Normally she showed no emotion at such times, and he was startled. 'What's 'appened, Princess?'

'Something . . . I'm not sure. I'll tell you back at the chalet. But I think the caper's off, Willie. I'm sorry.'

'Don't worry about that. What's the next move?'

'We have to make this look like a robbery. I've brought a

87

suitcase down for you. Collect everything portable that's worth anything. I'll do the same upstairs.'

'There ought to be a safe somewhere.'

'There is. A Bleddoes Miniature in Paxero's bedroom, but we didn't come prepared and I don't want to waste a lot of time.'

'They're good locks but small safes.' Willie smoothed a hand down the kitchen wall. 'This is soft stone, once you're through the skin where the air's 'ardened it. If I can find a cold chisel and club 'ammer in the garage I can cut the Bleddoes out from the other side of the wall. Say about ten minutes. I'll muffle the butt of the cold chisel, so there won't be much noise.'

'Right. Try it, Willie.'

Forty minutes later the black folding canoe glided away from the boat-house and was lost in the darkness of the lake. It was very low in the water, for everything they had stolen, including the little safe, now hung suspended from a rope and tightly wrapped in a sheet of heavy duty polythene Willie had found in the garage. He paid out the double rope steadily, and felt bottom at four fathoms. They were roughly fifty yards out from the shore now, and directly in line with the western corner of the villa. He jerked hard on the loose rope of the pair, and felt the double-loop highwayman's knot pull free. He drew in the rope, picked up his paddle and said, 'Right, Princess, it's there any time we want.'

*   *   *

An hour and a half later Willie Garvin stepped out from the shower and pulled a towelling wrap about him. He had already removed the stain from his face, the dye from his hair, and the brown contact lenses. Modesty was packing his case for him, ready to leave. Whether Paxero's description of the thief would eventually be tied in with the quiet man who had rented a chalet on the far side of the lake was an open question, but there was no point in waiting to find out.

She had changed into a dress for travelling and was securing the strap on Willie's case when he padded bare-foot into the room. She looked up and smiled, but there was still that odd look in her eyes as she said, 'No need for me to go back to the Métropole. I've paid a week in advance, and I only left a few clothes there. I thought we'd drive straight to Zurich, turn in the car there to the rental people, and get the first available flight out.'

'London?'

'Or Paris.' They had a pied-à-terre on the heights of Montmartre. 'Whichever we can get on first. I just want a place of our own, to sit and think. Do you mind if I leave talking till then?'

'It's me, Princess. Willie Garvin. Remember?'

She made a wry grimace. 'And I've spoiled your caper, but that doesn't mean I take you for granted.' She went to him, put her hands on his arms, and rested her head on his shoulder for a moment. 'Sorry, Willie. Now come and lie down while I see what Paxero managed to do.'

He slipped off the robe and lay down on the couch. There was bruising on his chest, forearms and shoulders, and a raw weeping graze across his ribs where the rope-sole had torn the skin badly. Very carefully she felt his ribs.

'Nothing cracked, Princess. I've 'ad worse than this from Siv when she was feeling romantic.'

'Siv?'

'Swedish girl I met in Florida. She wrestled alligators.'

'God, Willie, I don't know where you ever found the time. Now lie still. I'll clean the graze with Eusol and put on a light dressing to stop your shirt sticking.'

'You sure there's time?'

'Ten minutes isn't going to make any difference. They won't even wake up for another hour or so.'

Her hands were firm and felt good. On this occasion his

hurts were nothing, but he remembered the first time, long ago, when he had come close to death from an infected bullet-wound; remembered the shock he had felt to discover that she had sick-nursed him through a week of semi-conscious delirium. There had been other occasions since, when the roles were reversed. That was when he first saw her weep, from weakness. Nobody else had ever seen that. Later she had said that once you'd been lifted off a bedpan by Willie Garvin you were spoiled for life.

She said, 'How do you explain all the scars to your girls, Willie?'

'It varies, Princess. Sometimes I say I was an animal trainer, sometimes I tell 'em I was tortured by the Albanian Secret Service, sometimes—'

'Never mind. Turn over. Ah, he's given you rainbow shoulders. We'll try some Lasonil for that. I wish I'd hit him harder now.'

'Can't blame a bloke getting narked when 'e catches you robbing 'im,' Willie said philosophically. He was wondering what could possibly have happened in the villa to have such an effect on her. Presumably she had found something, but he could not begin to imagine what it might be. Even for him, who knew every nuance of her every mood, it was hard to define her response. Whatever she had found, it had not alarmed her, and she did not seem exactly troubled. But it had engaged her deeply, and he sensed something of bafflement and uncertainty in her, as if she were trying to resolve some rare problem for which there was no precedent.

'Right, Willie love.' She straightened up and began to pack the little first-aid box. 'Get dressed and we'll go home somewhere.'

Six

Two DAYS had gone by, and they were in Wiltshire, at Modesty's rambling cottage which lay in a quiet valley near Benildon. Tarrant said, 'I've been grossly deceived. I believed you to be in Switzerland, concocting some grotesque plot to show Paxero and friend the error of their unpleasant ways.'

He had been at the C W establishment at Porton that morning on official business. Returning after lunch, he had told his driver to take a cross-country route. As they passed a mile from Benildon, he had glanced across to the cottage in the valley and seen the unmistakable figures of Modesty and Willie moving from the stables to the cottage. Now, an hour later, he knew what Willie had planned for Paxero and Damion, but not why the project had been cancelled.

'Grossly deceived,' he repeated. 'And even more grossly disappointed.'

Modesty said, 'I know, and it's entirely my fault. But think how Willie must feel, and he hasn't complained.'

She wore a blouse and skirt, very little make-up, and her legs were bare. As she spoke, Willie returned from taking a tray of tea out to Tarrant's driver.

Tarrant said, 'I'm not greatly moved by how Willie feels.' He passed his empty cup to her. 'Still, if you found it prudent to move out after committing your felony, I'm glad you got seats on the plane for London rather than Paris.' He looked about him contentedly. 'Tea and cucumber sandwiches are so civilised, even if their purveyor isn't.'

'Their what? Oh, you mean me?' Modesty looked at him in surprise. 'I'm very civilised. And you're not usually rude to me like that.'

'I haven't felt the same about you since you virtually fell on the floor laughing when I told you about my night in the wardrobe. You're not civilised, my dear, and neither is that fiend Garvin. It's no more than a thin veneer.'

Willie nodded agreement and helped himself to a cucumber sandwich.

'May one ask,' Tarrant went on, 'what happened in the Paxero villa to make you cancel such a splendidly conceived enterprise?'

Modesty hesitated, then stood up. 'All right. I won't be a moment.'

She went out. Tarrant looked at Willie and said quietly, 'She's a little distrait.'

'Just thinking. She'll tell you about it.'

Modesty returned and put something in Tarrant's hand. He stared down at the splendidly proportioned timepiece with pleasure. 'A Breguet, surely? My dear, it's one of the most beautiful things I've ever seen.'

'I gave it to a man a long time ago.' She smiled briefly. 'This same watch. A sort of farewell present when I retired him from *The Network*. While we were searching Paxero's villa I found this in the drawer of Damion's bedside cabinet. That's why we had to make the whole thing a robbery. It wouldn't have done just to take the watch.'

Tarrant said, 'You're sure? I mean, sure that no other watch exactly like this exists?'

'Open the back.'

He flicked the thin gold disc open and read the inscription. *To Danny from Modesty.* Carefully he hid his surprise. This wasn't quite like her. There were men in her life, and he had known some of them, but he had formed the impression that her way with a man would be warm and generous but without intensity. This watch seemed to belie that impression. It was a very special gift, more sentimental than he would have expected.

Modesty said, 'His name was Danny Chavasse. He

wouldn't have sold that watch, he wouldn't have just lost it, and I don't think anyone could be smart enough to have stolen it from him. Not from Danny.'

'Surely that's possible, though?' Tarrant looked at Willie, who shrugged and said, 'I scarcely knew 'im. Danny left *The Network* soon after the Princess brought me in.'

'All right, it's possible,' Modesty said, and took back the watch, looking at it with a frown. 'But I don't think that's what happened. Call it a hunch.'

'Can't you find him and ask?' Tarrant suggested cautiously.

She looked up. 'He was on Paxero's yacht, on that caviar cruise when it was lost without trace. Until the other day I believed he'd been dead for three years.'

Tarrant sat up straight. 'And now?'

'He may be dead. But I don't think he died when the yacht went down.' She looked at the watch on her palm. 'And if Danny Chavasse had this with him on the yacht, which I believe is ninety-nine percent certain, then how did Damion come by it?'

Willie said, 'We thought it might tie up with that thing you told me the CIA computer came up with. About people vanishing.'

'The trouble is, we can't make sense of it,' Modesty said. She sounded a little annoyed with herself. 'Yet there's something . . . I don't know, something familiar about it.'

Tarrant looked from one to the other of them in astonishment. 'I can't make sense of it either, but of course there's something familiar about it. A man gets taken out of circulation but arrangements are made for it to appear that he's dead, so that nobody will look for him. I can give you three examples straight off. First, it's almost what happened to you and John Dall, isn't it? From what you told me, it was set up to look as if you'd both drowned in the river.'

Willie closed his eyes and winced. Modesty said, 'Oh, my God. That's why I had a sense of *dejà vu*. It's what Willie was planning to do with Paxero and Damion.'

'Which is my second example.'

'Of course.' She shook her head angrily. 'I'm getting senile.'

'You were thinking of other things and along other lines.'

'Don't make excuses for me.' She stared hard at Willie, who looked at the ceiling. 'Or for him, either.'

Willie grinned inwardly. That was a flash from the old days of *The Network*. If you failed for want of using your head, she let you know it. And if she were guilty too, you didn't make soothing excuses for her. She was looking at Tarrant through narrowed eyes now, thinking hard. At last she said impatiently, 'I give up. What's the third example?'

He sighed, and ran a hand over his grey hair. 'I am.'

'You?'

'Oh, for God's sake, girl, don't tell me you've *forgotten* last summer?' His nerves twitched at the memory of those endless days spent as a prisoner in Chateau Lancieux, the small, remote castle in Gascogne, under physical and mental torture. He was believed dead, his body lost in the Gorges du Tarn. Only his assistant, Jack Fraser, had suspected otherwise, and had taken his suspicions to Modesty.

She had found him, but that was only the beginning. Tarrant recalled the painful journey through the complex of caves beneath the castle. He closed his eyes, and saw again the great vaulted cave with the mass of stalactites glittering silver in the lamplight, and the naked girl, greased body gleaming as she fought for his life against a man stronger, faster, more skilled even than she, while Tarrant himself lay broken and exhausted on the edge of the underground lake, watching, helpless.

He opened his eyes to see her shake her head ruefully. 'Of course. We thought you'd drowned in the Tarn. It's the same pattern.'

'Only if you're correct in thinking that your friend Danny Chavasse is alive, my dear.'

94

Willie said, 'If so, what about the other people on the yacht? And the other people who've disappeared? You've got to reckon that maybe they're all alive, Sir G. So who's got 'em, and where are they, and why?' He shrugged. 'That's as far as we've managed to get—just working out the questions. D'you reckon the CIA computer could come up with any answers?'

There was a long silence. Tarrant said at last, 'I don't place a lot of faith in computers. For me, the bizarre situation you describe could only exist if it were true that Danny Chavasse is still alive somewhere in the world. Given that, then I'm bound to accept that the others who are believed to have died when the yacht went down may also be alive. And still others who've vanished singly or in two's and three's before and since.' He looked at the watch in Modesty's palm. 'Chavasse is the only key.'

'Yes.' Modesty reached out and put her hand on his. 'I'm sorry, I'm being a very poor hostess. Would you like some more tea, Sir Gerald?'

Tarrant smiled. Would you like some more tea? It was sometimes hard to recognise her as the girl in the cave who had fought and won, and risen from the black icy lake to carry him to safety. He said, 'I'd love to stay longer, but I have appointments and I'm late already.' He stood up. 'Thank you for the tea.'

When they were outside, on the little brick path with the scent of honeysuckle about them, he said, 'How will you go about discovering whether or not Danny Chavasse is dead?'

She looked across the valley. 'I wish I knew. It's tricky, but we'll think of something. I can't let it lie.'

Willie said, 'Damion 'ad the watch. We could start with 'im, Princess.'

'I don't know, Willie. He won't talk just for the asking, and we don't go in for the persuasion bit. We'd have to trick it out of him somehow, and that's a tall order.'

Tarrant said, 'I hope you won't be angry with yourself

again if I suggest a rather macabre notion which may have escaped you.'

She gave him a quick smile. 'All right, I promise.'

'What you need is an expert with specialist knowledge of the quick and the dead.' He bent to kiss her on the cheek. 'Now, why don't you go and have a word with your friend Lucifer?' He put on his hat and walked down the path to the waiting car.

*　　*　　*

Two hours later, when the New York call had come through, Modesty put down the phone and said, 'Dr Benson says Lucifer's just the same, and always will be. He thinks we can very probably get a reliable answer from him, especially with the watch for contact.'

'And with you, Princess.' Willie looked up from the airline time-table. 'You're 'is answer to St Michael, you're the fallen angel who saved the Kingdom of Hell from the rebellion of the godly.' He thought for a moment about the strange and handsome young man who believed that the world was the upper level of Hell, and that he was its fallen master, Lucifer, Prince of Darkness. 'Does 'e ever 'ave any girls now?'

'No. I was the only one, ever.' She gave a little shrug. 'Poor boy. He tells Benson, his new Asmodeus, not to summon me to His presence because I'm busy about the world doing His work. That's how he covers himself against never seeing me.'

Willie said gently, 'I don't suppose he's too un'appy most of the time. They look after 'im well, John Dall saw to that.' He scratched his nose thoughtfully. 'It's good that 'e remembers, and still feels that way about you. Might 'elp a lot.'

She made a small grimace. 'I hate using him.'

'I don't see why, Princess. All right, you're playing up to someone with an afflicted mind, but you can't change it and you'll be doing no 'arm. And there's Danny Chavasse to think about.'

'Yes.'

'Shall I try for a flight tomorrow?'

She thought for a moment. 'No, two or three days can't make any difference, and I'd like to pack so we can go straight on from there to Tenazabal.'

'The Colliers?'

'We were going there anyway, and when I've seen Lucifer I'd like to talk it over with Steve. He knew Lucifer as well as anybody and he's the psychic expert.'

Willie looked puzzled. 'I'm missing something. You mean Steve can give you a percentage chance on whether or not Lucifer's answer is right?'

'No, he'll have no statistics to work on. I was just thinking . . . suppose Lucifer says Danny's alive, that he hasn't been transferred to the lower levels. We still have to find him.'

'I know. I've been trying not to think about that one, 'oping it would go away. So where does Steve come in?'

'He doesn't, Willie.' She turned to him, laughing at herself. 'Dammit, if we're starting the hunt in a crazy way with Lucifer, we might just as well be consistent and keep it crazy, especially when there's nothing better to try. So what about Dinah? She has a gift, too. A gift for finding things.'

*   *   *

In the early hours of the morning Willie Garvin woke from a restive sleep to the sound of small noises below. He pulled on a dressing-gown, went down to the kitchen, and found Modesty in a shirt and denim skirt frying eggs and bacon. The kettle was coming to the boil, and a filter-cone was perched ready on the large coffee-jug.

She said, 'I thought I'd have breakfast and go for a walk. Want some?'

'M'mmm, please.' He rubbed his eyes. 'You can usually sleep with a gun at your 'ead.'

'I know. This Danny Chavasse thing has got to me a little.'

'Rather I left you alone, Princess?'

'No, I'm glad of company.' She scooped eggs and bacon on to a plate and set it before him, then put more in the pan and poured boiling water into the filter cone. 'What's new around these parts, Willie? I'm out of touch, what with six weeks in the States and your Paxero caper as soon as I got back.'

'Not a lot. I got theatre tickets for two or three new things I thought you might fancy. Oh, and the ballet. If we can't use 'em, Weng'll give 'em to Madge Baker to raffle for one of 'er charities.'

'Thanks. I hope we're here to use them.' She had never tried to stop Willie spoiling her, it was much too enjoyable. 'How's Madge?'

'Potty as ever. Oh, and she's found Mr Right at last. That makes the ninth in four years, unless I've forgotten a few. Now what else? Ah yes, I'm losing Doris, so I'll 'ave to get a new barmaid at *The Treadmill*.'

'Doris? I thought she was a fixture.'

'So did I, but 'er 'usband reckons they can do a lot better in Australia, so they're emigrating. That reminds me, I 'ad a night out with Jack Fraser a couple of weeks ago, and 'e told me a fabulous story about a cock-up made by the press bloke at the Ministry . . .'

They gossiped casually as they ate. When they had smoked a cigarette with their coffee Modesty said, 'I thought I'd go across country to *The Harrow* and circle back by the footpaths. About a couple of hours. Come if you feel like it, Willie.'

'Fine. Give me three minutes.'

When he came down wearing slacks and shirt she had put on a headscarf but her feet were still bare. He was not surprised. She had been into her teens before her feet had

98

known shoes, and her soles were still leathery enough to take any terrain.

As they moved past the outbuildings in the moonlight and started up the valley-side she said, 'Do you remember much about Danny Chavasse?'

'I only knew 'im for a few weeks, Princess, when you gave 'im the job of smoothing the rough edges off me. But I liked 'im. I think everyone did. Very *simpatico*, Danny.'

'Yes. I used him for women, and he was in a class of his own. He could get information you'd never get any other way.'

'So Garcia told me. What nobody could ever figure was 'ow Danny managed to end an affair without getting any come-backs. I mean, it's not easy to pick 'em up and put 'em down just like that.'

He heard her laugh in the darkness. 'He was a genius, I suppose.'

'It didn't show. After all, there were quite a few girls in the organisation, but they never went crazy over 'im.'

'He could switch it on, Willie. But when he switched it on it was genuine.' They moved in silence for a while, and when she spoke again there was a different note in her voice, a slight hesitation. 'Were you surprised by the inscription in the watch?'

'I was a bit.'

There was little he did not know about her past, or she about his. They had never recounted their stories as such, but over the years many fragments had emerged, and there were very few pieces missing from the jigsaws. He sensed now that one of those pieces was about to fall into place.

She said, 'If he's alive I have to find him, Willie. I'd be a cripple if it wasn't for Danny Chavasse.'

'A cripple?'

She slipped her arm through his as they made their way down a grassy slope. 'I don't mean a club foot. But . . . well, you know I had one or two bad experiences when I was young.'

By most standards her whole early life had been one un-ending bad experience, but Willie knew what she meant, knew that she had first been raped when she was twelve—as near as she was able to estimate her own age. The man had been a Bedouin outcast, a wandering mendicant, and for six days she had travelled with him, tethered like a donkey, a halter about her neck, carrying the sack of trash he would set out for sale as he squatted in some village market. On the sixth night she had killed him with a long nail wired to a short piece of wood.

Three years later she had been caught by a flesh gang in Port Said, to be broken in for a brothel, but had escaped after only two days.

He said, 'I didn't know 'ow badly it affected you, Princess. I mean, you've 'ad one or two pretty rough times since I've been around, but you never got knotted up.'

'I can ride it now, Willie, just wrap it up and let it dissolve. We've both learnt a few mental tricks with the years. But at the time I brought you into *The Network* I was an emotional cripple, only half a woman. I didn't hate men, but I was scared out of my wits at the idea of contact. One look, and I'd freeze.'

He stared into the darkness, astonished. 'You managed to 'ide it well. There wasn't even a whisper among the blokes.'

'I'm not surprised. I was running a gang, and they had to keep their distance anyway, so playing the cold efficient bitch filled the bill. But I *felt* crippled, Willie, and I desperately wanted to be whole. So I took the only chance I could see, and briefed Danny Chavasse for his last job.'

'You? When you went away for a few weeks that first summer?'

'Yes.'

He stared wonderingly at the pale blur of her face beside him. 'Well, I'm glad it worked, Princess. Any chance of passing on the Chavasse secret?'

She laughed again. 'There just didn't seem to be any particular secret. All I know is that when Danny switched on, it was total. I imagine it made no difference if you were plain or pretty, young or old. Nothing existed for him but you. And somehow he knew exactly the right thing to do at any particular moment. No hurry. We didn't go to bed together for the first eight days . . . and then somehow he wiped out all the bad times before.'

'You didn't mind ending it?'

'No. But don't ask me to explain that either. Maybe he just switches off, but there were no regrets, just good memories.'

They moved across a plank bridge and began to climb again. Willie was thinking soberly that if Danny Chavasse was the man who had made Modesty a whole woman, then he, Willie Garvin, owed him a great deal. Without Danny Chavasse, nothing would have been the same, and the splendid years past could surely never have happened. He felt a little cold at the thought, and said quietly, almost to himself. 'That's a heavy debt . . . I 'ope to God we can find 'im.'

'Yes. But don't feel bound to come in, Willie. It's not on your slate, you know.'

He shook his head. 'You can see it there all right from where I stand.'

*   *   *

Dr Benson sat in his large and pleasant consulting room, the bulky file open on his desk, and looked with open curiosity at the dark-haired girl and the big fair man with the rather rough-hewn face who sat across the desk from him. They had arrived an hour earlier, when he had been busy with a patient, and the girl had since changed into a red cheong-sam. He tried hard not to let his eyes wander to the length of superb leg which showed almost to her upper thigh, and said, 'You feel this is how Lucifer will best remember you from your—um—association with him in the Philippines?'

'This was how he liked me best.'

'Sure. I believe you were a prisoner there for a while with a Mr Stephen Collier?'

'Professor Collier. Yes.'

'And a group led by a man called Seff were using Lucifer's precognitive powers for blackmail purposes in some way?'

'Yes, but I think you must ask John Dall for any information about that.'

Dr Benson sat back and made a wry grimace. 'I've tried that, ma'am, but he told me to mind my business.'

Her grave face lit in a sudden smile which warmed him and made it even harder not to dwell on her legs. 'I'm very grateful to you for looking after Lucifer so well, Dr Benson. John Dall says nobody could do more for him.'

'My pleasure, ma'am. He's a very interesting patient.'

She took an old envelope and a small pencil from her handbag. 'Is he just the same?'

'Well . . . there's been no change since he first came here. He believes totally that he's Lucifer, Prince of Darkness, that this world is really the upper regions of his domain, and that people don't die but are transferred to the lower levels at his command, when they've completed their work for him here. The lower levels meaning our old concept of Hell, the pit and the fires and the torment.'

'Does he still have his power of predicting a person's death by psychometric contact, Doctor?'

Benson looked a little uneasy. 'It's not part of our treatment to encourage his condition by experimentation of that kind, Miss Blaise. But since all treatment is useless in his case, I must confess that we've permitted a reputable psychic investigator to make several test runs with him. It's entirely confidential, of course. We don't go around warning people that they have an eighty-three percent chance of dying within the next few months.'

Willie said, 'They might not take kindly to it.'

'That's so. But I assure—'

Modesty said, 'Don't worry, Dr Benson. The best you can do with Lucifer is to keep him happy, and if that means letting him perform what he believes to be his Satanic work, then I'm all for it. Does he know I'm coming?'

'Yes. He hides his feelings, of course, but in fact he's very excited.'

'Will this help or hinder his power?'

'I'd say it would help, but we're in a very sensitive area here.'

'How did you let him know I was coming?'

Benson smiled. 'I guess you're well aware that the way to handle Lucifer is simply to give him a bald fact and let him rationalise it in his own way. I simply said that his most loyal servant, Modesty, to use her worldly name, sought audience of him. He gave me a gracious nod and said he was expecting you, having summoned you himself by sending a messenger from the lower levels. Whatever that means.'

She said a little sadly, 'It means that often at night he hallucinates. That he goes down amid the fires and the screaming souls of his lower kingdom.'

Benson looked at her wonderingly. 'May I ask how you have knowledge of that, ma'am?'

'Because I've slept with him, and he's told me.'

'Oh.' Dr Benson looked embarrassed. 'I'm sorry, I didn't know that.'

'Seff ordered it. According to his tame psychiatrist it would either stimulate Lucifer's precognitive powers, or he might try to kill me.'

'You were fortunate.'

'I had to help him rationalise the idea of Satan indulging in a human pursuit, but it worked. He needed a lot of help.'

'I see.' Benson closed the file briskly, relaxing. The girl clearly felt no embarrassment, which made it easy for him to ask the next question. 'Mr Dall has provided a suite for Lucifer here. Do you plan to let him take you to bed, ma'am?'

'If he wants to. I imagine it would improve my chances of getting a good result from him.'

'By a small percentage, at least, I would think.'

Again she gave him that friendly, untroubled smile. 'So let's play the percentages.'

*   *   *

He was waiting for her in the small private garden, wearing black slacks and a flame-red shirt, a superbly built young man with a cap of short black curly hair and vivid blue eyes. As she came to him he extended both hands and gave her a sad smile.

'Modesty. Most faithful of all my servants.'

'I was happy that you summoned me, Lucifer.' She stood before him, and he put his hands on her shoulders. After a moment he leaned forward and kissed her gently on the brow. She felt his hands tremble a little. He looked down at her in the red cheong-sam. She wore nothing beneath it. As if by chance his hand slid down her shoulder to rest on her breast for a moment, then almost shyly he stepped away and put his hands behind his back.

'I have been much occupied on the lower levels, Modesty. How goes the struggle against my Celestial Colleague here?'

'Well, Lucifer. He loses ground everywhere. Chaos multiplies under the power of your servants.' And that was no lie, she thought.

'Good.' His smile grew brighter, and he took her hand firmly. 'You will stay with me for many worldly years now, Modesty. You have earned long rest.'

'Your words make me happy, Lucifer. I ask only one thing. The Enemy grows desperate, and his minions are cunning. If they foment sudden rebellion in your domain, in the next hour or day or year, send me against them. Let no other be your most trusted warrior.'

'It shall be so.'

'I am greatly honoured.' At least she had given him an easy way to rationalise the shock of disappointment when she went away.

He said, 'I have an inner sanctum here on the upper levels, Modesty. We will go there now.' He took her by the hand. 'For a few worldly hours I will put away the burdens that have lain upon the Fallen One since He and His angels cast me down.'

'Again you make me happy. It is good for Lucifer to lay aside his black wings and take human guise upon him for a while.'

Later, in the darkness of the quiet bedroom with the blinds closed, the armour of his paranoia dissolved and he became an urgent, uncertain, rather pathetic young man, striving wordlessly. But this he would forget, she knew. He was less gauche and inept than the first time, but still he needed her guidance, needed the whispered encouragements phrased to make it seem that it was he who dominated and she who was submissive.

Afterwards, as he had always done before, he slept as if drugged. She knew that when he awoke he would be brimming with confidence and a great sense of his power as Satan, Son of Morning. While he slept she took a shower, put on the cheong-sam again, then rang for the orderly to let her out of the suite, and went through to Dr Benson's private lounge in the main section of the nursing home, where Willie waited browsing through a large book.

'What's he like, Princess?'

'Just the same. We haven't done much talking so far, and he'll sleep for hours. I want to be there when he wakes, and I'll try him with Danny's watch then.' She sat down. 'I wish Steve was here. He could always tell when Lucifer's predictions were going to be accurate.'

'He'd fly down from Tenazabel if you asked 'im, Princess.'

'I know, but I don't want to do that unless it's necessary. I'm sure I'll be able to tell with Lucifer. At least I *was* sure but now I'm getting nervous. I wish I had Danny's signature for Lucifer to use as a psychic trigger, instead of the watch. He was always good with handwriting as a contact.'

'Better forget it for a bit.' Willie lifted the book. 'I'll read you some extracts from this, it'll make your mind boggle. Next time I walk down the street I'll be looking at people and wondering if they're the ones who like doing it upside down in a plastic dustbin full of bananas.'

She laughed and said, 'Remember it for me, Willie, I think I'll have a sleep. Wake me in two hours, will you? I've got to brief Benson on how to break up the party.'

'Right.' He looked at his watch.

She drew up her legs, settled her head in the wing of the chair, breathed deeply three times, and was asleep.

*　　*　　*

Lucifer stood in the open french windows and looked out upon the garden, stretching his arms. It was good to have laid down his monstrous burden of duty and suffering for a while.

Modesty sat on the side of the bed, watching him. She knew that he would now go into a reverie, for no normal conversation was open to him. He would sit, stand, or pace slowly, speaking seldom, gazing upon some distant vista of his own imagining.

She said quietly, 'I have a favour to ask of you, Lucifer.'

He turned, smiling. 'If it does not offend the Laws of my Principality, which even I must not break, then it is granted.'

She held up the watch. 'Will you tell me if this belongs to one who still dwells on the upper levels? Or was it owned by one you have already rewarded by transference to the true Hell of the lower levels?'

His smile faded. 'Why do you wish to know?'

'He is a very minor servant, but useful. I have lost trace of him, and my power is insufficient to find him. I fear the Celestial Enemy may have suborned him.'

Lucifer shrugged, frowning. 'A trivial matter, surely. Can the Son of Morning never rest?'

'I'm sorry, Lucifer. Forgive me.' She bowed her head and turned her face away from him. A moment later she felt his hand on her shoulder and looked up to see him smiling down at her indulgently.

'It would be ungracious to refuse my most loyal servant, who works only for my victory in the day of Armageddon. Come, give it to me.'

She put the watch in his hand, and studied his face as he gazed down at it. No flicker of uncertainty touched his eyes. He weighed the watch for a moment, then gave it back to her and said simply, 'A man close to forty, as mortals count time. He dwells in the upper levels still.'

Her mind raced. If his strange gift had given him any other clue it might be important. But she must phrase the question carefully, and not suggest any limitation of his power.

'Thank you, Lucifer. Now I know he is somewhere on this globe I can send minor servants to seek him out. Unless it is your Will to point the way.'

'My Celestial Colleague has long ceased to use supernatural powers in this earthly realm,' he said gently, 'and I have chosen to do the same. Let your minor servants find the man within the natural laws of the upper levels.'

So he had no more to give. She thanked him again, and they moved out into the garden. He was fingering something, a piece of paper, and said, 'This woman . . .' a hesitation, then more slowly, 'This woman I may soon decide to transfer to the lower levels. Very soon.'

He put the paper in her hand, turned away and began to pace slowly across the little lawn. She felt the blood drain from her cheeks. What she held was the envelope she had taken from her bag earlier, in Dr Benson's consulting room, ready to make notes. She had put it in the pocket of her cheong-sam, and it must have fallen out on to the bed. Inside the envelope, on thin airmail paper, was the letter she had received from Dinah Collier over two weeks ago now. It was type-written, for Dinah was blind, but her signature was scrawled in ball-point across the bottom. And Lucifer had always been good with handwriting as a psychic contact.

Trying to keep her voice casual she said, 'Lucifer, did you say this woman was soon to be transferred?'

He glanced at her as he paced past, a glance of kindly patience wearing thin. 'I have said what I have said. No more now, Modesty.'

She sat down on the teak bench and waited, feeling sick. Dr Benson came twenty minutes later. 'Lucifer, your pardon for this intrusion, but the rebellion in Cathay grows stronger.' Benson was rather proud of Cathay, he knew Lucifer liked ancient words.

'I am aware, Asmodeus, aware of all things in my domain.'

'Of course. And you will have heard Belial's cry for help. You will know that without Modesty, all Cathay is lost!'

Modesty stood up. If her mind had not been so troubled she might have admired Dr Benson's enthusiastic acting. Lucifer was showing signs of inner conflict. She said to Benson, 'Let Belial be told it is Lucifer's will that I return at once.'

Lucifer's face cleared, and he smiled his sad smile. 'The struggle is unremitting, Modesty. I will send for you again when the time comes.' He turned away and resumed his pacing.

Outside the suite Benson said, 'Hell, I could almost believe it myself sometimes. Did you get what you wanted?'

'More than I wanted. I'm sorry, but we have to leave right away. Are my clothes still in Room 12?'

'Sure, but—'

'I'll go and change. Please send Willie Garvin to me right away.'

Benson looked at her stiff face. 'On the run, ma'am.'

108

She had stripped off the cheong-sam and begun to dress when Willie knocked and entered. In a few short sentences she told him what had happened. He sat on the bed, the envelope in his hand, and tugged savagely at his ear. 'Oh Christ, not Dinah!'

'We'll go there right away.' She drew in a deep breath. 'Danny's alive, I'm certain of that, but he's been gone for three years now, so a little delay shouldn't make any difference.'

Willie dragged a hand down his face. 'Was Lucifer certain about Dinah? I mean, did 'e really say she's going to die soon?'

'I don't think it was quite that.' She fastened her bra. 'It took me by surprise, and I keep trying to play it back. He wouldn't repeat it. I'm sure he said he *might* decide to transfer her to the lower levels very soon.'

'Not certain, then?'

'Maybe not, but it means something. Lucifer was on top form, and it's my guess that if Dinah's not going to die she's going to come very close to it. Zip this dress for me, Willie.'

'She's healthy, and pretty rugged. But . . . I suppose it might be the baby?'

'Baby?'

'You said she was pregnant. Maybe something could go wrong there.'

'It could be anything. Car accident, lightning, falling downstairs, baby trouble, fever—anything. I couldn't get any more out of Lucifer, I don't think he knows any more. Just life and death.'

'Or a near miss.'

'Let's hope to God that's it.'

'Do we tell Steve?'

She looked at him as she slipped on her shoes. 'No. I've been thinking about that. It can't help, Willie. *We* can't help. Unless Lucifer was entirely wrong, something's going to happen. All we can do is . . . be around.'

Seven

DANNY CHAVASSE was on sanitary duty with Marker, the South African. Two of the big buckets were slung on a long pole between them, and a cloud of insects surrounded them as they plodded from the slave quarters to the down-river end of the valley. There a small jetty had been built out from the bank so that the sewage could be emptied in fast-moving water.

As they lowered the pole from their shoulders Marker said, 'I tell you man, one day I'll try it again.'

'The river?' Danny up-ended one of the buckets, then lowered it by a short rope into the tumbling water to clean it. 'She'll hang you next time, if there's enough left to hang.'

Marker had already tried to escape down-river. It was a suicidal gamble. If a man did not drown in the first few minutes he would be cut to ribbons in crag-strewn rapids; and if he managed to reach the bank before rapids claimed him, the unrelenting jungle would be his executioner. As it was, Marker had been trapped only four hundred yards down river by a seine of barbed wire which spanned the river and dipped below its surface. His body was still scarred by the lacerations. When they had healed sufficiently he had been flogged.

As he emptied the other bucket he said, 'Not the river next time. Kim says they've got those barbed-wire barriers every so often for a mile. I'll hit the jungle next time, Danny.'

They both knew that he was simply talking, talking himself through one of the fits of depression that from time to time came upon those who had not yet sunk into total resignation and inertia.

There was nothing to stop you stealing out of the slave compound by night and heading into the jungle. Without a machete you might get fifty paces into it, once you crossed the bare strip which was constantly cut and sprayed to prevent encroachment. If you had a machete, and were very fit, you might make progress at the rate of a mile a day. But after the morning roll-call the Specials and their dogs would come after you along the track you had spent all night hacking out. You would be back in the compound and lashed to the triangle for a whipping before noon break.

If by some miracle you could get a three or four day start, your first day's trail would vanish under new growth. If you could then find food and water to keep you alive, and strength to keep hacking for another three or four weeks, and you moved in a straight line, without once losing your way, then you might eventually reach the nearest inhabited area, which was the site of New Santiago. The men in charge there were Paxero's men, and some at least would know of the plantation. They would know you had escaped because there was a radio link between the development site and Limbo, but they would hardly be expecting you, because your chances of survival were so small.

Danny Chavasse hauled the clean bucket out of the river and said, 'The jungle's not a good prospect. Anyway, don't say it aloud in quarters, people don't like you too much already.'

Marker wiped his scarred face. 'It's mutual.' He looked along the valley, pointed, and said, 'New intake.' Danny shaded his eyes and saw the helicopter coming in along the river-line. North of the house and the Specials' barracks, the ground rose in a gentle slope to a little plateau half a mile beyond. This was the landing pad.

'More likely Paxero,' Danny said. 'Kim heard he was coming.'

'If I could just kill that bastard,' Marker said longingly. 'And Damion, and the old woman. Man, I'd die happy then.'

'You'd die. We all would. Don't go stir-crazy, Marker.

You might have an accident, like a hoe sunk in your head. And don't try the jungle.' Danny spoke quietly but his tone was not casual. 'The motto's one out all out. That's not just for the sheep and the God-fearing, it's the precept for people like Kim Crozier, Schultz and his wife, and Valdez. And me.'

Marker spat in the river. 'How do you get a whole bunch out, man? You tell me.'

'I don't know.'

The helicopter was closer now, dipping to land. Marker said, 'What about the supply helicopter?' This was the big Chinook which flew in every few weeks with supplies.

Danny sighed. 'Don't be bloody stupid.'

In the early days, before acceptance had dulled the fires of determination, there had been much discussion of plans to seize the supply helicopter and force the pilot to fly out the slaves. The Chinook had been in frequent use then, bringing in building materials and heavy equipment. There were three Land Rovers on the plantation, and a ten-ton truck which had been flown into Limbo in parts and assembled in the big workshop by the river. The truck had been used for earth-moving when the plantation was laid out, and was now used for maintaining the roads, spraying the perimeter to hold back the jungle, and any haulage work too heavy for the Land Rovers.

No plan to seize the Chinook had ever grown beyond the embryo stage, for there was a strict routine when supplies were flown in. Two hours before, all slaves were assembled in their quarters. The Specials, armed with automatic rifles, stood guard on them. The black overseers handled the unloading. After the Chinook had taken off, the slaves were sent back to work again.

Marker shouldered the pole and picked up his empty bucket. 'All right, so we can't grab the Chinook. Are you saying we just go on picking beans and carrying shit till we're dead?'

Danny squinted across the valley. A closed horse-drawn

carriage was coming from the southern end of the plantation, two Specials riding with it as bodyguards. He said, 'When Miss Benita goes, we're all dead.'

'So we wait for *that*?'

'I think that's the time when we grab our spades and hoes and see how we make out against guns.'

'Some chance, man!'

'No chance. We might just take a few with us. But maybe it won't come to that, if we get help from Outside.'

'Outside?' Marker turned to stare at him. 'Christ, have you been in the sun without a hat?'

Danny shrugged as they trudged along the road. 'You play bridge, Marker?'

'Poker.'

'Well, if you're playing a hand of bridge, and you can make your contract only if the adverse cards lie in a certain way, then you assume that's how they lie and you play accordingly.'

'Assume help from Outside?'

'It's the only way we can win.'

'Man, you depress me.'

They moved on in silence. Danny Chavasse allowed himself a brief indulgence in reverie. The hotel at Lanzarote . . . he had unpacked, changed and was sitting alone on the terrace, idly wondering what Jeanne Fournier would be like. It was not important. He would locate her tomorrow, perhaps, and then begin his usual slow approach.

He heard the rustle of a crisp cotton skirt, and a woman stood before him. He stared up at her in astonishment, then got to his feet. Her face was taut, her eyes blank. He glanced quickly about him, then said very quietly, 'Mam'selle! I had no message that you would be here. Has something gone wrong with the job?'

She shook her head, looking straight at him but with eyes not quite in focus. He realised to his utter astonishment that she was feeling some kind of fear. She said, 'No. There isn't any Jeanne Fournier. I'm the job, Danny.'

His mind turned somersaults as he slowly absorbed her meaning. 'Mam'selle . . . ?'

She shook her head. 'No, call me by name. I'm the job, Danny.'

Understanding dawned on him, and suddenly he saw her as if for the first time, no longer the cool, hard, frightening human being who happened to be young and female and striking; those last qualities had been of no significance, and he had been aware of them only as negatives, in that she did not happen to be old or male or ugly. Now she stood before him without armour, without confidence or magnetism, almost without hope, as perhaps no other man or woman had ever seen her.

In that moment he knew that his days with *The Network* were numbered, whatever the outcome. But that was unimportant. The familiar sense of challenge seized him, and with it came the old exhilaration as he felt the currents stir within him, his mind seeking, probing, judging her needs with the instinct that was his peculiar gift and was beyond all logic. A girl, an exceptional girl, probably unique . . . but young, emotionally scarred . . . in a strait-jacket, crying for release. Was there only a husk within the strait-jacket? No. Now that his antennae were tuned to her he sensed a potential response so strong that it amazed him.

Without effort, his entire being focused upon her. The job was begun now, and she would constitute the whole of his world until it was ended. He smiled and said, 'Modesty? That's an English name, surely? Is this your first trip to Lanzarote? If so I hope you'll allow me to—oh, forgive me. My name is Danny. Danny Chavasse. I hope you'll—'

Marker's elbow jabbed his ribs, jerking him back to the present, and Marker was muttering from the corner of his mouth, '*Wake up for Christ's sake! You want a sjambok across your back?*' They had reached the junction with the main track, and the carriage was about to pass in front of them. The Special who was riding on the near side was staring at them. Marker had stopped and put down his bucket. Danny hastily followed suit. The curtains of the carriage windows were drawn back, and they saw the greyish olive face with the skin stretched tightly over the bones, the curving blade of the nose above the small shrivelled mouth, the stringy neck rising from the high collar of the black dress, the little lace cap perched on thick iron-grey hair drawn tightly back from the brow.

The two slaves looked down at the ground and touched half-curled hands to their temples in a servile salute. Miss Benita looked straight ahead. The Special watched them, tapping the coiled whip against his leg as he rode past.

Marker picked up his bucket and shouldered the pole again. His back ached with memory of the lash and his face was stiff with hatred. What had once been arrogance in him had now been transmuted into a dour stubbornness which alone saved him from the apathetic resignation of all but a few of the slaves. Yet he had felt primitive fear as the old woman passed.

*   *   *

When Paxero and Damion entered the drawing-room, Miss Benita was seated in her usual high-backed chair near the wide french windows which looked out over the plantation.

She extended her hand. 'Ramon. It is good to see you.' Her voice, soft and beautiful, seemed out of place coming from the pinched mouth.

'Tia Benita.' He took her hand and kissed her dry cheek. 'You are not looking well.'

She ignored Damion. He waited for Paxero to sit, then took a chair in the corner and settled down with quiet, grave face to enjoy himself. Listening to the mad old woman never failed to fascinate him.

She said, 'I am well enough, Ramon. Disappointment is bad for me, Dr Crozier says.'

'I'm sorry I could not bring you the two new slaves you wanted, Aunt Benita. It is sometimes difficult.'

'You must try harder, Ramon dear.' She had been saying that to him for as long as he could remember, through all the years that she had worked like a beast of burden to keep him at school, to feed and clothe him, to pay the premium that secured him a job in the small import-export office in Guatemala City, and to save the tiny sum which had enabled him, at seventeen, to put through the first deal on his own account. He had bought and sold some timber, on paper and against the trend of commercial opinion at that moment, but it was young Paxero's judgement which had proved right, and he had made almost a thousand percent profit. He had flair, and his judgement had almost invariably proved right ever since. But for many years they had continued to live on tight purse-strings, allowing themselves plain but ample food as the only indulgence. *Eat. And save money. And try harder, Ramon.* He had heard the words a thousand times.

He said now, 'I always try hard for you, Aunt Benita.'

'Of course. You are a good boy.'

'Will you let me take you to New York, to see a specialist?'

'I cannot leave the plantation, Ramon. My work is here. Next year I hope to break two acres of new ground, so I shall need more slaves, at least twelve.'

Damion wished he had more than a profile view of Paxero, so that he could see his expression. *Twelve!* That was a tall order. You couldn't work a mass grab like the yacht business again.

Paxero said gently, 'You shall have them, Aunt Benita. It would help very much if you picked out a large number from your magazines, so that I have a range to choose from. Some are more difficult than others, you see.'

Aunt Benita pursed her lips and frowned slightly. 'Many are not suitable people, Ramon dear. And nothing in this world is easy, you know.'

'I always remember that, Aunt Benita. But today I've brought you many magazines and papers from all over the world, so perhaps that will help.'

'Very well. I shall try hard. Eight bucks and four females would be nice. Will you be staying for a few days?' The two men had their own quarters in the big house.

Paxero said, 'For two days, if that is convenient.'

'Only two? I see so little of you.'

'I have to go to Tenazabal, Aunt Benita, to see the English professor who is working on the Mayan calendar and its relationship to the planets for you. Are you still interested?'

The old woman gestured with a gnarled, workworn hand towards a long shelf of books. 'What a foolish question, Ramon. Surely a study of our own gods is more important than anything else.'

Damion almost grinned, but quickly clenched his jaws. This was a fairly new diversion of hers, which had begun a year ago. More than a diversion, perhaps, for it was now verging on religious mania. He knew, because Paxero had once told him, of that long-ago day of massacre when she had torn the cross from her neck and trampled it into the ground. From that day on, she had taught the boy to believe only in himself. Now there was a change.

'We are Mayans, you and I, Ramon dear,' she was saying. 'For centuries we have been trampled underfoot by invaders, and we have forgotten our heritage. But the old gods did not die. Perhaps they sleep, but if we turn to them again they will renew us.'

Damion detected a shadow of uneasiness in Paxero's voice as he said, 'They were harsh gods, Aunt Benita. It might be unwise to rouse them.'

'Of course they were harsh, silly boy.' Aunt Benita smiled, showing small white teeth. 'They are natural gods. Nature is cruel. Our old-time priests knew that, for it is one of the great truths, once known to us all, but forgotten by most of us today. It is those Christian priests who are to blame. They preach their milksop doctrine of love, yet their followers will tear a young girl's heart out for sordid gain as readily as our own wise ones would do it in the temple for worship.'

Damion thought, 'What the hell is she talking about?'

She sat brooding, her eyes distant. After a little while she went on. 'That was the good way, the way of truth. Let the slaves cling to their Jesus fables, poor fools. The gods are as tigers, not as sheep. Give them blood, and they will give back fine crops. Offer them sacrifice, and they will answer your prayers.'

Paxero said rather heartily, 'Well, the Englishman is at the Tenazabal Temple now, Aunt Benita. I hope he will be able to relate the Mayan gods to the different planets, and then to the old calendar, so that you'll know on which month each is in the ascendancy.'

Damion was well aware that Paxero scarcely knew what he was talking about. But then, neither did Aunt Benita. She had a rag-bag of assorted knowledge, gleaned from the books and cemented into a crazy jigsaw by her mania. He wondered if the English professor would be able to make any sense at all of whatever brief Paxero had given him.

Aunt Benita said absently in her beautiful voice, 'I want you to arrange a sacrifice in the temple, Ramon dear. That will help. The gods have health and strength in their gift, if one pays the blood-price.'

After a moment Paxero said, 'Very well, Aunt Benita. I'll get a goat and see to it myself.'

She leaned forward and patted his knee, smiling fondly. 'That won't please them at all, silly boy. It must be a girl. Not one of ours, of course. A gringo girl.'

Damion held his breath. *Jesus!* How would Paxero get them out of this one? A straightforward killing did not worry Damion. He had been in charge of the Specials when they gunned down the yacht's crew after the big grab, and he had rather enjoyed it, had felt heady with the sense of power. But . . . to sacrifice a girl in some ancient Mayan temple? He didn't much fancy that. It was crazy anyway, and crazy in a different way from the rather stimulating craziness of providing the old woman with her toy plantation and toy slaves to play with.

Paxero had turned his head to stare out of the window. His face held no expression at all, but Damion saw a gleam of perspiration on his brow. He swallowed, then said slowly, 'That would be very difficult, Aunt Benita.'

'Difficult? That is what we must expect in life, Ramon. Do you not remember how many difficulties I myself have overcome?'

'Of course, Aunt Benita. I meant that it might offend the gods rather than please them. We have no true priests now to perform a sacrifice. It would be blasphemy for anyone not initiated into the mysteries to do so.'

She said firmly, 'The act itself will be sufficient initiation, Ramon. The gods will be pleased. It is too long since they had blood.'

'Well . . . perhaps so. But I think we should wait until we have the Englishman's report, so that you will know that the time is right by the old calendar.'

'Oh, but this must be for all the gods, not one alone,' Aunt Benita said patiently. 'They are jealous gods, Ramon dear.' She picked up a book from the table at her elbow and flicked slowly through the pages. Paxero could see that it consisted of lined paper filled with notes in a small, crabbed hand. She rested one finger halfway down a page and said, 'Yes. Before the next full moon would be very suitable.'

Paxero stood up. 'It's too soon, Aunt Benita. There are some difficulties which cannot be solved quickly, however hard one may try.'

The beak of her nose came up like an axe about to fall as she lifted her head to stare at him. 'I see that you do not wish to do this for me, Ramon. I am . . . very disappointed.'

Her breath came more quickly, and her head fell. One hand moved feebly to her heart and she croaked, 'Tablets . . . on the shelf there. By the glass . . .'

Paxero moved quickly to pick up the glass of water and box of tablets beside it. He slipped a tablet into the half open mouth and held the glass to her lips. She drank, then lay back panting. Slowly the undertone of grey that tinged her bony face began to fade.

Paxero's face was wet with sweat. He held her hand and said, 'Shall I send for Dr Crozier?'

She shook her head feebly. Damion watched with uneasy fascination. She wasn't going to last long. If refusing her crazy demand was going to kill her, then the best thing was to get it over with quickly and close down the whole plantation. But he would never dare suggest that to Paxero, even when they were alone. He had once, long ago, spoken lightly and a little disrespectfully of Aunt Benita, and Paxero had hit him in the face.

Her breathing grew easier. Paxero crouched beside her, still holding her hand, and said, 'Now you must not upset yourself, Aunt Benita. I'm sure I can arrange everything just as you want it.'

She gave a long sigh and patted his hand. 'You are a good boy, Ramon, a good boy. The old gods will help those who serve them well.'

'Yes. You can rely on me.'

'I do, Ramon dear. And you will show me?'

'Show you?'

'Of course. You must arrange for a little moving picture to be taken.' She leaned back and closed her eyes. 'Send Manuela to me now, and I will see you at dinner this evening.'

Paxero stood up and wiped the sweat from his face. 'You are sure you are all right, Aunt Benita?'

'Quite sure. Go along and stop making a fuss of me, there's a good boy.' As they reached the door she said, 'Oh, you will be wanting a girl while you are here. I would rather you did not have one of the mestizo girls, Ramon dear, you seem to upset them a little. Just take your pick from the slaves.'

'Yes, Aunt Benita.' He hesitated. 'Perhaps I could take one back with me . . . for the old gods.'

The dark eyes opened. 'Oh no, Ramon. I really cannot waste one of my slaves like that.'

'It would save having to find a girl outside.'

'I do hope you are not becoming lazy, dear. We must all expect to be put to a little trouble now and again.'

'Of course, Aunt Benita.'

When they had mounted the broad flight of stairs and were moving along the corridor to the suite where their rooms were kept always ready for them, Damion said softly, 'Are you going to do it, Pax?'

Paxero lit a cigarette and inhaled deeply. 'Yes.' He paused by a window and looked out at a few distant white-clad figures weeding along the dwarf wall which carried the main irrigation pipe on the northern edge of the plantation. 'They all have to go when we close down. When Aunt Benita goes. One more life . . . what's the difference?'

Damion shrugged. 'It feels different.'

'It's just a gringo life.' Paxero gave him a half smile. 'You gringos owe us a million lives.'

Damion knew then that Paxero had absorbed the shock of this new madness and would see the matter through with the calm ruthlessness that governed all he had done for the old woman. He said, 'All right, Pax. Who shall I send on the job?'

'Martinez himself for one. He's Mayan, and that will please Aunt Benita.' Paxero drew on his cigarette. 'Who's the man who put the induction film together and handles the projector?'

'The American. Gregg.'

'Hard man?'

'He won't turn a hair.'

'Send him with Martinez. He can handle the lighting and the ciné-camera.'

Eight

PROFESSOR STEPHEN COLLIER knelt on all fours, twisting his head in an attempt to get his eye to the viewfinder of the camera, so that he could line up the lens on the long narrow aperture which pierced the rear wall of the temple. It was an hour past midnight. The lamp connected to a car-battery had been switched off so that he could see the night sky through the aperture. Moonlight angled through the wide arch of the entrance, throwing black shadows when he moved.

Beneath the aperture the temple floor was raised in a low dais between the wall and the massive rectangular block of stone which had once been what Collier called the only functional piece of furnishing. When he lifted his head he could see the shape of Modesty Blaise sitting on one end of the great stone.

Collier got to his feet. 'Another reason I hate you,' he said morosely, 'is that you never listen to a word I say.' He fumbled in his pocket for cigarettes. 'It's like casting pearls before swine.' He lifted a cigarette close to his face to detect which end was tipped.

Modesty said, 'Sorry Steve, what was that you said?'

'There you are!'

'What?' She played back the last few moments quickly in her head, registering the words. 'I never listen—? Oh, rubbish, I hang on your every word, darling. You know I do. Everybody does.'

'You tell lies, too. Wait a minute I think I've got a cigarette tipped at both ends here. Perhaps a collector would make an offer.'

'If you'd light the match first, you could see what you're doing.'

Collier sighed. 'Don't you start. Dinah's always doing that to me, pointing out some administrative simplicity that's escaped me.' He lit two cigarettes and held one out towards her. 'Now my vision's gone, I can't bloody well see.'

'Never mind, it'll soon come back. What were the other reasons you hated me?'

'I didn't actually state them. I just happened to vocalise the latter part of a mental train of thought.'

'Well now vocalise the former part.'

'If you insist. I was simply thinking that it's pretty creepy in here by day. By night it gives me the shivers, makes me want to call out for my nannie. But you just sit there on the sacrificial block and it doesn't bother you. I can't stand people who don't suffer equally with me. It's offensive.'

She looked about her. 'Some things spook me, but not this. I expect it's because I'm used to tombs.'

'How in God's name does anyone become used to tombs?'

'I mean old, disused ones. When I was small, and roaming around the Middle East, I used to sleep in them a lot.'

'A fascinating piece for Reader's Digest if you tweaked it up a bit. I Slept In A Tomb For the FBI And Found God.'

'Well I'm sorry if I'm being offensive. Anything else?'

'Yes. You're distrait, you're evasive, you don't pay me the attention my infinite charm merits, and in short you're acting very funny, you and Willie both.'

She flicked ash from her cigarette and said, 'Oh, nonsense.'

'All right, why are we out here while Willie stays with Dinah back at that collapsible edifice they please to call an hotel?'

'You had to come out here, and you were too windy to come alone, so I came with you. That's not acting funny, is it?'

'Ha! Likewise pshaw! Why isn't the Garvin boy with us? This is just the sort of lunatic activity he'd enjoy. But no, there's always one or other of you hovering around Dinah like a broody hen.'

'Broody hens don't hover.'

'You know what I mean.'

'Well, she's going to have a baby.'

'My sweet, I know that. I put it there. But Dinah's a healthy girl who doesn't need fussing, and neither you nor Willie suffer from the old-film syndrome where people start rushing around boiling water as soon as the girl announces she's going to have a baby.' He pointed his cigarette at her. 'You're acting funny, that's what.'

'Oh, rubbish,' Modesty said a little feebly. 'It's just that at a time like this Dinah needs a bit of extra fuss. All you ever do is insult her.'

'She'd be very hurt if I didn't. You know very well I only insult those I love. It's my weird way of demonstrating affection.'

She laughed. It was perfectly true. 'All right, you're being normal, but so are Willie and I. This Mayan job must be getting to you, Steve. You're imagining things.'

He sighed. 'You could be right. The whole thing's a complete dog's breakfast. But the bread's good, as we young swingers say.'

'Does Paxero come here much?'

'Only once, so far. I told him that now I'd started the job I thought it was a waste of time, and I didn't think I'd be able to relate anything to anything in the way he wanted. He just gave me a large cheque and told me to carry on.'

'Did you like him?'

'I was very polite to him.'

'I see.'

He dropped his cigarette, crushed it out and looked at the aperture in the wall. 'Suppose you get up off that excellent backside and tell me if the heavenly body coming into view out there is Mars. Must I do everything myself?'

She slipped down from the stone, patted his cheek, and

moved to the aperture. 'Yes, that's Mars. But even if the photograph comes out it could just as well be any one of a thousand stars.'

'Don't bandy words with me, woman. I'm simply trying to amass impressive data to justify myself. How do you *know* it's Mars?'

'I can't remember how. I've known a little about stars and planets ever since I can remember. We used to watch them a lot.'

'We?'

'That old man I looked after for several years. I told you.'

Collier remembered. During her childhood wanderings she had encountered an elderly Hungarian, a refugee who had once been a professor in Budapest but had spent years in a DP camp after the war. She had taken him into her care like a lame dog, and the strangely assorted pair had roamed the Middle East and North Africa for several years. She had protected and fed him, stolen when need be, fought when need be. He had given her education in return, greedily absorbed. She had buried him in the desert one day, shortly before she settled in Tangier and took the job which eventually led to her setting up *The Network*.

Collier knelt by the camera and said, 'All right, it's Mars. Get your great Neanderthal head out of the way.'

'Steve dear, you won't be able to see it in the viewfinder for another five minutes, so you might as well stop doing your dog-imitation for a bit, you'll get creaky knees.'

He laughed and stood up again. 'Christ, it's good to have you and Willie around. Like old times. Well, not exactly. Dinah and I didn't really enjoy the blood-and-guts stuff too much. I hope you're keeping well clear of that sort of nonsense these days.'

'We always try. There've been a couple of things, but they just sort of happened.'

'That's the trouble with you two.' He glanced about him,

peering into the darkness. 'Still, it's nice to have a hulking great girl with me to deal with anything that goes bump in the night. Now listen, while we're waiting for that idle planet I'll tell you about the Mayan calendar. And bloody well pay attention, because I shall ask questions afterwards.'

'Go ahead. It's something I've always wanted to know.'

'Who doesn't? Well, to begin with they had eighteen months of twenty days each, plus a sort of unlucky five-day spell when the gods made all sorts of nasty things happen if you weren't jolly careful. But the Mayans actually measured time by the Calendar Round. Ask me what that is.'

'Steve, what's the Calendar Round?'

'A fifty-two year span derived from two permutating cycles. The first cycle is the aforesaid 365 days, commonly known as the Vague Year. The other cycle is of 260 days, and this comes from applying the numbers one to thirteen against the twenty days of the month.'

'Twenty times thirteen is two-sixty?'

'Well done, young Blaise. Now, they didn't call their days Monday, Tuesday, etc., because over in England we were still wearing woad and hadn't started to spread the good word. So they gave their days silly names like Kan, Ik, Akbal. And, ho-ho, they called their months Pop, Uayeb and such-like, would you believe it?'

'There are certainly some funny people about.'

'Most are, apart from us. I hope you perceived that given a date like 2 Kan 3 Pop, it couldn't occur again for 52 Vague Years?'

'And a good thing, too.'

'There was also a refinement called the Long Count, which used more and larger cycles, and had a time-span of thirteen baktuns. Ask me what they are.'

'What's a baktun, Steve?'

'A period of 144,000 days. So their Great Cycle came out at something over five thousand years.'

'There's confidence in the future for you. And given all

this, why are you taking a photograph of Mars through a slit in this temple?'

'God knows,' Collier said gloomily. 'I think I want to reconcile their calendar with ours, cross-check against astronomical tables, and see which month Mars was top god.'

'Why?'

'Oh, shut up. Shall I do my dog imitation now?'

'I think Mars is just about ready for you.'

Laboriously Collier got down on his hands and knees again. Ten minutes later their equipment was packed and they were ready to leave. The lamp was on now. Collier took a last look round the temple, then bent to detach the crocodile clips from the battery. 'Torch ready? I don't want to break my neck going down those steps.'

'All ready.'

The temple occupied almost the whole of the square summit of the pyramid, and stood twenty feet high, including the roof-comb. The entrance, a square arch supported by two stone pillars, was set in the southern wall. From the ground, the truncated pyramid rose to one hundred and ten feet. There were fifty-seven deep steps, broken halfway up by a wide terrace, so that the effect was of a smaller pyramid set upon a larger. Collier complained loudly during the descent, theorising that the Mayans must have had legs like flamingoes to cope comfortably with the climb, and that they must have come down backwards.

Fifty yards from the base of the pyramid was their Jeep, standing on the turning circle at the end of the four miles of dirt road which led from the village of Tenazabal through dense jungle to the site of the temple. Each day a section of the road was cleared of encroachment by a small work-force from the village, and the whole length was covered each month. It was little wider than a truck, and driving along it at night was like going through a tunnel.

Collier drove at no more than twenty miles an hour, peering ahead for pot-holes. Low down, eyes of the night creatures glowed and vanished as the headlights caught them. He lifted his voice a little and said above the noise of the engine, 'Did Dinah tell you one of her old companies wanted her to go back and work for them?'

'No, she didn't mention it. What sort of job?'

'Just a one-off, for about three months. Small town in Florida somewhere, I forget the name. It was practically wiped out by a hurricane, and they're rebuilding with a Government grant, but all plans of the underground services were lost, so they want them located.'

This was the kind of job Dinah had worked at for several years before her marriage, this and locating minerals for mining companies. She was not unique. The art or mystery of water-divining had been expanding into other areas for many years. All kinds of enterprises used people with the gift for location now, because it had been found to work with sufficient certainty to make it worthwhile. Perhaps the fact that Dinah had been blind since childhood had sharpened her abilities in some compensatory way, for she was among the best in her field.

She used stiff wire bent at right-angles, with a leg of the wire inserted into a short copper pipe. With one of these in each hand she could detect water, metal, minerals; how she distinguished one from the other she could not explain. But she could trace an underground pipe that had once carried gas, or electric cable, or water. She could trace the run of a sewer, and specify the material of which it was constructed.

The gift had almost caused her death, and not only hers, when she had been seized and taken to the deserted Roman city of Mus, in the southern Sahara, by men who sought the great treasure buried centuries before. Collier still had occasional nightmares, reliving the macabre minutes when Modesty had been matched against the sword-master, Wenczel, in the old Roman arena there.

As the Jeep descended a slight gradient Modesty said, 'Dinah turned the Florida job down?'

'Yes. We want to be back home in England and settled down before the baby's due.'

'How did she get on with that job in South Africa last year?'

'Fine. They paid a lot of money and we made it a sort of holiday. Apart from that, the only work she's done is for me. Experimental stuff. I run controlled tests and collect all sorts of data, then try to make deductions from it, and get nowhere.' He shrugged. 'It's like all the rest of the psychic spectrum, you haven't a basis to start from.'

They crested a rise and she said, 'Easy, Steve, I think I saw lights coming the other way.'

'Lights? They're not going to bring a coach party out at this time of night.' He stared ahead. 'I can't see anything.'

'Neither can I now. I thought it was a car on sidelights, topping that rise about a mile ahead, but I suppose it can't have been.'

'We'll soon find out. There's a lay-by every half-mile, but they're so overgrown it's not funny trying to pass anyone. If you're right, somebody's going to have to back quite a way —what are you sniggering about?'

'Just hoping you're the one who has to back. I love it when you get mad with rage and start sounding off. I only wish Dinah and Willie were here.'

Collier stiffened with indignation, 'Oh, feel free, sell tickets!'

They passed an overgrown lay-by and moved steadily on, but there was nothing on the road. 'You're getting old,' Collier said smugly.

*   *   *

José Guardia, proprietor of the largest, most luxurious and only hotel in Tenazabal, sat in a cane chair on the porch. It was midnight, and he was idly wishing, as he had so often wished before, that his father had not been an idiot.

129

Fifty years ago, when the Tenazabal temple had been discovered, José's father had decided that the tiny village of Tenazabal had a great future. He had moved with his family from Poptún, and spent all his substance on building the fifteen-room El Dorado. The lower storey had been built in lime-stone, but then money had become tight, and the upper storey was of timber. During the building, the population of Tenazabal had grown from one hundred and twenty to three hundred and fifty, and there its great future had halted.

No travellers passed through Tenazabal, for there was nowhere to pass to. It was the end of the line. One road led to Poptún, twenty miles away. A few dirt roads ran out across the cleared ground where small-holdings had been established. The only other road ran to the great temple which had inspired José's father to believe that a new city would spring up on the site of the old. But the world had not beaten a path to Tenazabal. It was still no more than a cluster of houses, a church, a square, and a two-man police station. A few trucks plied between the village and Poptún. During the season, coaches brought parties of tourists to the temple, but very few visitors came to stay.

Five of the rooms in the El Dorado were occupied by José's family. At the moment, to his delight, no fewer than four other rooms were now occupied, for the hotel boasted six guests. Two had arrived only an hour earlier, two men who were sharing a room and had gone straight to bed after booking in for one night only. The other four would be staying for several weeks, José hoped.

He allowed his mind to drift away from wishing that his father had not been an idiot, and pondered idly on the strange ways of Americanos. These four Americanos who would be staying on were even more strange than usual, perhaps because they were English Americanos, though in fact the wife of the professor, Señora Collier, spoke with an Americano accent because she came from a similar country called Canada. José admired her. She was small, with a most

130

excellent figure. Her hair was the colour of honey and her face was very expressive and alive. Sadly, she was blind, but sometimes you almost forgot this, for she moved so freely. José stared towards the church. In the moonlight he could see her now, walking down the centre of the deserted main road towards the hotel. With her was the big fair man who was not her husband, but who had come a few days ago with the dark and attractive girl who was not his wife, and she had gone to the Tenazabal Temple some time earlier with the professor, who was the honey-coloured girl's husband.

Señora Collier and Señor Garvin had spent the time out in the patio, playing cards with a special pack which she could read by touch, talking, and evidently enjoying each other's company. Ten minutes ago they had gone for a walk in the moonlight, and now they were returning. She had an arm about his waist, his arm was about her shoulders, and they were laughing. At first José Guardia had thought it one of these Americano wife-exchanging affairs he had heard about, but now he knew that when they reached the hotel they would say goodnight, and Señora Collier would go to the bedroom on the ground floor which she shared with her husband, the professor. Señor Garvin would wait for the others to return. They would talk a little, then the professor would join his wife, while Señorita Blaise and Señor Garvin would go to their separate rooms. All most baffling.

As they came up the creaking wooden steps José Guardia rose and wished them a polite *buenas noches*, then settled again to his sleepy reverie. In the reception hall, with its two light-bulbs and two unmatched shades, Willie said, 'Feeling all right?'

'I'm great, honey. What with you and Modesty arriving and the morning sickness easing up, I feel human again. How do I look?'

'Sweaty but nice.' He prodded her stomach gently with a finger. 'You sure your old man didn't dream it? You're not showing much for four months.'

131

'I do pre-natal exercises for fifteen minutes every morning before I get dressed. Steve says it's an utterly obscene performance and pulls the bed-clothes over his head.'

'I can imagine. Him I mean.'

Her hand brushed across his chest, then moved up, and her fingers played with feathery touches about his face for a moment. 'You're not wearing your knives, so you're not expecting trouble. And if you were, you wouldn't have come here. So what are you and Modesty worried about, Willie mate?'

'Us? Nothing.'

'You feel worried and you smell worried. You smell like suede feels, but sort of crinkly.' She could identify people by her sense of smell, but usually described her impressions by reference to taste, touch or sound.

Willie laughed. 'It's just the humidity. Does the Princess still smell like brandy tastes?'

'Yes. But there's a touch of . . . of lemon in it now.'

'You're tired, and you're supposed to be sleeping for two, aren't you? Go on, Dinah, off to bed.'

Her sightless eyes looked past him for a moment, and her mobile face twisted in a mock scowl. Then she sighed. 'You're lying to me just a little bit, but I guess there's a reason. Goodnight, Willie. Sleep well.'

She turned her cheek for him to kiss, then moved away along the passage. He listened for the barely audible whistle from her pursed lips as she moved, and marvelled at the way she could use reflected sound to detect surrounding objects and chart her path so accurately. He looked at his watch. Normally he was relaxed and content in Dinah's company, but now it was becoming an ordeal. To behave naturally, in the face of her fine-tuned senses, was almost impossible when you were expecting bad trouble to hit her any day and had no idea what shape it might take.

His affection for Dinah was something special, and it was matched by his admiration. Modesty Blaise shared both, for they had seen the measure of the blind girl's courage and spirit. To be helpless in unending darkness, and to face horror and death as steadily as she had done, was no small matter.

A top Canadian gynaecologist was standing by on call in Guatemala City, and a private helicopter was ready to fly him to Tenazabal. That was the only preparation they had been able to think of. Perhaps Lucifer's prediction had been wrong, but Willie reckoned the chances of that at about twelve percent, much too small a margin for comfort. He shook his head, trying to thrust foreboding away, and went out to join José Guardia on the porch.

José raised a hand in welcome. Both Señor Garvin and the dark girl spoke good Spanish and were pleasant companions to gossip with. He said, 'Will you take a tequila with me, señor?'

'*Gracias*, José. A small one.'

'I will fetch them.' José went through to the bar. Willie pulled up a chair. What the hell was it going to be? Snake-bite? A virus? Rabid cat? He stood up suddenly and went into the hotel, calling to José that he would only be a moment. Upstairs, in his bedroom, he opened his case and took out the light leather harness with the twin-sheaths holding identical knives. He stripped off his shirt, strapped the harness in place so that the knives lay in echelon on his left breast, and put on the shirt again. A rabid cat? Or dog? He would mention that to the Princess . . .

José was waiting for him on the porch. They sat with their drinks, talking idly, sometimes relapsing into silence for a while. Twenty minutes later there was a noise from within the reception hall and two men came out, carrying luggage grips. One was tall and rangy, with thinning sandy hair, the other dark and bearded. They both looked angry. The dark man said in Spanish, 'We cannot sleep in this flea-pit. It is too hot, and it stinks.'

José stood up. 'My hotel is clean, señor. The night is hot,

yes, but it is always so at this time of year.'

The man threw some quetzal notes on the little table. 'It is not worth suffocating to see your god-forsaken temple.' He moved down the steps, the tall man lounging beside him. José stared after them as they moved round the corner of the hotel to the car park at the back, then he shrugged and picked up the notes.

'Not polite persons, Señor Garvin.'

'No. And they do not have the look of those who sleep only in silk sheets and air-conditioned rooms.'

'True.'

They heard a car start, and a few moments later saw it turn out into the road, a dark blue Ford. The rear-lights dwindled as it moved away down the main road, then vanished as it turned left by the church. The sound faded, and Tenazabal was quiet again.

José sat down and said, 'If I had anything worth stealing, señor, I would go to look.'

'Yes.' Willie Garvin's ears were prickling, and sweat suddenly filmed his brow. He stood up and ran into the hotel. The Colliers' room was at the back. He swung round the corner of the main passage and banged sharply on the door. 'Dinah!'

There was no answer. José came along the passage. 'There is something wrong, señor?'

'I'm not sure.' He banged on the door again. 'Dinah!' He turned the handle. The door was locked on the inside. He whispered, 'Oh, Jesus!' and smashed it open with the flat of his foot. The room was empty, the bed-clothes thrown back. Dinah's dressing-gown lay across a chair beside the bed.

Willie moved to the window. It was unlatched, and swung open at his touch. He looked out on to the hired Chrysler he and Modesty had arrived in. Dinah had been taken. Taken while he talked on the porch with José. The men had probably used ether or chloroform, had taken her out through the window, put her in the car, then picked up their bags and played out the brief charade on the front porch.

Willie turned, and the bewildered José shrank back at the look on his face. 'Señor Garvin . . . what . . . ?'

'Those men have taken Señora Collier.' He swung a leg over the sill.

'Taken? But in God's name, why?'

'I don't know.'

'I will call the police station at once, señor.'

'*No*!' From outside the window now, two terrifying blue eyes looked up at José. 'The police will ask a hundred questions, and there is no time. Do nothing, say nothing, until I have spoken with you again.'

José thought of the honey-coloured blind girl he respected and admired. He thought of the two men who had flung the quetzal notes down in front of him. A slow, shocked fury began to rise within him. He thought of the two policemen, whom he mildly despised, and watched as the big Americano with savage blue eyes got into the car. Better this way, José thought. Holy Mother, I would not wish for that one to come after me. Leaning out of the window he said softly, 'Trust me, señor. God be with you, and with the señora.'

The big man nodded, then the engine roared and the car swung away with a scrabble of tyres on the hard-packed dirt.

Nine

COLLIER SAID, 'Something I keep meaning to ask you and keep forgetting. Do you ever hear anything about how our old friend Lucifer is getting on?'

Beside him, Modesty said, 'I was in touch with his doctor not long ago. Apparently there's no change.'

'Hardly to be expected, poor devil. Poor Satanic devil indeed. I've sometimes been tempted to ask if I could run some precognition tests with him, but his line of prediction is rather gruesome. Hallo, who's this?'

They were emerging from the jungle road at the point where it entered the village, and a car was coming towards them fast, flashing its lights. They halted a few yards apart, nose to nose. Modesty said, 'It's Willie,' and felt a sudden coldness under her heart.

He came towards them, dragging the back of a hand across his brow. Collier started to speak, then saw the mask-like face in the moonlight. Modesty was out of the Jeep. She said, 'Dinah?'

Willie nodded. He looked at Collier, then at Modesty again, and his voice was raw and husky as he said, 'It wasn't an accident or sickness. Two men took 'er. They booked in earlier, and took 'er after she'd gone to bed. Christ, I could cut me throat.'

Collier thought he had mis-heard. He saw Modesty raise her hands to press hard against her temples as she said, 'Dear God. I didn't dream it might be this kind of trouble.'

Collier said, 'What the hell—?' Her hand fell on his wrist, gripping hard.

She said, 'Dinah's been taken by two men. But please,

Steve dear, please don't talk now. There's no time.'

'Taken?' he said incredulously. 'That's crazy!'

'*Please*, Steve.' She looked at Willie. 'How long ago? Which way?'

'About ten minutes. If you didn't pass 'em, I don't know which way. I thought they'd be on the Poptún road, so I went that way. A couple of miles out, there's Pepe's van coming back from Poptún. Got 'eld up by a breakdown. He said nothing passed 'im going out from Tenazabal, so I thought they must've gone your way, there's nowhere else.'

'They did,' she said suddenly, and swung round to the Jeep. 'You drive, Willie. In beside him, Steve, quick.'

Collier flung himself dazedly into the passenger seat as the Jeep leapt away in a tight circle. His heart was pounding with fear and he could feel rivulets of sweat running down his body. Savagely he sank his teeth into his lower lip to hold back words. Dinah? *Taken . . . ?* Oh, thank Christ they were here. The Jeep was hurtling along the road, its dipped headlights scything away the darkness. Modesty was saying, 'I'll ride blind, Willie. Warn me when we get to the last down-slope, and I'll take over.'

'Right.'

'You think it's the temple?'

'Can't think of anywhere else, Princess. You didn't see the car?'

'I thought I did, then it seemed I hadn't. They must have driven behind some undergrowth in a lay-by. You don't know why?'

'No. Could be like last time.' He was speaking of the time when Dinah had been seized by the monstrous Delicata, who needed her powers to locate the treasure of Mus.

Modesty said, 'If so, that gives us time. We'll have to make it a quiet approach.' She reached forward, ran a hand over Willie's chest, then said, 'Good. I wish I'd got a gun.'

'I didn't dare wait, Princess.'

'I know. Stop blaming yourself.'

137

After a little silence Collier said in a controlled voice, 'May I speak now?'

'Yes, but there's not much time, Steve.'

'You knew this would happen?'

'No. We saw Lucifer. By accident he picked up Dinah's letter. He said she . . . she might be transferred to the lower levels.'

'Oh, God.' He held his head in his hands. '*Might*?'

'Yes. So there seemed to be a hope of averting whatever it was. We thought . . . a natural event. Not this. I'm sorry, Steve. Sorry we were stupid.'

He shook his head slowly, understanding now why their behaviour had been strange. 'You weren't stupid. Oh Jesus, my poor little Dinah. You think they believe there's something hidden in the temple? Some sort of treasure?'

'Maybe. Quiet now, darling.'

Willie said, 'Going over the top soon, Princess.'

'Right.' She leaned forward.

A few seconds before they topped the rise, Willie cut the lights and ignition. Collier's stomach turned over, for the Jeep went plunging down the long slope in what seemed pitch darkness. Then, as his pupils adjusted, he saw that Modesty was half-standing, an arm over each of Willie's hunched shoulders, her hands on the wheel, staring ahead. It dawned on him that they had anticipated this moment from the start. That was why she had been riding blind, her eyes closed, ready to take over when the lights were doused.

He said to her very softly, 'What do you want me to do?'

'Follow if you want, but don't initiate anything, no matter what. Leave it to Willie and me.'

'Yes.'

They coasted on down the slope. Willie let out a long breath and said, 'There's someone up there, Princess.' The temple entrance faced away from them at an angle, but a light from within cast a diffused glow against the night sky beyond.

She said, 'And a car below. Black or dark blue.'

'That's them. Ah, I got it now.'

A minute later the Jeep came to a gentle halt fifty paces from the Ford. Collier climbed out, then felt Modesty's restraining hand on his arm. Willie ghosted forward, a knife poised in his hand. He circled the Ford, then lifted an arm to beckon.

Modesty said, 'Very quiet now, Steve, and keep well in the shadows. We know there are two, but there could be more, and if we're spotted while Dinah's in their hands it could be bad.'

Before he could reply she broke into a run. He saw that she had kicked her shoes off and was barefoot. Next moment she and Willie were moving up the steep awkward steps of the pyramid together. Collier thanked God he was wearing crêpe-soled shoes, and followed. An awful dread possessed him, and every nerve in his body had become a red-hot wire, twitching uncontrollably. By the time he had climbed to the broad ledge halfway up he was soaked in sweat and the air was rasping in his throat as he gulped it in. He paused for a moment to still his breathing, and looked up, but they were no longer in sight.

Steadily, racked by physical and mental agony, he climbed on. His head rose above the flat top of the pyramid at last, and he was looking at the western wall of the temple. To his right, beyond the corner, lay the glow of light from within. He could see nothing of Modesty or Willie, and could hear no sound.

Warily he moved towards the corner until he could look obliquely between the entrance pillars. Shock, terror, and a vast murderous fury burst like an explosion within him. A bright light from somewhere along the western wall, out of his range of vision, shone upon the great sacrificial stone. Upon the pitted surface Dinah lay face-down in an ungainly sprawl, naked, abrasions streaking her body. Behind the stone, on the raised dais, was a dark man with a moustache which circled down from his mouth to become a beard. He was in shirt-sleeves and wore a revolver in a shoulder-holster. Close to Dinah's head lay a large ornamental knife. The man stood on the edge of the dais, four paces from the narrow aperture in the wall behind him, unfolding what appeared to be a white sheet.

For a moment Collier was powerless, every muscle locked. Then he tensed to lunge forward, mouth opening for some primitive, wordless cry. A hand clamped over his mouth, slim hard fingers driving savagely into the hinge of his jaw. Another hand caught at his hair, dragging his head back. Lips touched his ear, and Modesty's voice breathed with chill ferocity, '*You want her dead? Quiet, goddam you, or I'll put you out cold.*'

The berserk fury drained from Collier, leaving him limp. He raised a hand, patted the hand on his mouth gently, and tried to nod his head. Her lips still against his ear, she whispered, '*She's alive, Steve, but it's tricky. We have to wait.*' Slowly she released him then drew him back a little. In the moonlight he saw her pointing to a small square hole in the wall where a plinth had once been socketed. He stood on tip-toe to peer through, and saw in the far corner of the temple a small camera on a tripod and an open leather case of accessories. Wires ran from a battery in the case to a pair of spotlights hanging from hooks driven into crevices in the wall.

A lanky man with thinning sandy hair stood looking off towards the dais and the altar, which Collier could no longer see. He wore no jacket, and his damp shirt clung to his body. A revolver hung low on his right hip, but it was only there for a moment. A hand moved in a blur, and the revolver came clear. It spun round the man's middle-finger smoothly, seemed to leap through the air and was spinning in his other hand. It leapt again, spun, dropped neatly into the holster, and a moment later was drawn again. The whole perform-ance was completely relaxed, almost absent-minded, the doodling of a man whose gun was a part of him.

Collier was calm now, reaching back for remembrance of past dangers, calling upon the small measure of experience they had given him, striving coldly to shut away all emotions that weakened control. Tricky, she had said. Yes. She was unarmed. Willie could have taken the man with a knife, but there was still the dark man beside Dinah. He wore a gun too, and there was no reason to think he might be less adept with it. And where was Willie anyway?

The lanky man laughed suddenly and said, 'Jeez, you're sure as hell putting on a show for the old girl.'

The other man's accented voice echoed from the dais. 'He said to make it look good for her. You be sure you got a film in the camera.'

'You just worry about the acting, Martinez old buddy.'

Collier's jaws ached from clenching his teeth. Somewhere within his numbed mind an incredible thought was dawning. He took two stealthy paces to join Modesty, and when he looked obliquely between the pillars he saw that the dark man had laid his gun down on the stone and put on some kind of white surplice.

From the far corner the other man's voice said, 'Hey, when they used to stick these girls, did they have 'em wide awake an' wriggling?'

Martinez shrugged. 'Who knows?'

'Those priest guys were your folks from way back, you oughta know.'

'I think maybe they stuck them awake. Better let Miss Benita see it that way.' He rolled Dinah on to her back and slapped her face hard.

Modesty's fingers bit deep into Collier's arm. He stood utterly still, clinging to sanity, and thought with terrible intensity, 'I will kill this man. Somehow I will kill him.'

The American voice said with a chuckle, 'I got a real good way to wake that piece of tail up.'

'Forget it. She is coming round.' Martinez slapped her again. 'Come, *querida*, wake up.'

Collier saw his wife's arm move. Her hand explored the surface of the stone. She shivered, and said in a wavering voice, 'Steve? Steve, honey . . . ?'

Collier closed his eyes, felt tears run down his face, felt his heart torn apart within him. Modesty breathed, '*Whatever I say, do it.*' He had no idea what she intended, but his trust in her was total. He groped to touch her hand in acknowledgment, and opened his eyes. Dinah had lifted her head a little, turning it to listen. He saw her nostrils flare as she took the scent of the man close to her. 'Steve?' Her voice cracked on the word. She tried feebly to sit up. Martinez took her by the hair and held her down. She gave a gasping cry at his touch. He said, 'Okay, Gregg. Start the camera. I'll give her a few seconds to wriggle.'

Casually he reached for the big ornamental knife. Behind him there seemed to be a sudden shift of light, a movement of air, something too fast for Collier's perception. The man's reaching hand twitched, and fell to his side. For a moment he stood upright. Then, astonishingly, he bowed from the waist and appeared to be kissing Dinah's stomach. Collier saw the black knife-haft jutting from the back of the man's neck, the blade entirely buried. He saw the narrow aperture in the wall behind, and knew at last where Willie Garvin was.

Modesty drew him back and said softly, 'Get round the corner, Steve.' At the same time he heard Gregg saying, 'Hey, Martinez. What the hell—? *Christ!*'

As Collier backed to the corner he saw Modesty step into the light. She said in a hard, clear voice, 'You're covered. Drop the gun or—' She hurled herself back into cover as the bellow of a shot filled the temple, and Collier realised she had drawn the man's fire to take his attention from Dinah. He saw her leap at the temple wall, one hand in the plinth hole, finding crevices with her toes, and even as he backed away round the corner he saw her reach the roof-comb and draw herself up.

There came the thud of running feet crossing the temple, and the change of sound as the man burst out through the entrance. A pause. A wary footstep, then a soft thud, a scuffle, the clatter of metal skidding across stone, and a gasping curse.

Modesty's voice snapped, 'Steve!'

He broke from behind the corner. The man called Gregg was rolling away, over the top step of the pyramid. He found his feet and started down without looking back. Modesty was coming to her feet, and Collier knew she must have flung herself at the gunman from the low roof-comb. She said, 'I didn't get him right, but he's lost his gun. Find it and cover the entrance.'

Willie came round the corner fast from the eastern wall of the temple, a knife in his hand. He peered at the figure running down the steps. Modesty said, 'Save the knife and cover Dinah. There may be others.' Willie swung through the arch, calling, 'It's all right, Dinah. We're 'ere.'

Collier fought down the desperate desire to go to her, and looked quickly about him. Almost at once he saw the gun, and moved to pick it up. Modesty was on her way down the steps now, and he tracked back in his mind for something she had said as he sought the gun. 'If it's only me, the bastard just might turn for a quick kill . . .'

Collier looked down the steps, trying to judge distances. The man had reached the halfway terrace already, and was moving fast. Collier heard Modesty call, 'Try me without a gun, yellow-belly.'

The man turned his head for a backward glance, then came to a halt. To Collier he was now a foreshortened black shape against the pale stone of the terrace below. The black shape turned, the head moved as if to peer. Then the figure stepped forward, waiting, and moonlight glinted suddenly on the blade of a knife. Collier felt his lips draw back from

143

his teeth in a snarl of vicious joy, utterly uncharacteristic of him. The man could see only one pursuer. A girl.

She's got him! Collier thought. *She's got the bastard!* He saw her dark shape move on down the steps. The man waited. Then, as she reached the terrace, he hurled himself at her, knife-hand swinging up in a slashing arc.

Collier strained his eyes. It was like watching some strange dance of shadows there below. Her long legs moved with swift easy grace, her body swayed and turned. He saw the gleam of her bare foot flashing out chest-high, saw the man stagger, recover, and come in again. Even when the figures merged and went down together he felt no alarm. His mouth was still stretched in that grinning rictus of hate when he saw the tall man suddenly flung high in the air on the swinging pivot of her leg. The sprawling shape flew clear of the terrace edge, well clear, then turned slowly, thrashing the air, to crash down headfirst on a step fifteen feet lower.

The figure bounced, then began to roll limply but quite fast, step by step, coming finally to a halt only half a dozen steps from the bottom. Collier dragged his eyes away and saw Modesty coming up the steps towards him. She called, 'Any trouble?'

'No.' His voice sounded strange to himself.

She reached the summit, took the revolver from his hand, and looked about her, 'I think we can relax. If there was anyone else they'd have shown by now.' She was breathing deeply, and he could see a trickle of blood running from a split lip.

He said, 'Thank you—' His voice broke. She took his arm and moved towards the entrance, calling, 'All clear, Willie.'

Dinah sat huddled on the big stone, wrapped in the surplice stripped from the dead man, clinging to Willie, her head pressed against his chest. He stood holding her close with one arm, a knife in his free hand, talking softly to her. She was shaking, her face screwed up tightly, mouth twisted, fighting for control. As the others appeared Willie lifted his voice and said, 'All finished now, 'ere comes Steve.'

Collier ran to her and gathered her in his arms. She clutched at him and croaked, 'You . . . all right?'

'Yes. Oh God, Dinah—'

'M-Modesty?'

'No damage.' He found it hard to utter words.

'I m-made Willie tell me. He s-said those men were going to—'

'Yes. Don't think of it, sweetheart. They're dead.' His voice rose, hoarse with new fury. 'They're bloody *dead*!'

Tears began to run from her blind eyes, wetting his chest. She said feebly, 'Get . . . get me home, Steve . . . I feel bad inside. In my stomach, low down. Where's Modesty?'

Collier said, 'Oh Christ.' His haggard face was grey.

Modesty moved forward and took Dinah's hand. 'I'm here, love. We'll get you home now.'

'Stay with me . . . *please*!' The last word was a sob.

'Every second, I promise. Just try to relax, pet. Willie's going to carry you down now, then Steve and I will take you back to the hotel, and we'll have a top doctor here within a couple of hours.' She gave a nod. 'All right, Willie.'

He picked her up gently, and said, 'Want me to stay and clean up, Princess?'

'Please. Any problems?'

'No. It'll be a couple of weeks before the road-gang reaches this end again, and everything'll be swallowed up by then. Oh, you might leave me the spade and machete from the Jeep.'

Five minutes later, as the Jeep moved off with Collier holding Dinah in his arms in the back, he said, 'What's Willie going to do?'

Modesty said, 'Bury the men, clean up all trace of them, run their car a little way into the jungle, then walk home.'

'God, it'll take him all night.'

'Willie won't mind.'

Dinah said in a strained, muffled voice, 'I . . . don't understand. Who were they, Modesty? Why did they want to . . . kill me?'

'I don't know, Dinah. But I'm going to find out.' She changed into top, driving smoothly, steadily, to avoid shaking the sick girl. 'There's one thing, though. You were due for close call. Lucifer told us. A close call at best. And now it's behind us.'

*   *   *

Two days later José Guardia stood in the reception hall of the El Dorado with a long envelope in his hand, thoughtfully riffling through the wad of American dollars it contained. A small fortune indeed. No doubt the Americanos could afford it. They had brought in a special doctor by helicopter, and now the machine had returned to take the whole party to Guatemala City. All the same . . .

Señor Garvin appeared with his luggage grip. José leaned on the reception desk and said, 'I am sorry you must leave, señor, and deeply sorry that Señora Collier has lost her baby.'

'It happens, José.'

'Yes. But how truly sad that she should walk in her sleep, and fall so heavily. It was the night those two men came and went, was it not? Perhaps their going disturbed her, and caused her to walk in her sleep.'

'I had not thought of that, José, but I expect you are right.'

'That is what I shall always believe, señor.' José held up the envelope. 'I do not require this to remind me that the two men drove away to Poptún, and that Señora Collier walked in her sleep.'

'Thank you, José. But keep it, please. As a token of friendship, no more.'

'If that is your wish, señor. And thank you. Señora Collier is a very nice lady. Those two were not nice men. I hope they will not come back.'

'It would be most surprising. Goodbye, José.'

146

'*Vaya con Dios, señor.*'

*   *   *

Dr Kimberly Crozier said, 'Martinez and Gregg went out on a special job ten days ago, and they didn't come back.'

Danny Chavasse put down the bundle of fresh laundry. 'What happened?'

'Nobody knows. It was a local job, at Tenazabal. They just vanished. Damion's looking into it, and the name of your friend Modesty Blaise has been mentioned.' He nodded. 'Yes, I thought that would get a reaction.'

Danny's lips were pursed in a soundless whistle. 'Jesus, Kim. Maybe she's getting close.'

'Maybe. That makes four Specials in less than a month. I just might start pipe-dreaming with you, Danny.'

'Just don't let Miss Benita die on us now. How is she?'

'Not too bad. Paxero's keeping her sweet with promises. If I read him right, he'll concentrate on getting your friend out of his hair, then try to pull off a nice big coup for Aunt Benita.'

'Good.'

'Good?'

'I don't know how much Modesty knows. Maybe very little. But if Paxero moves against her she'll have that much more to work on.'

'If she's still alive.'

'There's always that. But I know which one I'd bet on.'

'You almost persuade me. Danny, I've asked Schultz to wangle it so you draw Dawn for your next bedfellow, is that all right? She's at the bottom of a down-swing, and I think you can help.'

'You're just a medical ponce, Kim.'

The black man grinned. 'So long as it works. What is it you've got in your balls, Danny? Librium?'

*   *   *

In the house above Montego Bay, Paxero said angrily, 'So you've still no idea what happened to them?'

Damion shrugged. 'Sorry, Pax.' He had arrived only ten minutes ago, and was hot, sticky and travel-weary, anxious for a shower and a change of clothes. But he was being careful to hide his impatience, for Paxero was in a bad mood.

Four days ago Collier's cable had been forwarded from Paxero's office in Guatemala City. *Regret must withdraw from Tenazabal engagement. Wife ill. Will return all fees. Staying two weeks Casa Palmera Acapulco if you wish to contact. Apologies. Collier.* Damion had been sent at once to Tenazabal.

He said, 'Martinez was a bloody fool. He could have picked up a gringo girl anywhere, but he cut corners. Went to Tenazabal to reconnoitre, spotted Collier's wife and decided she'd do fine.' He threw his jacket over a chair and sat down. 'They didn't know Collier was doing a straight job for you there.'

'Do you *know* that's what happened?'

'I'm guessing, Pax, but it's a good guess. I talked to the hotel man, Guardia. He said two men booked in and left the same night. Martinez and Gregg weren't using their own names, of course, but that's who it was all right. He described them.'

'And the Collier girl?'

'Guardia said she went sleep-walking, fell down, and brought on a miscarriage.'

Paxero swore.

Damion said, 'I know he's lying, but you're not going to break his story.'

'So what happened?'

'I think Martinez and Gregg took the Collier girl. I think they're dead.'

'And Modesty Blaise was there, with this man of hers, Garvin?'

'Yes. It seems they're old friends of the Colliers, and they

148

were there all right. That's why I think Martinez and Gregg are dead.'

Paxero stared at him, tight-lipped. 'And she was there when the Hillbillies failed on the Dall job.'

'Yes. They're dead, too. She's becoming a serious matter, Pax.'

'You think she suspects something?'

'Suspects you? Suspects Limbo? There's no way. But I think she's unlucky for us, and we ought to take her out of circulation. Aunt Benita would like to have her.'

'Where is she now?'

'With the Colliers and Garvin. I went on to Acapulco and did some quiet checking.' Damion leaned back in his chair and smiled. 'Modesty Blaise goes scuba-diving for an hour every morning. Early. And alone.'

Paxero lit a cigarette, exhaled, and gazed with half-closed eyes at Damion through the smoke. 'And we have the cruiser at San José,' he said at last. 'All we need is two reliable scuba-divers.'

'We're as good as any I know.'

'Yes. I think it would please Aunt Benita if we handled this ourselves. But let's not underestimate the Blaise woman, there's been too much of that already.'

Damion stood up. He was still smiling. 'Hand-to-hand stuff underwater is a mug's game anyway. Too uncertain. I was thinking of a net, Pax. Suppose we go down with a thin nylon net, about ten metres by three. That way we could snare her without actually making contact, and there'd be no risk of drowning her, which is an important consideration.'

Paxero looked at his watch. 'Call the airport,' he said. 'We'll fly out today. You'll have time for a shower if you're quick.'

Ten

COLLIER SAID, 'Don't overdo it, darling.'

It was early evening, and still hot in Acapulco. In the house which stood high on the slope above Caleta Beach, the big windows had been slid back so that the living-room was open to the terrace. Collier had just made long drinks. Dinah knelt over a large-scale map spread on the floor. In one hand she held a thread with a tiny pointed plumb-bob of brass suspended at the end of it. In the other hand she held a slim Breguet watch which had once belonged to a man called Danny Chavasse.

Turning her head in Collier's direction she said patiently, 'Who's overdoing anything? Look, I got a bit shook up, I got a few scrapes, and I finished off with a miscarriage. It happens to people all the time, one way or another, but it's ten days ago now, so let's forget it.' She wiped her brow with the back of a hand. 'All old Collier needs to worry about is whether he's got another shot in his locker. I'm okay, and I'd be better still if everyone would get back to normal.'

Modesty stretched out long bare legs, rested her drink on the arm of her chair and said, 'Yes, but if you're feeling tired—'

'And you can shut up too, honey,' Dinah said amiably. Then after a pause, 'Isn't that man Garvin going to put his oar in?'

'He's sitting directly behind you,' said her husband, 'totally engrossed in the erotic swaying of your behind. And with that micro-skirt beach thing you're wearing, he must have a stupefying view.'

150

'True,' Willie agreed.

Dinah said, 'As long as it keeps him quiet, that's dandy.' She lifted the hand holding the thread with the small pointed weight at the end, and began to move it very slowly back and forth across the map. Modesty and Collier exchanged a glance. She made an apologetic grimace, and he answered by spreading a hand in a helpless gesture.

That morning Dinah had spent an hour with her locator on a series of maps. Now she was repeating the last of six trials on the large-scale map covering a fifty-mile square section of Guatemala, south of Lake Petén Itzá. They all knew that the exercise of her gift stretched her nerves, and were aware that she was tiring now. Her face was still peaky from her recent ordeal, and there was a dew of perspiration on her lip as she crouched over the map, face characteristically screwed up in concentration.

At last she said almost brusquely, 'All right, mark it.' Collier moved quickly to mark with a ballpoint where the pointer rested on the map. Dinah dropped the thread, stood up, moved to where Modesty sat, held the watch out for her to take, then wiped a finger along her upper lip and said, 'I'll have that drink now. Don't let's talk about the map for a minute or two till I've stopped twitching.'

Willie moved to put a glass in her hand. Collier said aggressively, 'Now look here, woman. While you were busy grovelling around for Willie's pleasure just now, I finally managed to construe that cryptic remark about old Collier having a shot left in his locker, a remark which would be grossly offensive if it weren't so absurd. Where I come from, the virility of the Colliers is spoken of with bated breath.'

Dinah giggled and said, 'He comes from Tring. When he first told me that, I thought he was joking.'

'Cast no slurs on Tring,' Collier said coldly. 'In Ivinghoe they regard us as the Reeperbahn of Hertfordshire. Oh yes, and what's this about *old* Collier?' He looked at Modesty and Willie. 'It's laughable, isn't it? I'm exactly three years

151

older than she is. Well, seven if you're going to split hairs.'

Willie said, 'And you always look so young. I sometimes wonder if you 'aven't got a portrait up in the attic, getting old and grey and wrinkled, like Dorian Gray.'

Collier sighed and looked at Modesty. 'You've been letting him read books again. It's a mistake, you know. He'll only get ideas above his station.'

Dinah sat down on the couch, let out a long breath, and said, 'All right. Despite the airy badinage, you're all crouched round that map now, aren't you? So how did it come out?'

'Pretty good,' Collier said quietly. 'One shot was wild, but the other five are all grouped within an inch, and four of them much closer than that, on this river.'

'I don't know whether I'm right or not. You're the theoretical maestro, so you'd better tell Modesty and Willie what you think.'

Collier got to his feet and picked up his drink, then moved to sit beside his wife on the couch, taking her hand. 'Item,' he said. 'Starting with a world map, you pinpointed Central America six times out of six. A hundred percent. Item: moving to a map of Central America, you hit central Guatemala five times out of six. Item: moving to the larger scale map, you've hit the same point, within a few miles, five times out of six.'

He leaned back and closed his eyes. 'Item: you have an absolutely proven gift for certain kinds of location or divining on site, using divining rods. Whether this is a psychic faculty, or whether different materials produce some kind of electro-magnetic emission to which you're sensitive is not yet provable one way or the other. Item: to please your lord and master, you've run a few experiments in long-range location—in other words, locating on a map instead of on site. It seems this would have to be a psychic faculty rather than a sensory faculty. The results of the experiments were very substantially above chance expectation. In those experiments you used the plumb-bob pointer and a small piece of whatever material you were required to locate. In today's experiments you used the same pointer and an object which is intensely personal to a particular individual. That object is the watch which we know was in the possession of Danny Chavasse for some years, but which for an unspecified time has been in the possession of another person, which may have diluted whatever unique essence it is that your e.s.p. works on.'

He opened his eyes and patted her hand. 'However, if your attempts at location were a complete failure, one would expect a wide variety of results on the map. And that's just what we haven't got. You've kept hitting the same spot. It doesn't necessarily mean that Danny Chavasse is there. There's gold in the watch, so maybe you've hit a patch of gold-bearing ore. Or diamond-bearing, because there are jewels in the movement. Or a brass mine, if the spindle or something is made of brass.'

Willie said, 'Jesus, you don't mine brass. It's an alloy.'

'Oh, bugger off, Willie. I can't stand people who know things like that.'

Dinah said, 'If it was a mineral I'd know, Steve. I can feel it.'

'Fair enough. I'm just saying that the way you've kept hitting the same spot is significant, but it may not mean what we want it to mean.'

Modesty said, 'We know it can be all wrong a dozen different ways, but let's have an opinion, Steve. You know better than anyone what Dinah can do, so forget statistics and just make an assessment on what you feel.' Still kneeling by the map, she tapped a finger on it. 'Lucifer says Danny Chavasse is alive, and I believe him. Now tell me what the chances are that he's here.'

'It's shooting in the dark, darling.'

'Just shoot.'

'All right.' He thought for a moment, then shrugged. 'Seventy percent, maybe a little less.'

'Thanks.'

There was a silence in the room. Modesty and Willie stared down at the map. Collier watched them gloomily and felt tension growing in Dinah's hand. After a little while she said in a small voice, 'What's the picture, Modesty?'

'Pretty murky. I'm going to assume Danny's there, which means assuming quite a number of other people are there, and that Paxero's responsible for putting them there.'

'But where?' Collier said irritably. 'That's virgin jungle. And how? And why, for God's sake?'

'*How* wouldn't be too difficult for a man with Paxero's resources. And if you're going to snatch a lot of rich people and keep them alive somewhere, then you're not going to set up shop in Poughkeepsie or Wigan. Somebody might notice. You need somewhere inaccessible, in the middle of nowhere. And it's interesting that the area Dinah located isn't too far from this big development site that Paxero's been carving out of the jungle for years.'

Willie said, 'I reckon that adds a few points to the above-chance percentage, Princess.'

'So do I, Willie love.'

Collier drained his glass and got up. 'All right. Let's assume that Paxero has built a sort of jail somewhere on that river in the middle of the jungle. Every now and then he snatches one or two or more people, arranges it to look as if they've died by accident in such a way that the bodies are never found, and whisks them off to his jungle jail. I agree that all sorts of tenuous evidence points to this. But there has to be a rational motive, so just tell me *why*.'

'It doesn't have to be rational,' Modesty said gently.

'All right. Name an irrational one.'

'To please Miss Benita.'

'*What?*'

'Steve, until now we've avoided speculating about what happened in Tenazabal, but ten days ago two men came out of nowhere. They took Dinah to an old Mayan temple and they were going to re-enact a human sacrifice. One of them put on a priest's robe. He even had a weird old knife for the job. The other man was going to film the scene. They wanted Dinah to be conscious because Miss Benita would like it better that way. You heard them say it.'

Collier pinched his eyes, rubbing them hard with finger and thumb. 'Yes. It's not that I'd forgotten, more that I try not to remember.'

'I'm sorry to raise it now. Does it upset you, Dinah?'

'No. It just doesn't seem real any more. Do you mean that what happened to me is connected with all this other business?'

Modesty paced slowly across the room holding her elbows. 'As soon as we got here I fixed for someone I know in New York to check Paxero's history. It wasn't difficult, they ran a big piece about him in one of the news magazines a couple of years ago. Paxero was born in grinding poverty, lost his family, and was brought up by an aunt. Her name was Benita.'

Dinah heard the change in her husband's breathing, and caught the odour of fury upon him. She reached up a hand and said, 'Steve, honey. Please.'

'Yes. All right, sweetheart.' He took her hand and held it, looking at Modesty, his face pale. 'Do you mean Paxero sent those men to . . . to do that to Dinah?'

'Somebody did. They were doing it for Miss Benita's bene-fit, and Paxero has an aunt of that name who brought him up. There's a record of her death in Guatemala City, quite a few years ago, but that wouldn't be hard to arrange. Those men spoke of her as alive, so maybe she's here, with Danny and the others.' Her foot touched the map.

'But why?' Collier said again. 'I mean, why would Paxero or his bloody aunt or anybody want to do such a terrible thing to Dinah? Or to anybody? It doesn't even tie up with all this rubbish about people being kidnapped and kept alive somewhere in the jungle!'

155

'I don't know why, Steve, but it ties up to the extent that Paxero is involved in both cases and the motive is irrational in both.'

'So he's got a barmy aunt who goes in for human sacrifice and keeps human pets in a jungle enclave?'

'Somebody wanted a human sacrifice, you saw that yourself. And there's quite a lot going for the pets-in-the-jungle theory. I'm not even trying to find explanations, just dealing with things the way they appear to be. But people do have barmy aunts, Steve. The difference here is that most barmy aunts don't have multi-millionaire nephews to humour them'.

Dinah said, 'But honey, Paxero would have to be crazy too, to do things like this.'

'Not crazy. Just totally ruthless and with a strong fixation.'

Willie said, 'Remember Delicata? And Gabriel? They weren't crazy.'

The names triggered in Dinah's memory the sounds and smells and dread she had known during the time she had been in the hands of those monstrous men, and after a little silence she said, 'Well . . . what are you going to do?'

Collier said quickly, 'That's simple. Modesty tells Tarrant, who tells the CIA, and they send an aeroplane over the area you've pinpointed. Then if they see something rum, they take action accordingly. As a matter of fact, if there *were* anything odd to be seen, surely it would have been spotted from the air long ago?'

Willie shook his head. 'It's right off the regular air routes. And anyway, suppose you're flying over Guatemala and you look down and see a building or people or something in the jungle. You just think, 'allo, there's some sort of project going on down there, and then you forget it.'

Modesty said, 'You can also forget about the CIA sending a plane over. They're in enough trouble already for sticking their fingers in the affairs of other countries.'

Collier got up and moved to where she stood leaning against the side of the long window, gazing out over the balcony to the sea beyond. He took her none too gently by the shoulders and turned her to face him. 'All right. So you and Willie fly over and have a look for yourselves. Take cameras, and shoot film of whatever you find. Maybe you'll get a shot of Paxero's barmy aunt and her jailbirds doing whatever it is they do. Then you pass it to Tarrant or the CIA, and they can pass it on to the Guatemalan Government, and that's that.'

She said, 'Dinah, did you know his nose twitches when he's angry?'

'Never mind my nose, just listen to what I'm saying.'

'I did and it won't work, Steve. Paxero's the biggest man in the country, with enormous influence inside the government.'

'He couldn't head them off from a thing like this indefinitely, once they had an official enquiry from a foreign power.'

'He can do it for long enough.'

'Don't talk in bloody riddles. Long enough for what?'

Willie said, 'If Paxero's got some weird kind of operation going, then it's dead certain he'll 'ave ready-made plans for wrapping it up quick if something goes wrong. If Danny Chavasse is there, if other people are there, then Paxero can't let 'em live to tell the tale. They're dead at the first whisper. Dead and gone.'

Collier let his hands fall from Modesty's shoulders and turned wearily away. In silence he poured himself a fresh drink, then moved to sit down beside his wife again. He drank deeply, and said, 'How do you plan to play it?'

'We haven't had time to talk much about it.'

'You and Willie hardly need to talk, and anyway, you've had plenty of time between Dinah's session this morning and her check performance just now.'

'Well . . . we thought we'd go in two different ways. It's

157

safer, when you don't have any idea what the score is. So Willie aims to go in on foot from British Honduras.'

'Through the same kind of jungle we saw all around Tenazabal? Oh, don't be ridiculous.'

'He'll manage.'

'And what do you do? Tunnel your way in from Mexico?'

A little laugh exploded from her. 'I love you when you're all bitter and twisted. No, I'm hoping to go in the way we think a lot of other people have gone in.'

Collier blinked. 'Construe that for the simple-minded.'

Dinah said, 'I guess Modesty's hoping they'll snatch her.'

'Jesus Christ! Why the hell should they do that?'

Modesty said, 'I think I'm a candidate. They tried to grab me with John Dall in Idaho. I told you.'

'But that wasn't necessarily the same lot, Paxero's lot.'

'I'm quite sure it was, Steve.'

'All right, why should they try for you again?'

'For the same reason they tried before, whatever that might be. Maybe to please Miss Benita.'

'And that's your present ambition?'

'I'm hoping. If we're guessing right, then Paxero will already know that Willie and I were at Tenazabal with you. He probably knows we're here with you now.' She frowned. 'I'm a little disappointed he hasn't already shown up on the pretence of persuading you to go back to the job in Tenazabal.'

Collier lifted a hand that was not quite steady, and pointed at her. '*That's* why you've been scuba-diving alone every morning! You're setting yourself up to be kidnapped!'

'I wanted to establish a pattern, and it offers him an easy snatch, Steve.'

'God Almighty, you're raving mad. If what you believe about Paxero is right, you've already knocked off four of his men, two in Idaho and two in the temple! How do you know he won't just kill you?'

'Well, I can't ask him for guarantees, darling, but I'm

pretty sure that if he makes a move it'll only be to snatch me.'

Collier rubbed his brow. 'And then you go down the pipe-line to . . .' he nodded towards the map on the floor, 'to whatever's there?'

'I hope so.' She moved from the window. 'Don't look so fraught, Steve. I keep adding up everything we know, and I honestly believe there's a better than eighty percent chance that it'll work out the way I've said. If I'm snatched.'

'And then what?'

'Willie's rigged a miniature transmitter, small enough to go in one of those plastic containers for shaving-sticks. But it's got enough power to squirt out a signal for a couple of minutes every day for three or four weeks, so he'll be able to home-in on me when he's on the last few miles.'

'I meant what happens after you get there? And after Willie gets there? If you both do.'

She paused behind the couch and put a hand on his shoulder. 'How can I answer that? It depends on what we find. I do wish you wouldn't worry so. It's making a little bald bit, just there.' She dropped a kiss on top of his head.

'Worry? Who's worrying? And don't think you can get round me by wiping your nose on my head.' Collier leaned forward, picked up his drink, drained it, then clapped his hands together and said in a brisk, bright voice, 'Well, how about a flutter at the casino after dinner? I've been bending my amazing mathematical brain to the task of devising a system.'

Willie said, 'For winning or losing?'

'That's right, sneer at your betters. A winning system, you bird-brained Cockney sod.'

Dinah touched his arm. 'Don't Steve. Willie might not understand.'

Willie gave a half-suppressed snort of amusement. 'What's the system?'

'You bet on even chances, of course. All you need, if

159

you're on five-dollar stakes, is a capital of a quarter million, and if you play for three days without missing a spin, you come out with a certain profit of anything from twenty-five bucks upwards.' Collier stood up. 'I'm now going to have a shower and then sulk for a bit, but if everybody keeps coaxing me and making a fuss of me I might well resume my endearing ways before the evening's out.'

Dinah said in a low voice, 'I hope it never happens.'

'My darling, I *need* a shower—'

'Oh, stop it, Steve. I mean about Paxero coming, and Modesty, and . . . everything.'

Collier paused in the doorway. 'Ah, yes. On that point I have some information to convey. You may remember that I took a phone call just after we returned from besporting ourselves in the ocean, when the rest of you had pre-empted all the loos and left me writhing in agony in the hall.' He smiled brightly. 'It was from Paxero's office. He's arriving here tomorrow, hopes Mrs Collier is fully recovered, and would like to call on us briefly while he's in Acapulco.'

*   *   *

Shortly after midnight, Modesty and Willie stood on the terrace looking out idly over a silver sea. It was half-an-hour since they had returned from the casino. Modesty wore a silver lamé blouse and black trousers, Willie a dark maroon tuxedo.

She said quietly, 'I won't have you go alone, Willie.'

'I'll manage, Princess. I can get all the gear together in twenty-four hours.'

'I know, but let's not throw away first principles until we have to. You don't climb mountains alone, you don't go into jungle alone.'

'You don't go scuba-diving alone, unless you're looking for trouble.'

'I'm looking for Paxero to try something there. But going

160

into the jungle alone is something else. I want you to have someone we can rely on, Willie, someone we know and who knows us.'

'They're not all that thick on the ground.'

'I know. I thought of Paul Hagan, but he's married now. Is there anyone who comes to mind from the old *Network*? Krolli? Franklin? Molinet?'

'I'd rather 'ave one of Tarrant's people, Princess.'

'I'm sure he'll play. Which one?'

'Don't think I've flipped, but I'd like Maude Tiller.'

She gazed absently out at the silver-purple merging of sky and sea for a full minute without speaking. Then, 'You're not trying to do two jobs at the same time, Willie?'

'Therapy for Maude? No, that'd be stupid. Oh, it might do Maude a bit of good, but that's not the reason I'm suggesting 'er. There's several really. For one, she's done a jungle survival course in Brunei, with the Ghurkas.'

'Maude?'

'Yes. Tarrant goes in for broad-based training. Rokesby was telling me, at *Three Meadows*. He'll attach an agent to some service unit that's on an initiative test or a survival course. Might be in the desert, the arctic or the jungle. Maude was jungle.'

'Well . . . that helps.'

'We know 'er well, Princess, we've worked with 'er before.'

'Yes. She's good, Willie. But this trip through the Petén jungle is going to be a fair imitation of hell, and Maude's a girl.'

He smiled. 'So are you.'

'Yes, but . . .' She grimaced. 'Maude's always been a girl. I grew up as a kind of hermaphrodite polecat, all sharp teeth and claws.' She gave a half laugh. 'It hardly dawned on me that I was a girl until I looked down one day and found I was growing knockers. But I went on being just as mean and nasty and bloody-minded as before. So I'm sort of different.'

She touched his hand as it lay on the balustrade. 'Not better. Worse if anything, but different.'

Willie looked at her curiously, but in the semi-darkness it was hard to judge expression from her profile. He said, 'I'm not saying she's you, Princess. But she's got your kind of fibre. She won't slow me down, she won't let me down, and she won't give up.' He tapped a finger to his chest. 'Maude's got stamina in 'ere, where it counts.'

She rested her chin on her hand and said nothing, but gazed broodingly out to sea. After a little while Willie said, 'You reckon we ought to think of somebody else?'

She turned her head to look at him, and there was sudden surprised laughter in her eyes. 'No. You're right, all along the line. But it's just hit me—for the first time ever I'm a bit jealous. How about that?'

He understood at once. Because of all they had been to each other in the years past, they were in many ways much closer and more intimately a part of each other than any physical relationship could have made them. You could sleep together, and a day or a year or five years later you could hate each other. But when the bonds of total trust had been forged, strand by steel strand, in the fires of hardship, danger, and eyeball-to-eyeball encounters with death, then those bonds remained unbreakable this side of the grave. And in a sense, Maude Tiller would be invading ground that was their joint and most precious possession.

Willie said, 'I 'adn't thought of that, Princess, but it figures. I expect I'd feel a bit funny if it was the other way round.'

'Good.' She punched him gently on the arm. 'But now forget it. I'll be in touch with Tarrant first thing tomorrow and ask for Maude.' She thought for a moment. 'Yes. I like it, Willie. She won't want any concessions for being female. I think it's one of your better ideas.'

'There's one other thing, Princess.' He rubbed his chin and looked sombrely out over the sea. 'If we're right, you're going to disappear sometime soon, missing believed drowned. And Paxero's going to be around—before it 'appens, certainly. After, maybe. Do you reckon Steve and Dinah can put on the right sort of act for 'im?'

'Steve will be great, but keep Dinah out of the way.'

'Right.'

'You think you can do the trip in three weeks, Willie?'

'Count on it.'

'By then I'll have had time to find out all about what's going on. I'll wait for you to make contact.' She put a hand to his cheek. 'Now don't *you* start looking worried.'

He gave a wry laugh. 'Sorry. I'll be okay once it all gets going.' But Willie Garvin knew he would not. It was impossible to avoid speculating on what might be going on out there in the jungle. His worst imagining was of a crazy old woman who believed herself to be the re-incarnation of a Mayan priestess, so Paxero had built her a temple in the jungle and was feeding her people to sacrifice. It was a wild fantasy, he knew, but would the truth be any less bizarre? He carefully nourished three small seeds of comfort. First, he believed that Danny Chavasse was still alive, three years after his disappearance. Second, he had learnt from Collier that the Mayans did not go in for priestesses. And third, the girl who stood relaxed beside him, subtly fragrant, powerfully feminine, had a capacity for survival that put her in a class of her own.

*   *   *

Dinah sat at the dressing-table, hands resting in her lap, wearing a wispy white night-dress. She had finished cleansing her face and brushing her hair several minutes ago. Collier lay on the bed, hands behind his head. He had passed through the bad phase and felt almost himself again, resigned rather than angry, hoping rather than fearing.

He said softly, 'Hey lady, I don't half love you. Come and have a cuddle.'

163

'In a little while, honey. I want to see Willie first.'

'They've gone to bed.'

'No, I haven't heard the sounds yet. They're still on the terrace.' She tilted her head, listening. 'That's the window sliding shut. I guess they'll be up in a minute.'

Collier sighed. 'It won't be any use, darling. You just have to sit back and hope for the best.'

'There's something I want to say to him.'

'You can apologise for me while you're about it.'

'You make your own apologies, buster. You were a real bastard this evening. Every time you opened your mouth, poison-darts came out.'

'It was a purgative, my sweet. Castor oil for the mental bowels. Besides, the last thing they want is for us to agonise over them.'

'You didn't have to ask Willie if you could have his tuxedo altered to fit you, against the probability that he wouldn't be needing it any more.'

'Darling, they *expect* such things of me. Fool's licence.'

She nodded a little tiredly. 'Sorry. I didn't mean to go on at you.' She rose, and moved to pick up her robe. 'Do I look all right?'

This was the automatic check-phrase she used half-a-dozen times a day. Collier grinned and said, 'If Willie complains, refer him to me.'

She half smiled, pulled on her robe, and moved without hesitation to the door, skirting the armchair in her path. Ten seconds later she was tapping on the door of Willie's room. As she entered at his call she smelt tooth-paste and heard the swish of water as he rinsed his mouth.

''Allo, Dinah. I thought it was Steve.'

'Can I talk for a minute?'

'Sure. Come an' sit down.' His hand took her arm. 'This way.'

She felt the bed give as he sat down beside her, and turned her head in his direction. 'Willie, do me a big favour.'

164

'If I can, love.' There was a hint of wariness in his voice.
'Persuade Modesty to drop it. She'll listen to you.'

She felt him pick up her hand. 'Dinah, you know I can't do that.'

'Please, Willie. Look, what happened in Tenazabal was done to *me*. You say Paxero was behind it, but I don't care who it was. I don't want you and Modesty going after them. I don't want any scores paid off. I just want to go home with Steve, and I want you and Modesty to go home and . . . and be safe. You're our very special friends. Oh, I know we don't live in each other's pockets, but you can't realise what it means to Steve and to me just to know you're . . . there.'

'We're not out to chop Paxero down, Dinah. We're just trying to find out what's 'appened to a lot of people who've gone missing.'

'If you're right, then do as Steve said, hand it to Tarrant or the CIA or somebody like that.'

'Big organisations can foul things up.'

'That's *their* problem! It's not yours or Modesty's. It's not your business.'

'Danny Chavasse is our business, love.' She was silent, and her shoulders sagged a little. He went on, 'Danny's important to the Princess, so that makes 'im important to me.' He took her by the arms, turning her gently to face him. 'Remember Panama? When I got you away from Gabriel, and 'e had a big team out looking for us? Remember I called Modesty . . . and she came? Now, suppose we thought Steve was in some crazy sort of jungle jail. Or you. I mean, instead of Danny. Would you want anyone to tell us it wasn't our business?'

After a long silence she said meekly, 'All right, Willie. Please be careful.' She groped for his face, kissed him, then stood up. As he guided her to the door he said, 'How's Steve?'

'All right now. He's just kind of switched off.'

'You do the same. Otherwise you'll get worry-wrinkles,

and then you won't be the most beautiful girl in the world any more.'

'We certainly can't have that.' She gave him an effortful smile. 'Goodnight, Willie.'

As she came into the bedroom Collier lifted his head and said, 'You don't have to tell me. He pitched you a load of schmaltz about Danny Chavasse.'

She picked up his mood. 'You hit it, tiger. Dear old pals. Hearts and flowers.'

'Ridiculous.'

'So naïve.'

'What are friends *for* if you can't let them down?'

'That's what I always say.'

She took off her robe, moved to the bed and lay down beside him, huddling close with an arm across his chest and her head on his shoulder. For a while they were silent, and then he said thoughtfully, 'Something important occurred to me while you were gone. I almost trotted along to tell Modesty right away, but then I thought the whole scene here was beginning to look like a French bedroom farce.'

'What was it you thought of?'

'Well, she said she'd be taking a miniature transmitter in a shaving-stick thing.'

'For Willie to home-in on. Yes.'

'But she expects to be grabbed while she's scuba diving. That means she'll end up with nothing but the swimsuit she's wearing, so she'll have nowhere to hide the damn thing.'

He felt Dinah's shoulders twitch slightly. She said, 'I wouldn't bother to mention it, honey.'

'But it's a point she's overlooked. And Willie too.'

'I doubt it.'

'My sweet, they must have done. Where on earth can she hope to hide the thing? I know it's small, but—are you crying?'

'No.' Her voice was muffled, her face pressed into his shoulder. 'More sort of laughing. I'm sorry, but you're so lovely and dense sometimes. I bet you'd score zero on those aptitude tests where you have to fit shapes together.'

'I fail to see—' Collier stopped, thought for a while, then said, 'Oh. Yes. That facility had escaped me.' He lifted his head and said with asperity, 'All right, but I hope you're not planning to convulse the company at breakfast with my alleged obtuseness.'

She gave a smothered snort and nibbled his shoulder. 'You haven't got a hope, buster. We're going to be short of laughs for quite a while, and this one's too good to waste.'

* * *

Three days later, in a Whitehall office, Tarrant looked grimly across his desk at Maude Tiller. 'Furthermore,' he said, 'I was confined in that wardrobe for several hours, believing myself to have been inextricably involved in a jewel-theft. I then suffered the indignity and humiliation of being released by an accomplice of your friend Garvin, and given this note.'

Maude's hand shook visibly as she reached out to take it. Her cheeks had become strangely hollow during the last few moments, and Tarrant was certain she was biting them inside to prevent an explosion of astonished laughter. She read the note, and her pursed lips drew even more tightly together, so that when she looked at him again it was from wide eyes in a clownish face. She seemed to be having difficulty in breathing—and was, since she dared not relax her diaphragm.

Tarrant said with a baleful glare, 'I shall assume you had no part in this disgraceful and distasteful prank. I shall also assume that you are distressed and horrified by it.'

Maude nodded vigorously, dragged in an agonised breath through her nose, and contrived to say, 'Yizzir,' without opening her lips more than a hair's-breadth.

'Very well.' Tarrant leaned back in his chair. 'I've recalled you from leave because I have an urgent job for you to do. You'll leave for Belize this evening. Go and see Mr Fraser now, and he'll brief you. That's all.'

'Thangyuzzir.' She turned away, and almost broke into a run. When the door had closed behind her, Tarrant relaxed and allowed himself to smile. Then he thought about Modesty Blaise, and the smile faded.

In Fraser's office, Maude staggered to a chair and collapsed against it, clutching the arm and doubling up in a painful release of mirth. Fraser looked at her over the top of his spectacles, then went on writing a memo in his neat, precise hand.

Two minutes later he looked up again and said, 'Feeling better now, Maude?'

'Yes.' She took a tissue from her handbag and wiped wet cheeks. 'Yes thank you, Mr Fraser. Sorry, but I just couldn't help it.' She gestured towards Tarrant's office. 'You . . . know what Willie did?'

He took off his spectacles and looked at her primly. 'Yes. But it stops here.'

'Yes, sir.' She was not deceived by Fraser's manner. It had been his cover persona during many years as an agent in the field, but behind it was a very hard, competent man. She took a mirror from her handbag and let out a gusty sigh. 'Oh, my God. Do you mind if I do a face-repair?'

'Go ahead. Then read this.' He pushed a file across the desk towards her.

Ten minutes later she rose from the armchair and put the file on his desk. Her face was quiet and her manner sober now. She said, 'Modesty and Willie really believe Paxero has something going on there in the Petén?'

'If that's not clear from the file, then I'm losing my grip.'

'I'm sorry, Mr Fraser. Of course it's clear. Does Sir Gerald agree with them, or is he sending me on spec?'

'He thought their deductions were tenuous, but he respects their hunches, so he was going to send you anyway.'

'Anyway?'

'Even before we had word yesterday that Modesty Blaise failed to surface when scuba-diving off Acapulco.'

Maude stared. 'So she was right, and Paxero's got her?'

'Let's hope so,' Fraser said dryly. 'And if so, let's hope she's being taken to the place she believes she's being taken to, and that she's still alive when you and Willie get there, if you and Willie get there.'

'He asked for me?'

'Specifically. And with Modesty's concurrence, I've no doubt.'

'That's quite a compliment.'

'They're not concerned with paying compliments, Maude. You'd better get along to Medical now. Then off you go to Belize. Good luck.'

She hesitated. 'Won't you be briefing me, Mr Fraser?'

'I have. Willie Garvin meets you at Belize. From then on you do what he tells you to.'

When she had left the office Fraser sat polishing his spectacles, wondering idly if she would come back. He hoped so, but sometimes they didn't. He had been one of the lucky ones himself. Even after several years behind his desk he still found it odd to be the one saying 'Good luck' instead of the one being wished it.

Nice girl, Maude. He hoped she wouldn't stay in the game too long, if she hadn't done so already. He settled his spectacles on his nose, picked up his pen, and forgot her.

Eleven

MODESTY BLAISE sat slumped in her seat, watching the un-mapped jungle below through half-closed eyes. Her head ached dully, partly from the effect of soporific drugs and partly as a result of the blow which had left her with a swollen cheek and a slit over the cheekbone.

To avoid suspicion it had been necessary to make a convincing attempt at resistance when opportunity offered, and she had done so as they were transferring her from the ship to the helicopter off Playa Grande two hours before. One of the crew had suffered a broken wrist. It was Damion who had hit her, and she now knew that he was very quick and very strong. She suspected the same could be said of Paxero.

They sat opposite her, in the two aft-facing seats of the Bell Long Ranger. The pilot's name was Jason. There was no co-pilot. One end of a thin nylon cord was noosed about her neck, the other end fastened somewhere behind the seat. Her wrists were handcuffed. She wore monk sandals, a thin yellow sweater too small for her, and a grey skirt too big for her, all provided by Damion. Beneath was the swimsuit she had been wearing when they netted her under the sea off Acapulco, thirty hours before.

She supposed that they were keeping silent as part of a general design to let uncertainty nourish fear, and sap her nerves. For a time she had considered the merits of showing agitation, asking questions, becoming in turn shrill, indignant, pleading. But withdrawal was far easier, and perhaps more plausible in a woman they suspected of having put down four very capable hirelings of theirs in recent weeks.

Now that she was launched upon her task she had slipped into a mental posture that contained elements of the mystical. Certain areas of emotion were virtually inert, and though she would be aware of fear, apprehension, concern, anxiety, and all the emotional weakeners, they would be heavily damped down. Other areas were finely tuned to heighten perception, sensitivity, and judgment. There was no conscious effort in achieving this mental posture. The ability had evolved within her during the enormously receptive years of childhood, and was now a part of her essential fabric.

Looking down, she saw a silver thread of river twisting frenziedly through the solid green jungle, and for a moment or two she thought idly of Willie and Maude. They would be on their way by now. A hard, brutal way, coming in across the remote border from British Honduras. The jungle could kill very efficiently and in many ways. But that was their problem, and no effort of hers could help. For the present, the immediate present, she had no problems. They would emerge soon, but until she could see what shape they took and in what circumstances they were meshed, there was no forethought to be taken, no merit in wasting mental energy on them.

Eyes open to warn her of any change in the terrain below, she slept.

*　　*　　*

When the long eliptical shape of the plantation broke the solid green jungle and roused her, she felt no surprise, only a touch of self-reproach at her failure to have envisaged this final piece of the jigsaw. She saw the big colonial house and outbuildings, the stables, the dirt roads, the miniature wooden church, and the long low huts forming three sides of a square and ringed by a wire fence. That would be where the prisoners were quartered. In the centre of the valley were the big rectangles of coffee-trees set out in neat lines, with the drying area and storage sheds on one side. She could see white-clad figures moving between the rows of trees, and two or three men on horseback.

The helicopter swept along the river, then turned to hang lazily above the landing pad. As it dropped gently down she saw two Land Rovers moving towards it along the track which led from the rear of the big house. The noise of the engine faded abruptly, and the dust settled. Without a word Damion unlocked the handcuffs, removed the noose, opened the door and got out, followed by Paxero. A man in a bush hat and wearing a gun appeared and said, 'Out.' As she emerged, one of the Land Rovers was already moving off with Paxero and Damion. The driver of the other Land Rover glanced at her without interest and pointed to the passenger seat. She climbed in, and the man in the bush hat sat behind her. The driver let in the clutch.

After half a mile Paxero's truck swung round in front of the big house. Her own carried on along the road which led through the middle of the plantation, and now she saw the slaves. They wore white cotton shirts, trousers or skirts, and most had floppy linen hats. Some were on steps, stripping the coffee cherries from the trees, some were filling wicker baskets with the picked cherries, some carrying baskets to a horse-drawn cart. Faces turned to stare as the Land Rover went past. Ahead she saw a man on low steps working on a tree near the edge of the road, at the end of a line. He took off his hat and wiped his brow as the Land Rover drew near, staring openly, but with no sign of recognition. She lifted a hand to push back a tress of hair, and flickered an eye-lid as they passed.

Danny Chavasse. So Lucifer had been right.

She said, 'What happens next? What *is* this place?'

The man behind her slapped the back of her neck. 'It's

Limbo, girl. And that's your last question, see?' He spoke with a Welsh accent, and with a note of relish. 'It's a slave you're to be now, and no asking questions. You'll find out.'

The truck came out of the plantation area and bore right, towards a prefab hut which was set apart from the main quarters within the wire fence. A black man stood in the open doorway. As the truck halted the man behind her gave her a push in the back and said, 'Have her ready in an hour, Doc.'

She got out. The Land Rover swung in a tight circle and moved off. The black man said, 'My name's Crozier. Dr Kim Crozier. Come in, please.' He turned back into the hut.

She followed, and found herself in a well-kept and seemingly well-stocked consulting room. Dr Crozier gave her a sober smile, put out his hand and said, 'Hallo, Miss Blaise.'

She took the hand, and looked at him vacantly. 'You know my name?'

'I'm not supposed to yet, but I get to hear about most things, and I knew they were bringing you in. Danny Chavasse is quite certain you're here by your own design, and I'm hoping he's right.'

'Danny who?'

White teeth showed in a broad smile. 'You're not quite sure where I stand in this set-up, of course.'

'I'm not sure of anything. I just know I've been kidnapped, and doped, and brought to this place. It looks like a slave plantation.'

'That's what it is. You're taking it very calmly.'

'So far I'm too numb to react.' She frowned, rubbing her brow with the tips of her fingers. 'You have to get me ready for something?'

'For induction. An explanation of why you're here.'

'How do you get me ready?'

He made a vaguely apologetic gesture. 'Medical check-up, Miss Blaise. A thorough one. I have to certify you free from infection. I'm sorry I've no nurse to be present, but Miss

Benita doesn't allow slaves that kind of privilege.'

'Miss Benita?'

'She's the Mistress of Limbo.'

'I keep thinking I'm dreaming.' She looked about her with dull eyes. 'I haven't washed in two days, and I'm dirty. Is there somewhere I could wash or shower before you start?'

'Yes, of course. At least we keep clean here, and as resident doctor I have useful privileges.' He opened a door. 'You'll find a toilet and shower at the end of the passage, last door on the right.'

'Thank you.'

As she moved past him he said, 'Do you know Danny Chavasse's hand-writing, Miss Blaise?'

'Who?'

Kim Crozier put a folded piece of paper in her hand. 'Danny thought you might not recognise it, so he gave me a word to say. Lanzarote.'

She unfolded the paper and read: *You can trust Kim all the way. Danny.*

When she lifted her head Kim saw that the dull expression had vanished, and her eyes were friendly now. She gave him a quick smile and said, 'Hallo, Kim. Safe to talk?'

'Sure.'

'I don't remember the handwriting, but the word Lanzarote's good enough.'

He said with sudden urgency, 'Have you got any sort of back-up laid on? It needs to be quick, like a platoon of paratroops dropping at dawn.'

'I've got two people coming overland.'

'Two?'

'Think about it. Nobody's going to send a force into Guatemala. And if the CIA or British Intelligence had taken this thing to the Guatemalan Government, you can bet Paxero would have been the first to hear about it. Don't tell me he hasn't got emergency arrangements to close this place down fast.'

'He's got them.' Kim put hands on his hips and gave a hopeless shake of his head. 'But what can you do with two?'

'I don't know yet, not till you've answered about a hundred questions.'

'All right, we'll talk while I do the medical. Go and get a quick shower, then slip on a robe you'll find behind the door.'

When she returned five minutes later, wearing only a white cotton wrap, she was carrying the clothes she had worn and a small grey plastic cylinder, domed at one end. She said, 'I was dirty all right, but this is really why I asked for a shower, before I was sure about you. It's a homer to guide Willie Garvin and Maude Tiller in.'

He stared. 'Another *girl*?'

'Oh, come on, doctor. She does beautiful needlework.'

He half laughed. 'Sorry. I'm no male pig, but there are physical differences.'

'Which sometimes helps.' She put the cylinder on the table. 'Don't worry about Maude. When the crunch comes, it's not going to be settled by muscle. And I'd rather have Willie than that platoon you mentioned.'

Kim Crozier studied her curiously. She stood relaxed in the thin cotton wrap, hair hanging loose, eyes quiet yet perhaps with a hint of ironic humour. She was tall, five feet six or seven he judged, and she was splendidly built. When she stood still, she stood completely still. When she moved, it was with the easy fluency that spoke of perfect co-ordination.

It suddenly dawned on him that this striking dark-haired girl with the bruised face was having a remarkable effect on him. It was foolish to think that her coming here could in any way break the grip that Limbo had on its slaves, the odds were far too great, yet for the first time in all the long years he felt his pulse quicken with a surge of genuine hope. She had given him no hardsell encouragement, no stirring call to arms, and it would have been crude to say that she inspired confidence. There was an emanation much more

175

subtle than that, and he could not have found words to describe its nature. He simply knew that he was in the presence of a unique personality, and the old equations were no longer valid. Soberly he decided that he had never known anyone, man or woman, with greater potential to achieve whatever would have to be achieved, if the slaves of Limbo were to outlive Miss Benita by more than a few hours.

She said, 'Can you hide the homer for me?'

He nodded. 'No problem. I live here, in a room at the back. When do you aim to operate it?'

'At midnight every night, for two minutes. Is that going to be difficult?'

'You'll be in the slave quarters. There are no stoolies, but any hint of an escape attempt is going to stir up a lot of trouble.'

She stared. 'As bad as that? All right, let's talk about it later. Could you work the homer from here?'

'What do I have to do?'

She picked up the cylinder and unscrewed the dome. 'Pull this aerial out here, and poke it out of a window if you can. There's only one switch, here on the side. Click it up for two minutes at midnight, then switch off and put the whole thing away.'

'That's all? Right, I'll see to it.' He took the cylinder, collapsed the aerial, screwed on the dome, and set it behind an array of bottles on one of the shelves.

'Thanks, Kim. Is that what I call you?'

He nodded, moved to his desk and took out a printed form. 'We all find ourselves with a single short name here, either family name, given name or in one or two cases a nickname. Like we have a Dutchman called Tonto, though I've forgotten why. I'm Kim, Danny's Danny. But Schultz is Schultz and Marker is Marker. Most of the women are first names. Oh, there's one exception, Mrs Schultz is Mrs Schultz. She's kind of the doyenne of Limbo. You'll get to know them all as you go along. You'll be Modesty, I guess.'

'Right.'

He pointed. 'Would you mind going through so we can start the check-up?'

She preceded him into the smaller room, looked about her, then moved to the examination table. 'Where do you want to start, top, bottom or middle?'

'First we fill in preliminary details on this form. Then I think we'll start with that cut on your face and work our way down.'

For the next twenty minutes he talked steadily about Limbo, its origin, layout, work-system, personnel, disciplines and customs. This was his own method of induction, designed to prepare new intakes for the official one to follow, and he had been through the routine many times before. She listened with total absorption, automatically doing whatever he required of her during the examination, and she was the first who asked no questions at all until he had finished his story.

Then, 'The Specials all carry handguns all the time, and automatic rifles most of the time?'

'Yes.'

'And each overseer carries a handgun and a carbine in a saddle holster?'

'Right.'

'Where's the armoury?'

'In the Specials' quarters. I don't know exactly where.'

She was interested in numbers—of slaves, of Specials, of overseers, of horses and dogs. She was interested in the water pumping system, the sanitation system, fuel supply, and storage of everything that came into Limbo. Above all she was interested in personalities.

'Tell me about the slaves, Kim. There are bound to be leaders who've emerged.'

'Yes. Stop talking for a moment, and breathe in. Out. In. Out. Fine. Yes, there's nothing official, but Schultz and Mrs Schultz head the committee.'

'The committee runs things?'

'Very loosely. There were some pretty brutal problems in the early years, but it's easier now that a pattern of behaviour has evolved. New intakes have a framework to conform to. Would you turn a little this way, please? Thank you.'

'Suppose you get a rebel?'

'Most of them are rebels at first. They want to form escape committees, like in the old war films, but everybody just goes to sleep on them, so it's like trying to stir tar with a teaspoon. Would you—? Ah, that's fine, won't be a moment now. Sometimes you get a very tough rebel, someone who just can't take it at first, and gets lippy with an overseer or a Special. That wins a flogging. We've got a man called Marker, a recent intake, who's been flogged three times. He's not broken yet, but he speaks soft and does as he's told.'

Kim Crozier straightened up and moved to the basin set against the wall to wash his hands. 'You can dress now. Clothes on the chair there. Shirt, skirt, sandals, and not very glamorous pants. No bra, though some of the women have made themselves one. You draw clean clothes every night and put your dirty clothes out for laundering every morning in one of three bins, small, medium, large. Danny said you'd be medium.' He began to dry his hands, watching her as she swung down from the table and began to dress. 'In case you didn't know, you're fit. By God you're fit. Oh, those are dry-season clothes, by the way. There's a different issue from September through November.'

'I don't expect to be interested in that, Kim. A little while ago you said any hint of an escape attempt would stir up trouble among the slaves?'

'Yes. It would frighten them. You'd draw a lot of animosity, and maybe worse.' He was silent for a few moments, ordering his thoughts, then went on slowly, 'Modesty, you have to understand the communal attitude that's evolved

178

here. It stems from several causes, but the main one is that after a little while people realise there's absolutely no hope of escape or rescue, none at all. There's just no way out of Limbo. So either you adjust to that, or you go crazy. If you go crazy you're put down, and as the human psyche prefers its host-body to survive, it tends towards adjustment.'

She buttoned the shirt and tucked it into the skirt which fell four inches below her knees. 'How much adjustment, Kim?'

He shrugged. 'Almost total. You have to take into account that in a sense the people here aren't treated badly. They have sufficient to eat, they work hard enough to give them a good night's sleep, but not savagely hard. They've developed their own simple ways of spending what leisure they have, and they get reasonable medical care. As long as they behave, they can live a life somewhat better than my great-grandpappy lived. He was a real slave, a genuine cotton-picking slave.'

She said, 'I think I see where you're heading, but you've had years to think about it and watch it happen, so fill it out a little for me. And can I borrow a comb?'

'Beside the wash-basin. You'll be issued with female basic possessions in your quarters.' He smiled. 'I thought you were going to tell me there's a difference, that my grandpappy was born a slave and these people weren't.'

'If there's no hope, it wouldn't take long to adjust.'

'Right. And remember, all the people here used to be rich. Some were idle rich, some were sixteen-hours a day rich, but they all had problems. Pressure problems, rat-race problems, tax problems, you name it. In Limbo, you've got no problems. Oh, you can get tired, bored, miserable. Everybody gets a bad patch now and then, when they stop just thinking about today and get hit by the full impact of being in Limbo for ever. But it passes.' He looked at his watch. 'I think ninety percent of the people here would be just a little bit scared of being dumped back Outside now.'

She had combed her hair and was now plaiting a pigtail, her head a little on one side, watching him. 'You feel that way yourself, Kim?'

'A little. Look, I've no money problems, I'm doing a job I like, and I'm a privileged member of this community. What happens to me if I go back?'

'Are you saying you don't *want* to?'

He shook his head. 'No. I'm saying it scares me a little. I've had to adjust too, Modesty. I guess it's a sort of Big Brother syndrome. When you've been looked after for too long, you lose a little mental sinew. But I want out, honey. My God, I want out. I want all the things I haven't let myself think about for six years.'

She began the other plait, and said, 'Who can I talk to safely, apart from you and Danny?'

'You mean who's safe to be told that you worked your way in here and that you're aiming for a break-out or a rescue?'

'Yes.'

'Schultz and Mrs Schultz. Marker. Teresa—I forget her other name, but she was an Italian actress.'

'Teresa Labriola? Supposed to have drowned off Capri?'

'That's her. She's bitchy, but she's still got some fire in her belly. The only other one is Valdez. I can't tell you how any of the others will react when it comes to the crunch, I just think it's safer if they know nothing about you until the crunch really comes. Nobody's going to squeal, but you'll have big trouble.' He looked at his watch again.

She said, 'It can't be a negotiated crunch, Kim. There's going to come a time when we have to go for broke and take control of Limbo. Will the ones you've named actually fight?'

'Marker will, and I guess you can count on Danny, though he says he's no fighting man. That's the trouble, we're none of us fighting people.'

'Anybody will fight if they're desperate enough.'

180

'Yes. But they're not, for reasons I've just been telling you.' He moved to stand closer to her and added softly, 'And they won't get desperate until it's too goddam late, Modesty. The old woman you're going to see soon, Miss Benita, she could die tonight or she could die in another six months. No longer, in my opinion. When she does . . .' He dropped his hand edgewise, like an axe. 'We go with her.'

'The Specials won't baulk at a massacre?'

'The Specials are conditioned, too. We're slaves, lady. Not much more than a hundred years ago, you could kill a nigger as of right, with no more come-back than if you killed a pig.' He put a hand on her shoulder and smiled. 'I'm not starting an old argument, just telling you that this is how the Specials see *us* now. The day Miss Benita dies is going to be the last day in Limbo for all of us.'

'So it's a matter of striking first. It has to be.'

He shrugged. 'I know that. So do the others I've named. But somehow we can't react to it. We're in Limbo, where you don't think about tomorrow.'

She stood relaxed, gazing at him absently, and he had a sudden sense of bewilderment, as if waking from a strange dream. A little while ago he had felt a new confidence, but now it had vanished. This scrubbed, pig-tailed girl with the quiet and beautiful face could have no more effect on Limbo than a feather falling from the sky, no matter what Danny Chavasse said. It was a pipe-dream, and only a fool could have drawn hope from it.

Behind her eyes, something suddenly flared. Her face did not change, but it was as if some potent aspect had possessed her, an emanation of force almost tangible in its effect, so that the impact of it made him catch his breath. The midnight-blue eyes focused upon him, and her gaze hit him with the tingling stimulation of a cold needle-shower. For a moment he seemed to hear the beat of drums, and a strange, reckless exhilaration bubbled in his blood.

She said quietly, 'Jesus, I'm slow. When the old woman

dies, you'll either be there with her or they'll send for you right away to confirm it. So what happens to you then, Kim?'

He stared down at her, his black face impassive, visualising the scene. At last he said with professional calm, 'I hadn't thought about it before, but I guess the massacre begins with me.'

'You said she could die any time, and that's the moment when the crunch comes. I hope to God she lives long enough for Willie Garvin to get here so we can fix some sort of pre-emptive strike. But if not, we'll just have to do the best we can, and to start with you have to have a stopper, Kim.'

'A stopper?'

'A defence. Something to stop them simply putting a bullet through your head.' The moments when that extraordinary aura of strength and will had seemed to radiate from her were now past, but the effect was still with him. He half smiled and said, 'I'm all for stopping that. But how?'

She crossed her arms and began to pace, holding her elbows. Again he looked at his watch. They would be coming for her soon. She said, 'If I could be with you at the time ...'. She looked at him. 'I'm a good nurse, and experienced. I once took out an appendix, under guidance. Any chance of you taking me on?'

He shook his head. 'No. In an emergency, if I need another pair of hands, I can ask permission for Mrs Schultz to help, but that's all.'

'Pity.' She fiddled thoughtfully with a plait. 'You told me the general sex customs here, but what about you? Could you have me here as your woman?'

He spread a hand ruefully. 'Wish I could, but no again. That was my own rule to start with, I figured that whether the doctor had a permanent woman or just went on the roster it was bound to cause trouble. So I ask for one of the mestizo girls to spend the night now and again. Miss Benita wouldn't let me change that now.'

182

'How often do you see her?'

'Miss Benita? Every day now. And a report goes to Paxero over the scrambler radio.'

She stood with her lower lip caught under her teeth for a moment, frowning, then gave a little nod. 'All right, you'll have to cope on your own when it happens. But here's how you start preparing for the stopper, Kim.'

* * *

The old sepia photographs thrown on the screen were fuzzy, the old clips of film were grainy, but both made their grim impact. Dull-eyed Indian peasants with scrawny children, watching their hovels burn; soldiers on horseback, jockeying their mounts back and forth to trample a patch of earth in which living men had been buried with only their heads protruding; a coffee *finca*; a man in a frilled shirt, posing with a gun held to the head of an Indian with hands bound in front of him; another picture of the same scene as the gun was fired; a cotton plantation; film of starving babies, squalor, desolation, with the counterpoint of the great houses and vast estates of the wealthy plantation owners and *finqueros*.

Modesty sat in the darkened room, watching. A commentary in English came from a speaker set in the wall. Two men stood behind the wooden chair in which she sat.

'. . . when a plantation was sold, the Indians were included in the sale, so that for all practical purposes they were merchandise, mere slaves . . .

'Here is a communal farm hacked out of the jungle by a group of Indian families, who grew corn, fruit and coffee. When the farm had been established, the military commissioner of the area ordered the Indians to move out, on the grounds that the land belonged to a wealthy family named Varilla. The peasants refused, soldiers were sent in, their homes were burned, their crops ploughed up, and ten

183

Indians were killed, as shown in this next piece of film . . .

'The year is 1935. The debt peonage, the system of inherited debts, has been abolished. But here is a man who has just been hanged, because the *finqueros* were permitted to kill any peasant who entered a plantation or demanded his rights by force . . .

'These peasants are dying because their master had the crops sprayed with a deadly insecticide but did not withdraw the peasants during the spraying . . .'

The story continued for over thirty minutes. It was neither new nor unique, and within its own time-span could have been paralleled in many countries, but it was still a brutal and tragic story.

The lights came on and one of the men behind her said, 'Stand up.' He had a languid English voice, eyes that were sleepily vicious, and carried a riding crop. When she obeyed he said, 'After you've gone through that door on your right, you'll be in the presence of Miss Benita. You stand still and bow to her. You say nothing except to answer questions. You address her as "Miss Benita" or "Mistress". If there's any insolence, disobedience, or dumb insolence, you'll be taken out, stripped, and publicly whipped. You understand?'

'Yes.'

'All right. Move.'

The room was high-ceilinged and full of sunlight. The old woman sat upright in a beechwood armchair by the open window. Paxero stood behind her, his hands resting on the chairback. Damion sat unobtrusively in the corner. When Modesty was two paces into the room the English voice behind her said, 'Stop.' She stopped. The butt of the crop jabbed hard against her spine. She bowed from the waist, then straightened and looked without expression at Miss Benita.

The old woman's face was a bad colour, but the eyes were still quick and sharp. She studied Modesty in silence for a while, then said in Spanish, 'What does she weigh, Ramon?'

184

Paxero picked up the medical form from a small table beside her, looked at it, then said, 'Sixty kilograms, Aunt Benita.'

'She seems healthy. More so than most you bring me.'

'Yes. You'll get plenty of work out of this one.'

'I am very pleased with you, Ramon, you are a good boy. I hope you will bring me the man soon, the one who was with her in the photograph.'

'I'll try, Aunt Benita.'

The old woman tapped the floor with her stick and addressed Modesty, speaking slow English in the beautifully mellow voice which was at such odds with the bony face and shrunken frame. 'You have seen the induction pictures and film, girl?'

'Yes.' There was sharp pain as the riding-crop cut across her buttock. 'Yes, Miss Benita.'

'This plantation, Limbo, is my small offering to the men, women and children who were murdered, starved, or worked to death by the rich and greedy. You understand?'

'Yes, Miss Benita.'

'Now it is your turn. You will not be murdered, starved or worked to death, but you will be a slave. You now belong to me, and you have no rights of any kind. Work well, give no trouble, and you will have a life the poor people in that film would have envied. If you are a bad slave, we shall first try to correct you by punishment. If that fails, then I shall have no further use for you. Do you understand?'

'Yes, Miss Benita.'

The stick tapped on the floor again. 'Very well. Take her away now, Mr Sinclair.'

The riding-crop touched her shoulder. She turned and preceded the Englishman out of the room, passing the other man who had stood guard in the projection room and who was now to one side of the door, a hand resting on his holstered gun, watching her with the relaxed readiness of the professional. Her stomach felt taut, and she knew her pulse rate had risen. The Limbo operation was huge and daunting beyond anything she had even vaguely imagined, and her support was small and uncertain. For a moment she felt very much alone, and her mind reached out to Willie Garvin; then with cool anger at herself she accepted her aloneness, and wiped away all useless wishing and hoping and seeking for comfort.

This was likely to be a long haul rather than a short sprint, she told herself dourly, and there would be a lot of time in which to think. She would have to be careful not to let the weakeners get at her.

*   *   *

Schultz said, 'You're bound to be in a state of shock at the moment. When that passes, you'll have a pretty bad time, but we'll do our best to help you through it.' He was a man who had once been fat but was now lean, with face and arms burnt almost black by sun, and close-cropped grey hair.

Modesty said, 'I'll try not to be any trouble.' Mrs Schultz, a small compact woman with grey hair tied back in a pony-tail, looked at her sharply.

Because of the heat, benches had been carried out of the dining hut and most of the slaves were taking their noon meal in the open under the cane awnings, eating with spoons from bowls containing a mash of mince, potato and green vegetables. Some of the slaves had greeted her sympathetically, some had looked at her warily, others had taken no notice.

She had been shown the living quarters. The huts were partitioned to provide a common-room, and bedrooms for two, four or six. Privacy was minimal. Each slave had a locker, basic toilet equipment, and basic eating equipment. She had seen no reading material except a worn bible carried by an American called Berry who was apparently the leader of the church group.

She said, 'What does everybody do when they're not working?'

Schultz gazed about him. 'Different things. Some just sleep. Others have gotten to be pretty smart with their hands. Miss Benita doesn't allow us knives or tools, but there are still things you can do. Eddie over there, he's the best whittler you'll ever see, carving soft wood with a split stone. Julie, she gets an old box-lid and does mosaics of river gravel set in mud.' He turned to look across the courtyard at a group of five men and three women, aged from thirty to sixty, their heads close together. 'That's the choir doing a little quiet practice. They sing good close harmony for us most nights. And there's always patching and mending for the girls to do.' He shrugged. 'You'll find something.'

Danny Chavasse came slowly to where she sat with Schultz and Mrs Schultz. Beside him was a tiny girl with black hair cropped short and huge dark eyes set in a small brown face. Danny said, 'Thought we'd say hallo to the new girl, Schultz.'

'Sure. She's called Modesty. Modesty, this is Danny and Teresa.'

The Italian girl said, 'Ah, shit. We just get the sleep-around roster going smooth, then comes-a some pretty-face girl like this to make it go bad.'

Mrs Schultz said, 'Give her a break and don't be so hostile, Teresa. She won't be going on the roster till she's settled in, and then only if she wants to. We've explained all that.'

Teresa sniffed. 'She'll want to.' Her gaze rested coldly on Modesty. 'You play straight, kid, or I kick-a your arse.'

Danny grinned and said, 'And Teresa weighs in at damn near a hundred pounds, with her clothes on.' He put out his hand. 'What section have you been put in, Modesty?'

She looked a query at Schultz, who said, 'Mr Sam's section for her first week. Same as yours, Danny.'

'Right, I can show her the ropes.'

Teresa said impatiently, 'Listen Schultz, has Kim asked for

us to have new decks of cards yet? What's-a so tough? Four decks in a *year*, they not going to kill him for asking.'

Schultz said, 'He applied to Sinclair, and said it was medically important. Sinclair wouldn't play.' He glanced at Modesty. 'That's the English guy with the riding crop. He's Miss Benita's secretary and handles all administration.'

'Bastard.' Teresa spat out the word. 'I like to stick a knife into his belly.'

'He's bad medicine,' Schultz agreed. 'But if Kim goes over his head and asks Miss Benita direct, Sinclair won't like it one bit. You want Kim in trouble?'

She glared sullenly, then shrugged and turned away. Mrs Schultz said, 'Poor Teresa. She worries me sometimes. She's never really settled down here.' She looked at Modesty. 'You worry me a little too, honey. We've seen folk come in blustering, or whimpering, or hysterical, or very quiet, like zombies with shock. You're quiet, but I don't figure that's from shock.'

Danny Chavasse said very softly, 'Mrs Schultz . . . will you please not say that again out loud? Not until we've had a chance to talk privately, or until you've talked with Kim.'

Twelve

MAUDE TILLER stopped hating Willie Garvin long enough to yell 'Tree!' and to paddle furiously with the aluminium oar in an attempt to slow the rubber boat a little as it rushed down upon the fallen ramón which blocked the whole fifty-foot width of the river. Behind her in the boat, Willie whirled the grapnel. It flashed out into the dense undergrowth along the bank, dragged for a moment, then caught hard. The rubber boat slowed and swung sideways. Willie eyed the massive tree-trunk, five feet in diameter, and said, 'See anywhere we can get the boat under it, Maude?'

She ran her eye along the length of the tree, managed to prevent her shoulders slumping wearily, and said with brisk unconcern, 'No chance.'

'Right.' He began to haul the rubber boat towards the bank. Today was their seventh day on the river, and this would be the fifth time today they had been forced to unload the boat, cut a way through the jungle to by-pass a barrier or cascade, then reinflate and reload.

It seemed to Maude more like a year since the night when the small helicopter had taken off from near Benque Viejo and crossed the western border of British Honduras into Guatemala, piloted by a naval officer in civilian clothes. Maude and Willie had been set down with their gear on a small bare *playa* twelve miles upriver from where they were now, the only safe landing-place within the circle Willie had inscribed on the map.

When he had met her in Belize and briefed her, Maude had felt quiet exhilaration at the prospect which lay ahead.

Now she felt differently, for in her mind was a cold suspicion which had grown from seed to cankered fruit in the past seven days.

She sat holding the boat steady while Willie swung the machete to cut a path into the thick undergrowth of the river-bank. Ten minutes later they were moving slowly through the jungle. Both wore camouflage trousers and fatigue-jackets, peaked jockey-caps and combat boots. Maude carried a frame pack weighing twenty-five pounds, and dragged a sisal-hemp bag holding the deflated boat. Willie's pack weighed fifty pounds, and across the top of it, in waterproof cases, were strapped the two Stoner 63 Carbines with folding stocks.

Once in the jungle they were in a twilight world, beneath a roof of hundred-foot tall trees, coroso and guano palms, ceiba, ramón and sapote. Below this roof were smaller trees, the chapai with its vicious spines, the bulls-horn with its great steel-hard hooks, and a tangle of vines and giant ferns.

After half an hour of steady hacking, Willie cut towards the river again, cleared a small space on the bank, and set down his pack. 'We'll take ten minutes,' he said, and uncorked his waterbottle.

Maude dropped the boat, slipped her pack off, and sat down. She felt her stomach stir, and hoped desperately that she was not going to get the runs again. Willie squatted with the much-thumbed map spread in front of him, his back towards her. She slipped two fingers in her mouth, stretching it, stuck out her tongue, crossed her eyes, and made a wild, idiot grimace at him.

He was only pretending to study the map, of course. She was certain of it now. During the night hours when she lay sweating in her nylon hammock, mosquitoes buzzing about her head-net, muscles aching, hands cut and swollen by thorn and spine, she had had time to think.

The story in the file Fraser had given her in London stated that suspicions of Paxero's involvement with a number of people who had disappeared over the years was now very much stronger. One of those who had disappeared was an old flame of Modesty's, a man called Danny Chavasse, who owned a very special watch which Modesty had given him and which Damion had stolen, and which, by chance, Modesty had re-stolen. Now zip-pan to America, where a madman who believed himself to be Satan had informed Modesty that the said Danny Chavasse was alive and well and living in the world somewhere. Modesty and Willie had then gone to a friend of theirs, one Dinah Collier, who had carried out a kind of psycho-location which indicated that Danny Chavasse was at the spot marked X in the jungles of the Petén. So Modesty had permitted herself to be kidnapped by Paxero, in order to join the lost tribe of vanishing people, while Willie Garvin was to approach the spot marked X by way of the jungle. And he had asked for Maude Tiller to assist.

Just so.

Maude unzipped her fly, pushed down her pants and inspected the red spots on her belly. River bugs, Willie had explained, tiny little ticks called *arradores*. But the spots would not start to itch until the eggs laid under the skin began to move.

She zipped up her fly, deciding that what she hated most after Willie Garvin was the insects. She had been frightened by a large and dangerous monkey called a *saraguate*, by a night-prowling jaguar, and by *murcielagos*, the small vampire bats with anaesthetic in their bite, which allowed them to strike unfelt. But the insects were a ceaseless plague. She took a repellent cream from one of her pouches and began to rub it on her face and hands, watching Willie.

He was still studying the map, pretending to be anxious because there was no such thing as a reliable map of this area. His story was that the river they were on was not the river Dinah Collier had psycho-located when pin-pointing Danny Chavasse, but was a tributary of the Santa Amelia.

At one point it would bring them to within fifteen miles of where X marked the spot, and then they would leave the river and strike across a broad, low ridge of thick jungle to reach their final destination.

Maude put the insect repellent away and checked that her machete was firmly strapped to her thigh. She had taken it off once, in the boat, and Willie had given her a tongue-lashing which had come close to making her cry, though she would have preferred to die, given the choice. He was right, of course, and she should have known better, which only made it worse. The boat could always capsize going through a cascade, and you could lose your gear. You stood a chance of surviving in this jungle, for a while at least, without the food you carried, the halazone tablets for purifying water, your gun, your spare clothing, your hammock . . . almost anything. But without a machete, you were dead.

From another pouch Maude took what looked like a chunk of drooping wood and began to chew it. This was *cambó*, the heart of the coroso palm, tasteless but with a certain amount of sustenance. Willie was hoarding their concentrated foods for the trip on foot through the jungle, and as far as possible they had been living off the land. Yesterday she had eaten iguana meat, and the day before that, part of a small monkey, both victims of Willie's unique skill with his throwing-knives. Both had nauseated her, but she had managed to keep the stuff down.

The jungle course she had taken with the army in Brunei had been hard, but this was in a different category. Not that she had any complaints about the rigours she endured and had yet to endure. Pain and weariness, insects, heat, humidity, fear, the whole range of discomfort and suffering that the jungle could impose, these she could bear stoically enough. But she was being conned by people she trusted, and this was a bitter thing.

Willie Garvin moved to squat facing her, the map folded in his hand. She saw that his shirt was black with the sweat from his tireless hacking with the machete, and his face was lumpy with insect-bites. During the first day or two of the journey he had been relaxed and cheerful with her, the good-humoured Willie Garvin she knew, but gradually a strained atmosphere had gathered about them, and there was no humour in his blue eyes as he looked at her now.

He said, 'Another two miles of river. I'm 'oping we can do that tomorrow.'

'Then we head into the jungle?'

'I do, Maude. I'll leave you one of the rifles and all the gear. Rig you a shelter before I leave. You can manage for a week or two till I pick you up.'

Shock hit her. She said, 'Have you gone bloody mad?'

'No.' He gave a small shrug. 'It's not working, Maude. I made a mistake.'

'Not working?' Her voice rose and began to shake. 'Just tell me what I've done wrong!'

'Nothing. You've worked like a pack 'orse, and there 'asn't been a breath of a moan. But you're not with me, love. You're a million miles away. And what little gets through to me, it's got bad vibrations.' He shook his head. 'The jungle does funny things, an' I guess that's the trouble. Maybe you're not seeing straight, maybe I'm not, but we're right out of tune, and that's no good. Worse, it's dangerous. I wish I 'ad time to take you back, but there's no way, and I've got things to do.' He stood up. 'I'd sooner do them on me own now, Maude.'

She rose, glaring at him, her whole body shaking. 'So that's how the charade works out? Dump little Maude in the jungle for a couple of weeks, and she'll soon get over what that nasty Paxero did to her.'

He blinked, startled. 'Charade?'

'Christ, you don't think I *believed* it all, did you? All right, I did at first, but not for long.' She swallowed hard. 'So maybe you all thought it was for my own good. The Help Poor Maude Society. Well, thanks very much to you and Tarrant and Modesty and whoever bloody else, but now you can all go and get stuffed!'

Willie Garvin studied the blotched face gleaming with repellent cream, and understood many things which had baffled him during the past days. He bent to pick up the burlap sack containing the boat and said quietly, 'All right, Maude, let's get the boat pumped up.' He dragged the folded rubber out, and unstrapped the small foot-pump from his pack.

She stood watching, disconcerted, then said uncertainly, 'No arguments?'

'Waste of time.'

'Right. But you can forget the bit about dumping me on my own for a couple of weeks. I don't need any therapy.' When he did not answer she said, 'Willie, I said you can forget the bit about dumping me on my own.'

He looked up from connecting the pump, his gaze mild and remote. 'Maude, you can disbelieve anything else you like. But you'd better believe *that*.'

She watched him pump up the two sections of the boat and methodically load their packs aboard. He checked the machete strapped to his leg, glanced at her own, then coiled the grapnel line and put it in the well of the boat.

Maude said in a small voice, 'Have I been wrong?' She looked dazed.

He glanced at her thoughtfully. 'You want an answer?'

'Please.'

'You've been wrong. You got to be a bit jungle-crazy if you even begin to believe I'd do a snow job on you. Or that Modesty would, or Tarrant.' He nodded towards the northeast. 'I don't know for sure what's 'appened to Modesty, but I know Paxero and Damion grabbed 'er, and with them around I don't suppose she's 'aving the time of 'er life, any more than you did when you were with 'em.'

Maude saw a little spasm touch his face. It was gone in an instant, but the effect on her was more potent than any

words, for in that second it was as if a dark nimbus of cold
ferocity played about Willie Garvin. He seemed suddenly
huge, implacable, and very deadly. Yet his voice was still
casual as he squinted up at the sky for a moment and said,
'I expect I'll find Modesty waiting for me when I get to
wherever it is, but I don't want you along with your bad
vibes, Maude. I'm not asking you to believe it, any of it, but
just don't get in my way, that's all.'

She stood marvelling at her delusions of the past few days.
He had been right in saying that the jungle must have got to
her. You hated it for all it did to you, but the jungle was
neutral, and an unsatisfactory target for hatred, so you
found a convenient human target and built yourself a case
against it. She wondered how she could have failed to detect
the gnawing anxiety behind his amiable and unruffled
manner. He had the mental resources to subdue that anxiety
by starving his imagination, but it was still there. And she
knew, better than most, what Modesty Blaise meant to him.

He slid the boat into the water, holding the rope fixed to
the bow, and said, 'All right, let's get going.'

She moved to stand in front of him, put her hands on his
arms and said, 'Willie, I'm sorry. No more bad vibes. Will
you give me a break?' Looking up at him, she twisted her
face in a clownish grimace and rolled her eyes coquettishly.
'Go on. Give me a break and I'll show you the spots on my
belly.'

*   *   *

When Tarrant had finished speaking, the Minister sat
gazing at the map in front of him for a full minute in silence.
He was a pale, paper-thin man who gave an impression of
vague stupidity to those below him, and reserved his genuine
brilliance for dealing with those above him.

'It's all rather tenuous, isn't it?' he said at last.

'Up to a point,' Tarrant agreed. 'But all the tenuous implications led to the same conclusion. And then there are the personalities involved.'

'You mean this woman—er—what's her name?'

'Modesty Blaise.' Tarrant was well aware that the Minister had sent for the *Sabre-Tooth* file an hour before this interview and had made a well-informed assessment of Modesty Blaise. 'The fact is, Minister, that she laid herself open to being seized by Paxero, and it duly came to pass. I find that very convincing confirmation of what was perhaps a tenuous theory.'

'She could have drowned by accident, I suppose.'

'It's possible, but an extremely unlikely coincidence.'

'So you've had this man Garvin and one of your agents enter Guatemalan territory illegally from British Honduras?'

'Yes. Quite a lot of my agents have no legal right to be where they are, of course. And I understand,' he added apologetically, 'that the country is now called Belize.'

'It says British Honduras on this map.'

'I expect map-makers are fighting a losing battle against change these days, Minister.'

'Yes.' The Minister leaned back and gazed absently at the ceiling. 'I'm told we have a garrison of about six hundred men there.'

'Yes. I'm asking that a platoon should stand by to be flown in by helicopter when the call comes. If it comes.'

'Garvin is in contact by radio?'

'Not exactly. There's a limit to how much he could carry. He has a small gadget which will send out a signal for ten minutes or so—the letter G repeated again and again. I've two people in Benque Viejo on constant listening watch.'

The Minister frowned. 'I'm sure I've read something about Guatemala laying claim to Belize.' He smiled distantly. 'Isn't that why Belize is about the only colony opposed to independence, because they know they'll be invaded?'

Tarrant pretended to consider. Then, 'Would you like me to check on that, Minister?'

The Minister gave him a quick look and said more briskly, 'No, no I'm sure I'm right. In which case we don't want an incident with Guatemala, do we? If the CIA started this hare, why can't they put in some soldiers?'

'They've rather gone off the idea of putting in soldiers anywhere these days, Minister.'

The Minister looked at his watch. 'It's a messy business. I can't say I think much of your back-up arrangements, Tarrant, or of the whole operation for that matter.'

'It isn't really my operation. Modesty Blaise has been kidnapped. Garvin and another have gone to look for her. I'm trying to arrange for back-up now.'

'I can't authorise the use of troops, even a single platoon. Not for this.'

'I thought an exercise might be arranged, Minister. The border runs through the Maya Mountains, and isn't too well defined. An error in compass reading could easily take a helicopter fifty miles or so off course. One doesn't quite know what they'll find, but it must be some sort of . . . habitation. And whoever's in charge of the exercise might actually land there in response to an SOS of some sort— believing it to be in the Belize jungle, naturally.'

After a short silence the Minister said, 'It's a pity we can't do anything. If what you suspect is true, it would give us a lot of valuable kudos in useful areas. But there you are. I simply can't authorise the use of troops.' He looked at his watch again. 'Thank you Tarrant.' He stood up, switched off the tape recorder, and accompanied Tarrant to the door. 'You'll keep me informed of any developments, of course.'

'Certainly, Minister.'

'And I'm sure you'll pick a thoroughly reliable pilot for the helicopter.'

*   *   *

The oil-lamp in the small wooden church was always lit.

It hung above the simple wooden altar. There were no pews. Those who used the church either stood or knelt. At this moment, an hour after the evening meal had been eaten, there were seven in the church. Danny Chavasse stood by the slightly open door, on watch. The rest stood in a close group behind him, keeping their voices low.

Marker was saying furiously, 'You're telling us Modesty *knew*? She knew before she came here? Then why the hell didn't she get some real action started?'

Kim Crozier said, 'She didn't know, she guessed. And if she'd tried to get any official action started, we'd be dead by now, every one of us. Danny's already explained all that.'

Valdez said, 'She is what I have been waiting for, and thought would never come.'

Schultz said, 'How do you mean?'

'There is a need for somebody very strong, with much force. Somebody to make things happen, but with experience.' Valdez shrugged. 'Once I thought it could be Marker, but no. You beat your head against a wall, my friend. This one is different. I have watched her all this week.'

Teresa said, 'I don't like her. But that's-a nothing. I don't like any woman too much. What you say, Kim?'

The black man looked round the heavily shadowed faces. 'Danny knows her well. He says he'd rather have Modesty up front than any man alive. If Danny says so, I'll buy that. And there's this side-kick of hers, Garvin. He's on his way.'

Marker made a contemptuous sound. 'Through the jungle? He's already dead, man.'

By the door, Danny Chavasse said, 'Not Willie Garvin. She picks the best, Marker, believe it.'

Schultz said, 'If we're away from quarters too long, people are going to notice, so let's tidy this situation up a little. Kim says that when Miss Benita dies, we all die. And she could go *any* time.' He looked slowly round. 'Anybody disagree? Right, so we need to act soon, if we're not just going

198

to stand still for it. This girl came to Limbo deliberately, because of Danny. She asked Kim and Danny to pick out the slaves who could be trusted not to panic, and put them in the picture. Okay, that's done. I guess what she wants now is our agreement to let her run things her own way when the time comes. Is that right, Kim?'

The doctor nodded. 'Somebody has to decide how, where and when.'

Mrs Schultz said, 'Has she a plan of any kind?'

Heads turned towards Danny, who shrugged. 'She's waiting for Willie Garvin and the girl to arrive. Then she aims to do a night job with Willie, taking care of the Specials. They're the ones we have to beat.'

Teresa stiffened. 'Don't talk shit. They'd never get past the dogs.'

Kim said, 'She's thought of that. I've been storing meat in my medical fridge, and I've got plenty of dope.'

There was a little silence. Valdez said, 'Suppose Miss Benita dies before this man Garvin comes? What happens then, Danny?'

'That's what she wants to talk to us about. If we're not ready for it, we're going to be running around like a lot of headless chickens.'

Marker said, 'All right, we're here if she wants to talk. Why isn't *she*?'

'I thought everybody knew,' Kim said slowly. 'Paxero and Damion dropped in this morning. They're based at the development site now, and keep flying in to check on Miss Benita. They sent for Modesty just after siesta time at the big house.'

'What for?'

Teresa looked at the South African. 'For one big kinky screwing session, you dumb-a bastard. What else?' She gave a little shudder as if someone had walked over her grave. 'Poor bitch. She never come straight back and talk-a sense from that.'

199

Danny said, 'She was glad of the chance to see more of the house. I think she has in mind that next time or the time after might be the right moment to strike.'

Schultz ran a hand over his cropped hair. 'How do you mean, Danny?'

'After Willie Garvin gets here. Suppose Paxero and Damion send for her again. She kills them, then goes gunning for the Specials with Willie coming in from outside.'

Marker said incredulously, 'She kills them? Just like that?'

'Yes.'

The Italian girl looked at Danny Chavasse curiously. 'You never make wild talk, Danny. Okay. If you and Kim want-a for her to run things, I go along.'

'And me,' Valdez said.

Marker shook his head. Schultz said, 'I'd like to hear what she has in mind, but we can't wait too long tonight.' He looked at Teresa. 'They'd be through with her now, and getting ready for dinner, huh?'

She nodded. 'They take me twice last year. Siesta to dinner both times.'

'We'll wait ten minutes, then.'

Marker said, 'I'm out. I never took orders from a woman in my life.'

He turned towards the door, and found Valdez in front of him. 'Teresa is right,' the South American said softly. 'You are a stupid bastard, Marker. We *all* take orders from a woman, here in Limbo. I think this girl Modesty is our one chance, so wait for her now . . . or try to walk through me.'

*   *   *

Modesty buttoned the shirt and tucked it into her skirt, put on her sandals, and looked without expression at Sinclair, who lounged in the open door of the ante-room, watching her. All that had happened in the past few hours was already shadowy and unreal, fading into the void.

Her mind was occupied with appraisal, with visualising what she had seen and had been able to deduce of the layout of the house, and with estimating how long it would take her to reach the nearby building where the Specials lived. That was the key to control of Limbo, the place which held the weapons and the men who knew how to use them. If she and Willie could get inside, the crucial battle could be fought and won there.

Sinclair stood away from the door and jerked his head. She went out, along a passage, down a flight of service stairs which passed the kitchen, and out of a back door into the night, with Sinclair following.

Damion had had a gun, Sinclair had a gun, the man in the waiting Land Rover had a gun. So another time, if this pattern was followed, she could by now have destroyed four of the opposition and have three guns. And if Willie Garvin were waiting here, ready . . .

Sinclair thumped her in the back, pushing her towards the Land Rover. He had been lounging in the ante-room ten minutes ago when Damion had pushed her out of the suite with her clothes bundled in her arms. For a moment she remembered what Sinclair had made her do before allowing her to dress, and she felt a touch of raw satisfaction at the notion of his lifeless body lying at her feet. There were some men who made you wish there was a hell to send them to.

Five minutes later the Land Rover stopped outside the slave compound. A few people were strolling in the night air or sitting about as she went through the open gate. From the far end, in a corner where the long huts joined, came the muted sound of singing, a plaintive tune she did not know.

Martha appeared and said, 'You've had a bad time, honey. I know. Now just you sit and let me take care of you.'

'No, I'm all right. Truly. I'd like to see Mrs Schultz.'

'I think she went across to the church, but John said it's a sort of private meeting.'

'She's not back yet?'

'No.'

'I'll wait outside till they've finished. I want to be on my own for a while.'

'I know how you feel. They make you just want to die.'

Danny Chavasse swung the door open as she entered the church porch, then closed it behind her. The others stood in a little group on the hard-beaten earth that was the floor of the church, watching her.

Teresa said, 'Bad luck, kid.'

She nodded, moved forward, and looked at Kim. 'Who's with me?'

He said in a neutral voice, 'Danny and myself. Teresa and Valdez. Not Marker. Schultz and Mrs Schultz haven't said either way yet.' As he spoke he saw that there were still traces of crude, heavy make-up on her face, giving her a bizarre look in the yellow lamplight, but her eyes were serene and untroubled.

She looked at Marker and said, 'Because I'm a woman?'

'That's about it.' He shrugged. 'No hard feelings.'

'You're tougher? Smarter? Better equipped?'

His eyes hardened. 'That's right.'

She folded her arms and stood looking at him from beneath long eye-lashes. Her eyes seemed black, and he found her gaze oddly disconcerting. She said, 'Marker, where are the sight-lines between the big house and the nearest safe cover? Where's the dead ground? How is the armoury guarded? Is the ammunition for the overseers' carbines and the Specials' automatic rifles interchangeable? How would you cope with the dogs? What's your arrangement for knowing the moment Miss Benita dies? Which of the bucks among the slaves have ever handled a gun? Can you pick a lock? What's your emergency plan if Miss Benita dies tonight? Or tomorrow, while we're at work? How do you—?'

'Shut up and listen.' His face was flushed. 'I'm not saying *I* want to run the job. I'm just saying I'm a loner, and I don't want a woman telling me what to do.'

'It's no time for loners, and we're going to need you, Marker.'

'Too bad.'

She considered him broodingly. 'It's difficult. I could knock you cold, but all that proves is that I can knock you cold.'

For a moment he stared unbelievingly, then jabbed a warning finger at her. 'Don't talk bloody stupid, girl. I reckon you've had enough for one night, but you try anything with me and I'll whip your arse till you can't stand.'

Schultz drew breath to speak, but said nothing as Danny caught his eye and gave a quick shake of the head.

Modesty said, 'Are you a gambling man, Marker?'

'I gamble. Mostly I win.'

'What would you bet that I couldn't put you out in twenty seconds?'

'Christ, you're really asking for it, girl!'

'What would you bet?'

He gave a huff of angry laughter. 'Name it.'

'Co-operation.' She moved a pace nearer, holding his gaze.

'You're on. What are *you* staking?'

Her shoulders moved in a shrug. 'Whatever I've got that you want.'

He said grimly, 'I'll think of something.' Every moment he was becoming more angry and confused, yet was not sure why. True, she had thrown him on the defensive from the start, and had then steadily driven him into an untenable position, but her manner had been without hostility or challenge, almost friendly.

She was even smiling a little now, arms still folded, saying, 'Ready?'

'Any time,' he growled, and started to take a pace back, to drop into an attacking posture.

203

She said, 'Don't pull any punches,' and as she spoke something quite impossible happened. In his younger days Marker had fought many a brawl, using fists, feet, elbows and whatever came to hand as a weapon. In his experience, there was no way that you could stand flat-footed, square on, with folded arms, at less than arm's-length from an opponent and deliver a kick with the ball of the foot to the solar plexus.

It was over before his mind had time to interpret what his eye perceived. She seemed to fold back, leaning away from him, then came a flash of white skirt from the lower periphery of his vision and in the same instant a hammerblow took him under the heart, paralysing the whole nervous system. He came up on his toes under the impact, mouth agape, then fell twisting to the ground. As he fell his blurred vision caught another white flash of movement, then a smooth hard arm closed about his neck from behind, there was the pressure of a hand on his skull, he could feel her breath across his ear, her breasts against his back. He made one huge, undirected effort to struggle, and remembered no more.

Modesty rose, turned him on his back and began to massage his solar plexus. Kim knelt beside her. She said, 'It was just a sleeper-hold, I didn't want him concussed.'

'That's nice.' Kim lifted one of Marker's eyelids. 'Okay, I'll take over.' He looked at her soberly. 'He's going to be impressed, if that's what you wanted, but he's going to hate your guts.'

She sat on her haunches, and pushed back a tress of hair. 'He will at first, but it doesn't usually last long. And the main thing is I don't think he'll welsh on his bet.'

She stood up. The others were looking at her with a variety of expressions, Valdez amused, Danny relieved, the Schultzes startled, Teresa grinning openly. The Italian girl said, 'Shit! If we ever get out of this, come do that to some director I know.'

Schultz glanced at his wife, then at Modesty and said, 'Do

you know the answers to all those questions you asked Marker?'

'Yes, except for which men can handle guns. That's tricky, but I know three or four now. Whether they'll be any use when the crunch comes is something the rest of you can judge better than I can.'

Marker gave a long, wheezing groan. Modesty kept looking at Schultz. He was the key man now, the father figure of the Limbo slaves, and his commitment would be vital when the time came. She understood his problems. He had been in Limbo a long time, and it was hard for him to adjust to the strange idea that anything could ever change, that time was running out. She could almost see the effort he was making, trying to force his heart to accept what his intellect could not doubt.

He gave a little sigh, put out his hand to grasp his wife's and nodded slowly. 'All right, young lady. Somebody's got to play the hand for us, and it looks like you're the best we've got for this kind of game.'

Thirteen

JOHN DALL watched with respect as Dinah Collier set the drink down at his elbow without fumbling. 'Thank you, Mrs Collier.' He looked at her husband. 'And this was how long ago?'

Collier and Dinah said together, 'Sixteen days.' Collier added, 'We mean since Willie left.'

Dall nodded. It was now seventeen days since he had received a cable which simply said, *'Don't believe it. Love. Squaw.'* Three days later his secretary had brought him a clipping from a Mexican newspaper reporting the death by drowning of a woman called Modesty Blaise. He had flown to Acapulco, to discover that the friends who had been with her there had now left. He had rung Sir Gerald Tarrant, who had been blandly uncommunicative. Willie Garvin had disappeared without trace. Nobody seemed to know anything. Then Dall had thought of Collier, the man who had been caught up with him in the Lucifer affair. Collier and his wife, whom Dall had not met, were the friends who had been in Acapulco with Modesty and Willie. It had taken time to track them down, but he had found them now in a small hotel in Belize.

Dinah said, 'They told us to go home to England, but we just couldn't.'

'I know how you feel, Mrs Collier. Do you know if Tarrant's arranged any kind of back-up?'

Collier said, 'I rang him a day or two ago, and he just said he was doing everything possible. We couldn't talk freely, of course.'

206

'How does he expect to know when it's safe to send in any kind of back-up?'

'There's a man in Benque Viejo waiting for a signal.'

'What happens when it comes? If it comes.'

Collier made a sour grimace. He looked tired and harassed. 'I don't know. That's the bloody trouble with anything Modesty gets involved in. You're left biting your nails and wondering. I remember the day she got herself into a rapier duel with that sword-mad Hungarian in the arena in Mus. I'll never be as old as I felt that day.' He drank moodily. 'It's no way to treat your friends.'

Dall said thoughtfully, 'I could put a team in by air. If it's the way we think, Guatemala's going to be too busy apologising for what Paxero's done to think about territorial rights.'

'No.' Dinah's voice was sharp. 'If the timing's wrong, you could foul everything up. Willie's the only one who can act safely off his own bat. They've got twin minds when they're on a job.'

Dall sighed. 'I know.' He frowned down at his drink. 'How long do you propose waiting here?'

Collier said, 'Something ought to happen in the next week or two.'

'Suppose it doesn't. Suppose just nothing happens.'

'Christ knows, John. We hadn't thought that far.'

'I don't want to either. But I think I'll set some very able people to start keeping close tabs on Paxero.'

'What's the object?'

Dall's slate-grey eyes were very cold, his high-cheeked Indian face like brown stone. He said quietly, 'There could come a time when the only thing left would be to ask Paxero some questions.'

*   *   *

Maude smeared a film of oil carefully over the action of

207

the Stoner carbine, wrapped the weapon in a piece of polythene, and slipped it into the case. Water was boiling on a small fire. Willie Garvin was shaving by touch with a safety-razor.

For eight days now they had been edging their way through the jungle, in the eternal twilight beneath the roof of trees. Towards the end of their last day on the river, the boat had turned over going through a seemingly innocuous rapid. They both had their packs attached to their waists with twenty feet of nylon rope. Willie had found himself chest-deep in the racing water, and had lost nothing. Maude's pack had sunk into a deep gulley, dragging her down at the end of the rope. She would have drowned if she had not slashed herself free with the machete strapped to her leg.

The lost pack had contained ten pounds of canned food, her spare clothes, a Smith and Wesson .357 Magnum, her hammock, a rubber flashlight, toilet bag, and the small transmitter which was to have sent the signal to the agents waiting in Benque Viejo. When Willie had dragged her to the bank, a tiny strip of rock and gravel, she had wept from the combined effect of shock, dismay and guilt. He had left her to it until he had checked through his own pack, making sure that the interior water-proof bag had not leaked. Then he had picked her up briskly, stood her on her feet and said, 'Come on, Maude, you're a big girl now. Can't expect to 'ave it easy all the time.'

'But . . . the transmitter . . .'

'Forget it. I've never felt too sure those blokes in Benque Viejo would stay awake. We've still got the carbines, Modesty's 'and-gun, all six grenades, eight 30-round magazines, and both machetes, apart from a bit of food and some general gear. Just let's get our clothes off and see 'ow you look in a spare pair of my Y-fronts. And blow your nose, it's running.'

When they struck into the jungle, Maude carried the two carbines and the long coil of nylon rope which before had been fastened to the outside of Willie's pack. At the first halt he fashioned a wide-meshed hammock from the rope, and at midnight, for the first time, he set up the little receiver with the directional loop-aerial, to listen for the homing signal. When nothing came, he made no comment, but climbed into his hammock and went to sleep. Maude lay awake, troubled by dark imaginings.

In the days that followed, Maude Tiller learned many things that she could not have put into words, and what she learnt was not taught, but in some strange way imparted. Their routine was for Willie to lead for an hour, hacking a path with the machete. Maude would rest, and carry the gear forward every hundred yards or so. Then she would take the machete for half an hour. They spoke very little as they travelled, but what lay between them was easy and companionable. When twilight turned to darkness and they made camp for the night, they talked of many things but never the task in hand.

She learned the way of holding her mind alert and quiescent at the same time; of withdrawing from awareness of pain, weariness and discomfort; above all, of living only in the actual present, a span of moments, so that what had been and what was to come made no impact upon her and drained no energy from her.

On the fourth day, when they reached the crest of the long low rise of jungle, she crouched holding a flashlight for Willie as he set up the little receiver for the midnight schedule. He switched on, pressed the earplug into his ear, and began to turn the loop aerial slowly. Maude tried to watch his face in the outer diffusion of the light. He put his wrist in the beam to check his watch. One minute past twelve. Again he turned the aerial, very slowly. Even as his head jerked, she heard the shrill sound herself. He snatched the plug from his ear, holding it a few inches away, carefully rotating the aerial to seek the strongest reception. Several moments later he said, 'Right, take a bearing on that.'

She lay on her belly, holding the compass just below eye-level, and sighted along the loop of the aerial. 'Got it, Willie.'

He switched off, and together they peered at the compass. Maude swung the flashlight along the narrow trail they had cut in the last hour before making camp. Willie said, 'We're a couple of points off course.'

'Not bad.'

'Not bad for me. The Princess would've walked it in a straight line without a compass.'

'Ah, come on now.'

'No kidding. She's got an instinct.'

Maude sighed. 'If I didn't like her, I'd bloody well hate her. Tell me what she does badly.'

A ghostly chuckle came out of the darkness. 'Sing, sew, paint, deal with salesmen, socialise, suffer fools, make meringues, write letters, grow plants, forget favours, stay out of trouble . . . you name it.'

Maude looked at the small receiver. 'I guess the hump of ground was killing the signal till now. But anyway, she's alive.'

Moving the flashlight a little, she saw Willie nod, then wipe beads of sweat from his upper lip, dragging his hand across. 'I was beginning to get a bit worried,' he said.

On each night since, the signal had come through, growing stronger. For two days they had struck a path of thinner jungle, and had pushed forward five miles in that time. Water was no problem. There were many pools in the dark jungle. It had to be filtered through nylon and boiled, for half their supply of halazone tablets had been lost with Maude's pack, but they had not gone thirsty. The canned food had been eked out with a pheasant-like bird Willie had brought down from its perch on a branch at twenty paces. It had a four-foot wingspan, weighed twelve pounds and the meat had lasted them for three days.

Now Willie estimated that they were no more than four days march from their destination, whatever that might be.

When they had eaten a can of stew, swallowed some vitamin tablets, and had been settled in their hammocks for ten minutes, waiting for the midnight schedule, he said, 'Suppose there was time-travel, Maude.'

She relaxed in the darkness, and wondered vaguely how it was that she felt a greater contentment, a more positive happiness, at this moment than she could easily remember.

'All right, I'm a time-traveller, Willie. What's the next stop?'

'That's the point. You got two choices. Either you can go five 'undred years into the past, give or take ten years or so, and 'ave a look at what the world was like then. Or you can go five 'undred years into the future, and see what it's going to be like.'

'Candidates must specify their choice and give reasons for same?'

'Right.'

She thought for a while, absently scratching the now fading spots on her belly. 'Anywhere in the world? I mean, I don't see much point in late fifteenth century North America. Just Indians and buffalo. What was happening in England?'

'You're on the ten-year run-up to Henry the Seventh and the Tudors.'

'Never mind the kings. I'd like to see how ordinary people lived, but I expect it was pretty dull. On the other hand, there might be only insects left five hundred years ahead.'

'You're talking like a lawyer—on the one hand, on the other hand.'

'Shut up, I'm just doing my preliminary thinking aloud.' A long pause. 'Which did Modesty choose?'

'She didn't. I only just thought of this one, but I'll ask 'er sometime. I reckon she'd choose to go forward.'

'Why?'

'I dunno, Maude. Because it'll be more scary, I suppose. You figure what Walter Ralegh would feel if you dumped 'im in the middle of Piccadilly Circus on a Saturday night. And we're going to move x-times as fast in the next five 'undred.'

'If we last. What's good about being scared?'

'Getting through it. Best tonic in the world. Candidates will lose marks for wandering from the point.'

'All right. Can I have one small irrelevant wander before I decide on going back or forwards, and state reasons therefor?'

'Just a small one.'

'It's just a simple question, really. When we get through this dose of tonic, how about taking little Maude away somewhere warm and wicked and exotic for an orgy of sex?'

'You don't mean . . . ungovernable lust?'

'That very thing.'

'With little Maude? Big red spots on 'er belly and all?'

'Oh, you rotten bugger. They're nearly gone.'

'We'll make it St Thomas. You'll like it there.'

'Where's St Thomas?'

'One of the Virgin Islands.'

'Ha! We'll soon change that.'

*   *   *

At two in the morning Dr Kim Crozier heard tapping on the shuttered window of his bedroom. He got out of bed, eased the window open, and watched Modesty Blaise slip quietly into the room. Her face, hands and feet were black with a cream Kim had made with charcoal. She wore a shirt and trousers which the ever-ingenious Mrs Schultz had contrived to dye a patchy black.

He said, 'How did it go?'

'Pretty good. I can get close enough to the dog compound to throw your doped meat in.'

'I was getting worried.' This was the fourth night she had been out, but tonight she had been gone well over two hours.

She said, 'I went right up to the landing pad and beyond. They *must* have a set-up for damming the river, and that means there's a whole lot of explosive planted somewhere and wired up to a control in the house. Gelignite, probably. If I could find the stuff it would be useful.'

'No luck?'

'Not this time. It may be planted the other side of the river.'

He had followed her out of the bedroom and along to the shower as they spoke. Now she stripped off her shirt and trousers and began to wash the black camouflage from her skin. He grinned and said, 'You should be my colour. Save a lot of trouble.'

'That's a fact. You sent out the midnight signal?'

'As ever.'

'I was wondering about getting to the radio they have in the house, but it's no good.'

'I told you. The big house is better protected than the Specials' quarters, every door locked at night, every room wired with alarms.'

'It's a better defensive position, too. The best chance we've got is if Willie and I can get into the Specials' quarters by night. The lock on the back door's easy, I practised on it tonight.'

He handed her a towel. 'You scare me.'

'I'd scare myself if I thought about it. Can you fix me a cup of coffee, Kim?'

'Sure, but won't it keep you awake for what's left of the night?'

'No, I can go to sleep any time.'

He moved away to his little kitchen, and she began to dry herself. Carefully, not allowing the thought to penetrate dangerously, she acknowledged that in all probability she had bitten off more than she could chew this time. The whole situation in Limbo was too complex and unpredictable to yield to any fixed and clear-cut plan, certainly until Willie

213

arrived. She knew that the big mistake had been made three weeks ago, when she had set herself up for Paxero to snatch. It was obvious now that she should have launched Willie and Maude on their way first, and given them time to get in position before letting Paxero take her. As things stood, she had nothing like the support needed to seize the initiative, and from long hard experience she knew that to hold the initiative was the best of all advantages. There was nothing to be done but wait for Willie . . . unless the flashpoint of Miss Benita's death came earlier.

And then? In the time available, she had made every preparation possible against all combinations of events, but there was no telling how her little group of followers would react when the moment of crisis came.

They could seize-up, wait a few seconds or minutes too long before striking, or look about them for others to move first. Even if their spirit held, their lack of experience augured ill for their chances against the hand-picked killers who made up the Specials.

She felt a flutter of panic, took hold of it, and twisted it into a thread of hard resolve.

Eighteen days now. If all had gone well with Willie and Maude she might hope for some sign of their presence in only three more days. They would come upon the valley from the east, on the other side of the river, and would look down upon Limbo. That would be quite a moment. In daylight they would study the plantation, and Willie would surely pick her out among the slaves. Then he would make contact by night. She decided that from tomorrow, when the day's work ended, she would walk twice round the church before going to the compound for the evening meal. That would give Willie a place and time.

She put on her white shirt, skirt and sandals, and took the black clothes through to Kim. He gave her the cup of coffee and said, 'Any of the slaves know you're down here every night now?'

'Just our own people. I'm supposed to be sleeping with Marker this week in a two-bunk room, so nobody misses me.'

'He's standing by his bet, then? Playing it the way you want?'

She nodded. 'He'll always be a chauvinist male pig, but I'm special to him now. It's funny . . . but if he ever speaks to you about that night in the church, you'll find him almost boastful about the fact that I knocked him cold, as if it held some kind of cachet for him. It usually works that way with the hard men, I don't know why.'

'Fascinating piece of psychology.'

She smiled. 'If you ever work it out, let me know. How's Miss Benita?'

He shrugged. 'Any time. She was pretty bad this morning. Sinclair radioed the site, and Paxero flew in with Damion tonight.'

'I wonder if they'll stay a while. Willie should be here soon, and if they send for me for a kink session, it could be a nice chance.'

He looked at her curiously. 'It doesn't bother you?'

'I'm not even there, except in a remote sort of way. How's Miss Benita's mania for the old Mayan gods?'

'The same. They shot a fake film in a studio somewhere, sacrificing some girl. I think Paxero's chary of sending out any more Specials to do a real job now.'

'That's something.' She put down the mug. 'Thanks for the coffee, Kim.'

When she had gone he lay on his bed gazing into the darkness for a long time. While she was with him he always felt a quiet exhilaration, an illogical confidence that all would be well. When he was alone, he sometimes wondered if his mind had begun to play tricks at last, and if her coming to Limbo was no more real than a dream.

*　　*　　*

215

When Sinclair had supervised the morning roll-call, the slaves moved out in their usual sections under the three overseers on morning duty. This was the time of year when the crop had been picked and dried, and each section in turn would be engaged in the laborious task of hulling by hand, working by the big sheds on the western edge of Limbo. The other two sections were busy on the plantation, one working each side of the central road, hoeing, weeding, cleaning out the shallow pebble-filled irrigation trenches fed by water pumped from the river.

At ten o'clock, in the big main bedroom with the Venetian blinds slatted against the sun, Paxero looked across the shrunken figure in the bed and said harshly, 'Is she dead?'

Dr Kim Crozier straightened up and took the stethoscope from his ears, keeping his face a blank and trying not to remember that he might be living his last moments in this world. Damion stood by the closed door.

Kim said, 'Miss Benita's in coma, sir. It's what I've been telling you might happen.'

'A coma? But . . . she's not breathing.'

'It's not perceptible. I can try that injection I spoke about. It might give her a few weeks, sir.' Kim had rehearsed the words many times now, and hoped frantically that they sounded natural. This was the stopper Modesty had given him.

Paxero said in a low, hard voice, 'A few weeks, a few days or hours. *Try it!* Don't stand there and let her die, you black bastard!'

'I have to get the ampoule from my surgery, sir.'

'What?' Paxero's face became mottled with fury.

Kim said hastily. 'I couldn't take it out of the fridge before. It has to be used right away, at not more than two degrees centigrade.'

'Get it!' Paxero said. 'Take him down, Damion. *Move!*'

Kim snatched up his bag and made for the door. Damion followed, one hand on the gun under his jacket. Thirty seconds later a Land Rover roared away from the big house and went snarling down the road. One of the Specials was at the wheel, Kim Crozier beside him, Damion in the back. The truck crested the low rise which ended at the northern border of the plantation, then hurtled on down the long slope towards the slave quarters. Between the lines of trees, slaves turned to stare. Kim took out a square of dull red cotton, dyed with mulberries, and began to wipe his face with it.

Danny Chavasse lifted his basket of weeds, swung it on to his back, then moved towards the horse-drawn cart which stood between two lines of trees. Modesty straightened up to wipe her brow as he passed and said quietly, 'Was that it?'

Danny nodded, his stomach tight and cold. 'Miss Benita's gone. Kim was showing the red handkerchief.'

She looked along the strip being worked. Valdez and Teresa were in this section, east of the central road, and must have heard the urgent sound of the speeding truck, for they were looking towards her. She took off her floppy linen hat, and waved it as if dispersing insects. 'We'll need to co-opt one more pair of hands, Danny. When I've taken care of Mr Joe, you quieten the section down so there's no panic, then get hold of Bissau and follow me down to the road. I think he'll be all right.'

Mr Joe began to walk his horse towards them. 'You-girl. Git workin'. I don't allow no idle-talkin' trash in my section.' He let the coils of the lash fall, and gave a practised crack of the whip. Danny moved towards the cart. His mouth was suddenly dry, his heart pounding, for in Modesty's right hand he had seen a small, crudely carved wooden dumb-bell. The kongo.

She moved towards the overseer, her left hand held out, calling anxiously, 'I got a bad cut, Mr Joe. Can I go for Dr Crozier to fix it?'

Idly, expertly, he flicked the whip. The lash leapt out,

its tip laying a red weal across her upper arm. She jumped and gave a satisfactory yelp of pain. Mr Joe said, 'Don't like stupid trash who git 'emselves cut. Lemme see.'

Danny saw her move closer, showing wary apprehension. She extended her left hand, palm up. Mr Joe leaned down a little, peered, then reached out. Her hand darted, fingers clamping round his wrist, and in the same instant she jumped. Danny saw her right arm move in a blur, and heard the muted sound of wood on bone. The overseer fell sideways. She caught the horse's bridle as he hit the ground and said, 'Danny. Valdez.'

Danny took the reins. Valdez was there, face taut, sweating. She drew the carbine from the saddle-holster, a .30 Winchester M2, bent to take the Colt .45 from the man's gunbelt, passed both weapons to the Paraguayan and said, 'We'll join you as soon as we can.'

Valdez said prayerfully, 'Sweet Jesus,' then turned and moved up the slope towards the northern edge of the plantation which faced the big house.

With a heave she turned the unconscious man on his back, doubled his feet back and lashed them to his wrists with the whip, then passed the thong round his throat. Teresa came running up, eyes enormous in a face white under the tan. Most of the slaves had noticed nothing yet, and were still working. A few had stopped and were staring without comprehension, or with dawning terror.

Teresa was launching a kick at the overseer's head when Modesty caught her, swung her away and slapped her face hard. 'Keep it cool, cool, cool!' she said urgently. 'Lose control, and we're sunk. Christ, you *know* what you have to do, Teresa, so pretend you're acting in a film if you can't manage any other way.' Turning, she started towards the horse and cart, throwing a last word over her shoulder. 'Talk to them, Danny, and make it good.'

Fourteen

IN THE big house, Paxero took the hand-mirror from Aunt Benita's parted lips and looked at it. There was no sign of misting. He dragged at his jaw. She looked dead. He could find no pulse, no sign of life. But Crozier was a good doctor, and had insisted this was a coma. Paxero had read of people being certified dead who were in deep coma. Perhaps Aunt Benita had not yet gone. All the same . . .

With sudden decision he picked up the house-phone and pressed one of the buttons. 'Sinclair? I want all the Specials and off-duty overseers in the big hall right away, fully armed. Correction. Leave two Specials in their quarters to deal with the mestizo women if I give the word. Yes. We may be closing down.'

In the plantation on the western side of the road, Marker saw Teresa coming. He had heard the roar of the speeding truck, guessed what it might portend, and levered the head from the handle of his hoe. The end which had been hidden in the metal sleeve of the head was whittled to a sharp point and had been hardened by charring.

Teresa trudged along with the usual slow gait of the slaves. She was acting now. The cameras were upon her as she Carried The Vital Message. When she passed the bit-player, Marker, she whispered without moving her lips, '*Action.*'

Marker picked up his basket, the hoe tucked under his arm. He fell in behind the girl. Mr Sam glanced at her and ignored her. She was not of his section. At six paces distance. Marker dropped his basket and began to run. The overseer barely had time to register that something was wrong before the fire-hardened spear drove into his body with all Marker's power behind it.

Teresa heard the gasping grunt and the sound of the fall. She spun round, registering for the zoom close-up; flash of revulsion succeeded by grim acceptance of the brutal necessity. Marker was taking the carbine from the saddle-holster, the handgun from the dead man's belt. A two-shot now, Teresa coming into camera, catching the reins as the horse moved nervously. She said in the throaty voice that had been familiar to millions, 'Get to the drying-sheds and take care of the overseer there . . . *and keep it quiet, Marker.*'

It was a pity he had wrenched out the make-shift spear and begun to run well before she had finished her lines. There would have to be a re-take of that. From the corner of her eye she saw Mr Sam lying on his back, his shirt horribly blotched with red, and thought that the make-up men had done a good job on him. Turning, she swung up into the saddle of his horse, hitching her skirt high. The slaves were frozen, most of them. She waved an arm, beckoning them to gather about her, riding a little this way, a little the other.

Hart, the flaxen-haired Texan, said in a low ragged voice, 'In God's name, has Marker gone *crazy*? They'll hang him! They'll flog the whole section!'

Teresa rested her hands on the horn of the saddle and looked slowly round the half-circle of shocked faces. 'Listen to me very carefully,' she said, and though her voice was quiet every word was clear as a bell. 'Miss Benita is dead. Limbo is finished. They will kill us now, in the next hour, unless we save ourselves. But some of us have been ready for this moment . . . so listen quietly, calmly, while I tell you what must be done.'

*   *   *

The Land Rover swung away from the surgery, turned on to the main road with spinning wheels, and roared north towards the big house. As it reached the point where the upper windows and roof of the house were hidden behind the crest of the long upslope, a white-skirted figure leading a horse and cart emerged from the trees, moving slowly across the road, blocking the way.

The Special at the wheel swore violently and braked. The horn was dead, for Miss Benita allowed no horns in Limbo. As the truck slithered to a scrabbling halt Damion yelled, 'Out of the way, you stupid cow!'

Kim Crozier, in the passenger seat, watched Modesty. His nerves taut, he suddenly knew the reality of what she had called 'stab-fright', the natural fear that held you back in the moment of committing yourself to action. Above the throb of the engine she was saying something urgently as she moved forward, passing the offside wing of the truck, looking at Damion, gesturing. There was a brief moment when Kim realised that she was either speaking gibberish or a language unknown to him. He heard Damion say furiously, 'What?' Then she was past the driver, and as the man turned his head to watch her, Kim threw off the paralysis of stab-fright and reached out to switch off the engine.

Her right arm swung, and the little wooden dumb-bell struck under the driver's ear. Damion's reaction was faster than she had catered for, faster by a long way. Even as the driver slumped over the wheel Damion half rose, drawing back towards the nearside, his hand flashing beneath the light jacket he wore, lips stretching in a grimace. Hand on the door, she vaulted high, pivoting on the fulcrum of her arm, then her body snapped into full extension and her heels smashed into Damion's face and throat even as the gun came clear. He was flung from the truck, arching backwards in a sprawling dive.

As he hit the ground, Modesty landed in the back of the Land Rover. She reached to take the gun from the driver's holster and said, 'I want them right out of action for hours, Kim.'

'I'm all set.' He opened his bag, hands not quite steady. 'What about your overseer?'

She got out of the truck. 'Here.'

Danny and Bissau came from the cover of the trees, carrying the bound figure of Mr Joe between them. Bissau's heavy face was a pale mask, but his jaw was set hard against the fear that gripped him. They heaved the overseer into the back. Kim opened a box of ampoules. Danny said, 'You needn't worry about Mr Sam, Marker killed him. We don't know what's happened at the drying-sheds yet with Mr Brad.'

Kim drew chlorpromazine into the hypodermic. 'I guess we can stop calling them Mister.'

'Just habit.' Danny tried to smile, tried to relax the aching tension within him.

Modesty rose from beside the sprawled figure of Damion and said, 'You won't need to keep this one quiet either, Kim.'

'I thought not. Neck?'

'Yes. I must have been feeling more grudgy than I knew.' She picked up Damion's gun, a Smith & Wesson .357 Magnum, then moved to rummage in the truck. 'Didn't you say the Specials always carry spare magazines for their BARs, Kim?'

'In a rack, off-side.'

'It's empty. Ah, well . . .' She lifted the .30 calibre Browning Automatic Rifle from between the seats. The difference between having one twenty-round magazine and perhaps three or four was possibly the difference between having a small chance of winning and none at all, but her face betrayed no sign of the dismaying blow.

Danny said, 'There's a machete in the back here.'

'Good.' She gathered up her skirt. 'Hack this off short. It slowed me down just now, and we've got all the handicaps we need. Bissau, give Kim a hand getting Damion and that Special into the back.'

222

Bissau said, 'What is to happen now?'

She turned as Danny sliced his way round the skirt. 'Kim takes these three back to his surgery and gets ready to cope with casualties. Our casualties, not theirs. We head for the ridge at the north end of the plantation, where we can cover the house from behind that dwarf wall carrying the irrigation pipe. Valdez is there now, waiting for us. It won't be long before Paxero makes a move. He'll be starting to wonder already.'

Bissau helped Kim lift Damion's body. 'And then?'

'We've got a few weapons now. Enough to keep them pegged back in the house.'

Bissau heaved Damion's legs into the truck and wiped his brow. 'And then?'

Modesty unbuckled the gunbelts of the Special and the overseer. 'I'll let you know,' she said.

* * *

Valdez lay behind the eighteen-inch wall, watching the big house two hundred yards away. A three inch pipe, mounted on brackets, ran along the top of the wall, carrying water to the irrigation reservoir from which it was gravity fed to the plantation. Peering through the gap between the wall and the pipe, Valdez felt utterly alone.

When the Specials had poured out of their quarters a few minutes ago, all carrying automatic rifles, he had known sheer terror. His task was to hold them, if need be, until Modesty and the others joined him with more weapons, and Valdez was quite certain that his chances of surviving for more than two or three minutes were zero. The revolver was useless except at short range. He had hunted small game in both North and South America, and was a better than average shot, but doubted that the M2 carbine was acurately sighted.

When the Specials had gone straight into the big house

instead of moving towards the plantation, relief had almost loosened his bowels. Now a strange calm had come upon him as the minutes passed. Short of a miracle, he thought, he would soon be a dead man. Well, that was not so terrible. He had little enough to lose, and at least he would take two or three of them with him. The idea made him feel almost cheerful.

A quarter of a mile away, Marker crouched against a tree, a long stone's throw from the sheds, seething in an agony of frustration. The section overseer, Mr Brad, must have heard or sensed something to make him suspicious. He had dismounted from his horse, and had made the whole section line up facing the wall of one big shed, their hands flat on the timbers. Carbine held at waist level, menacing the slaves, he kept looking uneasily about him.

For two minutes now Marker had been trying to devise some way of getting close enough to silence the overseer. He had the carbine and handgun taken from Mr Sam, but a shot would trigger instant reaction at the big house, and for the moment Valdez would be covering it alone.

Marker bit his lip, then stood up, leaving the two weapons where they lay. Slowly he began to move forward, limping heavily, supporting himself on the hoe-handle.

Mr Brad saw him and called, 'What you doin' here, boy?'

'Accident, Mr Brad.' Marker limped on. He saw Schultz, against the shed, half turn his head to look over his shoulder. Mr Brad's carbine swung slowly from the line of slaves to Marker, and back again. At twenty paces he said, 'You git in line against the shed, boy.'

'Got a message for you, Mr Brad,' Marker said desperately, and limped on towards him. 'Mr Sam sent me.'

The overseer's suspicious gaze fastened on the bloody base of the hoe-handle, and his eyes widened. 'What's that? What's that blood?'

'Accident. Mr Sam sent to tell you.' Marker heard himself babbling the words. He knew he was doomed, for the
224

carbine steadied on him now. Ten paces. He could never make it. But he knew his own strength, and if the bullet hit no vital spot he might yet bring down the black man and give Schultz a chance, a small chance.

Mr Brad said loudly, 'You come closer, I kill you, boy!' There was a hint of panic in the overseer's eyes and voice. Marker moved on, tensing himself for the final effort, braced against the shock of the bullet. Something flickered in the air, angling between him and the other man. He heard the sound of a soft impact, and blinked dazedly at the black thing which had leapt suddenly from Mr Brad's chest and stood jutting there like . . .

Like the haft of a knife.

Mr Brad folded at the knees. Instinctively Marker lunged forward and caught the carbine as it sagged from nerveless hands. The overseer fell, breath rattled in his throat, and then he was silent. Marker turned, stupefied, and saw a man in jungle-green camouflage drop from between two gables of the shed roof. He was a big man, with fair hair curling from beneath a green jockey-cap, clean-shaven, a carbine slung on his back, ammunition pouches on his chest, a small pack on one hip, and field glasses hanging from his shoulder.

The man said quietly with a strong Cockney accent, 'All right, 'ands down everyone and no noise.' He moved towards Marker, jerking his thumb to the roof where he had been hidden. 'I've just seen Modesty Blaise take care of a couple of blokes in a truck, so I reckon some sort of balloon's gone up.'

Marker dragged a great breath of air into his lungs and said hoarsely, 'Garvin? You're Garvin?'

The big man nodded, bent to jerk his knife from the body, wiped the blade, and slipped it back into a sheath under his open jacket. Schultz moved forward, holding his wife's hand. The other slaves stared blankly, some with dawning hope, others with dawning fear.

Schultz said, 'Miss Benita's dead? It's started, Marker?'

225

Willie Garvin said, 'Just a minute. Tell me 'ow Modesty Blaise reckons to play it.'

Marker gathered his wits with an effort. 'She'll be heading for the ridge with one or two others. Aims to hold a line there with the guns we've collected.' He looked at Schultz. 'Teresa's bringing the other two sections in. You keep them quiet in the sheds.' He pointed. 'She wants Gasparro as a runner, and Stavros to handle a gun—'

From the north there came the sudden chatter of small-arms fire. Willie Garvin started to run.

* * *

She had arrived only one minute before the Specials emerged from the big house and began to move towards the plantation. Now she lay against the dwarf wall, barrel of the automatic rifle resting between the wall and the irrigation pipe. Bissau lay beside her with the Colt. Fifty yards away along the wall, Danny Chavasse was with Valdez.

She had seen her first shot with the BAR go a few inches wide of its target, hitting the butt of the rifle the man carried. Her next shot, adjusted for inaccurate sights, had found its mark. Valdez hit a man in the shoulder with his second shot. Some of the Specials threw themselves flat, others darted for cover.

A burst of wild firing raked the trees behind her. She signalled Valdez to hold his fire. They had only one magazine each. A Land Rover crept out from behind the house, and three men darted to gather behind it. The driver was crouched low, out of sight.

She realised bleakly that the battle, barely begun, might soon be lost. Marker and Stavros should have been here by now, each with a carbine and revolver to give added firepower. Bissau, watching her, saw her eyes burn suddenly. She said, 'Give me the Colt, and take the rifle, I'm going to move a little way right. Wait till that truck's really close,

226

then engage them. I'll come in fast and gun them down with the Colt, then we'll have some more BARs to play with—'

She broke off, head cocked at the sound of a steady *yap, yap, yap,* a weapon firing single-shot, but from a distance. From the east. From somewhere on the high slope across the river.

The Land Rover swerved drunkenly and stalled. The three men, exposed, turned and ran. *Yap. Yap.* One went down hard. The other two vanished behind the western corner of the big house. The rest of the Specials had already pulled back inside.

She rested her head on the butt for a moment, and let a surge of relief and exhilaration wash through her. The incomparable Willie Garvin was here, two days ahead of her best expectations.

Bissau said shakily, 'Who . . . ?'

She lifted her head, smiling. 'An old friend, from Outside.'

''Allo, Princess.' His voice, from a little way behind, was startling. Her head snapped round, and she saw him wriggling towards her, keeping low. He pointed, and she looked along the line of trees to see Marker, with a carbine, crawling up to join Valdez and Danny Chavasse. Behind Willie came two white-clad figures. Stavros, also with a carbine, and Gasparro.

Willie came up beside her and unslung his Stoner 63. 'That was Maude.' He jerked his head towards the river. 'We got 'ere a couple of hours before sun-down last night.'

'Hallo, Willie love. Welcome to Limbo.' She reached out a hand. He took it, and touched her knuckles briefly to his cheek.

'It's quite a place you've got 'ere.' He rolled on his side to look her up and down, still euphoric with the relief he had known since he had seen her through the glasses yesterday and felt the burden of anxiety and responsibility lift from his shoulders. 'You look like Robinson Crusoe in pantomime,' he said, grinning at the ragged mini-skirt.

'What trap-door did you spring from?'

'I crossed up-river before dawn. Left Maude in a nice commanding position on the other side. I figured to lie low and make contact soon as I got a chance, but then things started 'appening.'

'Yes. I'll fill you in later. Let's back off from here and get ourselves a position in the laundry.' She nodded towards the north-western corner of the plantation, beyond where Danny, Marker and Valdez lay. 'That way we'll have the open ground in a cross-fire. Have you got communication with Maude?'

He held up a black tube, seven inches long and as thick as his thumb. Attached to one end was a lead with an ear-plug. 'She'll be listening out.'

'Tell her what we're doing. She can cover the open ground while we're moving. And tell her thanks a million.'

As Willie slipped the plug in his ear there came the sound of a muffled shot from somewhere in front of them, then several more, irregularly spaced. Warily they lifted their heads, peering through the gap between the dwarf wall and the irrigation pipe. Three mestizo girls came running from the Specials' quarters, one staggering and holding her side, two screaming as they ran. Two men came in pursuit. There was a rattle of fire and the girls went down. Willie slid his Stoner through the gap and shot one man dead. Modesty's bullet plucked the other's hat away as he flung himself across the gap and vanished behind the wall of the big house.

She said furiously, 'Bastards! They were killing off their women.'

Willie nodded. During two hours of studying Limbo through glasses yesterday, he had built up a fairly clear pattern of its structure. He pressed a button on the tube and said, 'Maude. Nice shooting, love. Yes. I've made contact. We're in cover be'ind the irrigation wall, and we're moving to that place on the north-west corner. Keep their 'eads down if they try to move out, but don't waste any shots.'

228

He listened. 'Yes, fine. She sends you 'ers, and says thanks a million. Call you in ten minutes.'

*   *   *

In the larger store-shed the slaves sat in rows on the floor, listening to Schultz, who stood on a crate at one end. He looked very tired and his manner was laboured, which was unusual.

Long ago, in the world Outside, Schultz had been a steel magnate, but for years now he and his wife had found themselves with the task of maintaining a kind of peace in Limbo; peace between slave and slave, peace between the slaves and those who controlled them. In the main, and with a huge indebtedness to Kim Crozier, they had succeeded. It had meant preaching acceptance, obedience, passivity, and it had meant creating a new kind of society. But now, in a moment, the whole world of Limbo had changed, and Schultz felt disorientated and inadequate. His task was to prevent a panic. Modesty had said, 'Keep them from under our feet, Schultz. On the last day in Limbo, there'll be nothing more important than that.'

Schultz was deeply afraid of failing. He glanced at his wife for support, saw her quick encouraging nod, and went on doggedly, '. . . so that's how we stand, friends. When Miss Benita died, it was closing time for Limbo, closing time for *all* of us. But Modesty came in a few weeks back to make sure things didn't work out that way. I guess we're all pretty scared. I know I am. It's a pity there's nothing we can do to help the folks up front, but like Modesty says, you can't fight guns with coffee beans. All we can do is sit tight . . . and pray.'

The church group, in a corner, were already doing that. Among the rest of the slaves, emotion ranged from fevered excitement through numb bewilderment to open fear.

Schultz went on, 'They're pretty good folk up front, so we

229

don't have to worry too much. There's Marker, and you know he's tough. There's Valdez and Teresa likewise. We've got two people from Outside, good enough to get here through the jungle, and armed up to the eyeballs. We've got Danny and Bissau, real sound folk. And then there's Modesty. Well, she's been pretty quiet since she got here, but if a mixed bunch like Kim and Marker and Teresa are all backing her to win, that's quite something.'

Schultz indicated the dark, sparely built man who had arrived breathlessly a few minutes earlier. 'Now, Gasparro here and Teresa are acting as runners, so we're kept in the picture as to what's happening. Gasparro's just brought the latest news, which is that Paxero and the Specials are all holed-up in the big house. They've killed off the mestizo girls, which shows you what they'd have done with *us*, and they've probably killed all the domestic staff as well. The dogs are still shut in the compound, and nobody can get to them without crossing open ground. Our folk have killed four Specials and wounded one at least, and Modesty broke Damion's neck for him, which I guess a lot of you women will be glad to hear.'

An Englishman with greying hair stood up. His name was Thurston, and for most of his two years in Limbo he had been universally disliked for his aloof manner and unreadiness to co-operate. He had once been handsome, but his face was now hollow and his body wasting. For several weeks he had been dying, but he was doing so without fuss, and had been better liked in that time than ever before. He said politely, 'I was an army man for a time, Schultz. It seems there's a deadlock situation at present. But Paxero and the Specials have the fire-power, and after dark they can get out, free the dogs, and take up positions anywhere they like. If they're spread round the perimeter by first light, they can slaughter anything that moves in Limbo.'

With a tremendous effort Schultz smiled a confident smile. 'I was coming to that,' he lied, 'and there's no need to worry.

230

The two folks who came in from Outside have sent off a signal, and we'll have a back-up of military coming in by helicopter long before dark.'

*   *   *

Modesty leaned against the stout timbers of the laundry, watching through one of the slits Danny had hacked with the machete. She said, 'So there's no back-up?'

Willie shook his head, 'We lost the transmitter.'

Marker said, 'Christ, that's great!'

Willie gave him a pleasant smile. 'I'll be more careful next time.' He looked at Modesty. 'They're waiting for dark, Princess. We'll 'ave to finish it before then.'

'Yes.' She spoke absently. Some element in the situation was troubling her deeply, but she could not pin it down.

Willie slipped the barrel of the Stoner carbine through a slit and sighted experimentally on an upper window of the big house. Teresa watched him with interest. After a moment she said, 'We should arm all the slaves, with spades and clubs-a and anything, then attack in a great-a mass.'

Danny Chavasse, sitting on the floor beside her, said, 'We're not on location, carissima. They'd like nothing better than a chance to slaughter us in a great mass.'

'Okay, so tell me when you got a good script.' The Italian girl folded her arms on her drawn-up knees and rested her head on them.

Modesty said, 'Teresa, I want you to go down to the sheds. Send Gasparro up here in case we need him, then go on down to Kim's surgery, put him in the picture, and bring back the clothes of the Special he's got there doped. Keep the laundry between you and the house till you're far enough down the slope.'

Teresa got up. 'You don't-a have to tell me the last piece, kid. I was a girl partisan in *Destination Salerno*.' She grinned and went out.

Still watching through the slit Modesty said, 'Take over

231

from me here, Marker. And Valdez take over from Willie. We want to check something outside.'

A minute later, in the angle formed by the L-shape of the laundry, she leaned back against the wall, blew out a long breath and looked ruefully at Willie. 'I just wanted us to be on our own for a bit. It's hard to think with everyone waiting for you to come up with a master-stroke.'

He nodded. 'It's a big one, this.'

'Too big.' She grimaced. 'Too many people, too many factors, too many imponderables. But let's deal with the bits we can deal with. We've got to clean up the big house before dark, and that's something you and I will have to handle. I've got an idea that could help a lot—' She stopped short, and her face went blank. 'Oh, God. I've just caught up with why I sent Teresa down to the surgery. I thought it was only to keep her busy.'

'Something else?'

'Willie . . . Paxero isn't just waiting for dark. He's got radio communication with the development site at New Santiago, *and he's waiting for more men.*'

Willie looked at the sky to the west. Top management on the site would be picked men who knew Paxero's secret, who arranged the ferrying of supplies. With a thousand or more construction workers living there, cut off from the world, it would take only a few hours to pick out a score of hard men ready to earn a thousand dollars apiece for whatever they were called upon to do, and to fly them to Limbo.

Willie said, 'We can't get past the 'ouse to the landing pad from 'ere, but Maude could get to it in about 'alf-an-hour from across the river. It's only running at about twelve knots.'

'There's a barbed-wire net across it, Willie, some way beyond the landing pad. If she wraps her hands up she can haul herself across on the down-river side of it.' A pause, then a little shake of the head. 'But Maude can't handle the whole job on her own.'

232

'No. I was just thinking, Princess. If I went in the river at the south end of the plantation, I'd be down at the barbed wire in about five minutes, and I don't think they'd see me from the 'ouse. I could pad meself with coffee-sacks to save a few scratches.'

She stood leaning against the wall of the laundry, BAR cradled, long brown legs angling out from beneath the ragged cotton skirt, head turned to gaze distantly away. After a few moments she looked at him and smiled. 'No, I can't spare you, Willie. It's either Marker or Valdez.'

'Marker's pretty tough.'

'Very. But Valdez is cooler, and this has to be played right. What's more, he speaks Spanish. We want that helicopter and pilot, Willie.' She took his arm and they began moving towards the door. 'That must be why I sent Teresa to pick up those clothes the Special was wearing.'

Two minutes later Valdez said wryly, 'Please do not think I wish to chicken out. I have used up my ration of being afraid for today, but the fact is that I cannot swim.'

Willie appeared round the corner, trundling one of the big laundry barrels. 'I got a better idea. If we weight this right, you can go down with the current. Easier to keep your gun dry, too.'

Ten minutes later, in the big store-shed, Schultz said, 'Can I have your attention, friends? Gasparro's just brought word from Modesty, and we have work to do. We need some nice thick timbers, and I suggest we start by ripping down part of that end wall.'

*　　*　　*

Maude Tiller dragged herself out of the river and fell in a panting heap. When she had regained her breath she sat up, sucked at a gashed wrist, then drew the polythene-wrapped Stoner 63 carbine from its case and began to check it carefully.

Twenty minutes later she saw a barrel swing round the bend of the river. It was floating with no more than a foot of freeboard, and two wooden outriggers had been lashed to it at water level to prevent it tipping. When it hit the barbed wire she unwound the rope from her waist, threw the end to the man who crouched in the barrel, and hauled the strange craft into the bank. The man passed her the Colt .45 he carried, and a bundle of clothes wrapped in a piece of oilskin, then clambered out.

The wet, dirty, jungle-worn girl with the insect-bitten face said, 'I'm Maude Tiller.'

'I am Valdez.' He drew an arm across his brow, staring at her. 'Sweet Jesus, I did not think there could be another like Modesty.'

'There isn't, so we just have to try harder.' She gave a lopsided grin. Valdez felt a swift, stimulating empathy with this girl. He felt almost happy as he knelt and began to unwrap the bundle of clothes with the hand-grenade in the centre.

Fifteen

PAXERO HAD twelve Specials with him in the big house now, and three overseers. The serving staff had quickly been disposed of, soon after the shooting began. For a time he had been shaken badly, but now he was confident again. The slaves could not attack. Reinforcements would arrive soon, and when darkness came he would have every advantage.

His men would move out in pairs, spread round the perimeter, and wait for first light. One or two might be picked off, but Blaise could have less than a handful of slaves with the will and ability to fight. It would all be over by soon after sunrise.

He looked at Aunt Benita lying with hands crossed on her breast, checked that the candles burning on each side of the bed would last for some hours yet, crossed himself, then went out into the passage.

Sinclair emerged from a back room and said, 'The big helicopter's coming in.' As he finished speaking there came a shout from one of the front rooms. 'Señor Paxero! Venga rápido!'

He broke into a run. There were two men at the window of what had been the bedroom of Aunt Benita's personal maid. Paxero joined them, peering warily round the edge of the frame. The big truck used for heavy work and maintaining the roads was emerging from the western perimeter road. Long timbers had been lashed to the top of the canopy frame, shorter timbers blocked the whole windscreen, presumably leaving a small aperture for vision, and uprights lashed to the bumper shielded the engine.

Paxero sprang for the door, shouting. 'Sinclair! They've rigged an armoured truck to get in close! Get all the men downstairs, and split them to cover front and back. *Hurry!*' He turned back into the room. The two men there had risen to go, but he waved them back and said in Spanish, 'No. They will not all be in the truck. Stay here and be ready for a follow-up.'

He stood watching the approach of the great lumpy monster. There might be the chance of an oblique shot at the driver if it turned . . . and it *must* turn sooner or later, either to move round the back or to pull along the front of the house. The slaves in the back of the truck would be huddled behind earth-filled sacks or more timbers, but they would have to get out. And then . . .

Modesty Blaise crouched against the front of the truck's interior. She wore the belt, holster and Colt .38 Willie had brought for her. On her left hip was a pouch with two grenades. Willie had three. The sixth was with Valdez.

A huge ragged hole had been hacked in the back of the cab to give access to the truck. Through it she could see Willie sitting to one side of the wheel, steering with one hand. Two hoe-handles were lashed to the steering, and she held the ends loosely.

Willie said, 'Eighty yards, Princess.' He pressed the accelerator hard down for three seconds, then turned to scramble through the hole. There was an inch-wide slit in the windscreen timbers for vision, and through it she could see a strip of the western half of the house, from the big porch to the corner. The truck began to veer slightly, and she brought it back on course with the long handles.

In the bedroom, Paxero pressed his face against the wall to watch obliquely. If the fool at the wheel didn't turn or start to brake soon he'd run straight into the house—

Understanding exploded in his mind like a flashbulb. He lunged for the door, burst into the passage and raced for the head of the stairs, bellowing a warning. Then came a great crunching impact, and the whole house shivered as he was flung to the floor.

Within the laundry, Marker and Danny, Teresa and Bissau watched through the slits. Not a word was spoken or a breath drawn as the great truck ploughed into Miss Benita's house like a tank. Its offside extended partway across a big ground floor window, and only seconds before impact they had glimpsed a man there, firing on automatic as the truck lumbered down.

The sound of crumbling masonry and tortured beams came clearly to their ears, and when the truck finally halted it had driven half its length into the house. They saw Modesty swing out of the back and up onto the roof-timbers of the truck, running for the crazily leaning balcony. Willie followed, then both were lost in swirling dust.

Marker said, 'They made it. Let's go.'

Stavros put a hand on his arm. 'She said five minutes.'

Danny nodded. 'It only needs one man at a window to pick us off. We do it her way, Marker.'

To the south, Schultz was leading the slaves up the hill, all but a few who had mentally withdrawn from everything that was going on and now sat listlessly in the big store-shed. On Modesty's word, Schultz had given everybody the hard truth now, for it could do no harm.

Half a mile to the north, Valdez stood well clear of the landing pad. He wore a check shirt, cord trousers and a bush hat. Maude stood against a tree on the fringe of jungle, thirty paces away. The big Boeing Chinook, with its twin rotor pylons, was slanting down to land. Five seconds earlier, even above the clamour of the Lycoming turboshaft engines, they had heard the thunderous noise of the truck hitting the house.

Valdez lowered his gaze to stare down the valley, then glanced at Maude. She grimaced, lifting a hand with crossed fingers. He nodded, then looked up again and waved to the descending helicopter.

The room served by the balcony was empty. They crossed the sagging floor. Willie wrenched the half-jammed door open and Modesty went out fast, spinning as she flew across the broad passage to the far wall, the Colt .38 in her hand. By the stairhead, Paxero was getting to his feet, staring towards her. As he lifted the automatic she shot him through the head at fifteen paces.

Willie was in the passage now, against the other wall. He held a knife by the blade in his left hand, a carbine in his right. Handguns were anathema to Willie Garvin, and by his own admission he was useless with them, but he was very expert with a long barrel, even from the hip, and strong enough to use the eight-pound Stoner one-handed. They began to move towards the stairhead, Modesty facing forward, Willie facing back. From below came sounds of turmoil, shouting, and running feet, laced with the sound of a man screaming in pain.

Modesty glanced down at the automatic lying by Paxero's body. It was a Colt Commander nine-shot .38 and would be a useful addition to her fire-power. She crouched, and was reaching towards it when two men stepped out of a room further along the passage. She saw them first as undefined movement on the edge of her vision, refocused instantly, saw the BAR aimed from a man's hip, another coming up to the aim, and fired across her body, under her left arm, with the revolver in her right hand. A single shot came from the BAR as the man jerked and spun, lurching against his companion, and in the same moment Willie turned and fired. Both men went down in an ugly tangle of limbs and rifles.

For a moment the house seemed to fall quiet, then somebody shouted, 'Señor Paxero!' Feet sounded in the hall below, and Sinclair's voice snapped, 'Get up there and see!' There was an edge of panic in it.

238

Willie saw Modesty kneeling up, a hand pressed to her stomach, a red stain spreading over the rag of a skirt. As his mind froze, an automatic circuit cut in smoothly. He took his knife in his teeth, pulled a grenade from his pouch, jerked the pin free, and tossed the grenade over the balustrade. It was bellowing its death-cry below when he snatched Modesty up in his arms, moved along the passage, and set her down in an open doorway from which they could see the stairhead.

Face rigid, he cut the waistband of her skirt, pulled it gently away, and eased the top of her pants down. She took the skirt and mopped blood from her stomach, peering down.

'I . . . don't think I'm gut-shot, Willie. Too much bleeding, and not enough shock—'

'Let me see. Lean back.'

She obeyed, taking the carbine, and swivelling as she lay supine, sighting upside down on the head of the stairs. Ten seconds later Willie let out a long exhalation, and wadded her skirt over the wound. 'In and out, through a fold of flesh when you were bending over. You got two 'oles about four inches apart, level with each other.'

'Get a dressing on, quick.'

He was snatching the field dressing from his thigh pocket as she spoke, then tearing the plastic cover away with his teeth, spreading the medicated pad over her belly, pressing down the plaster backing round the edges. She rolled over, got to her feet, moved a tentative pace or two, then nodded.

'All right. It might slow me down a little, though.' She gave him the carbine. 'You take the service stairs and start working through below. I'll hold the stairhead.'

He visualised the house plan she had shown him, drawn by someone called Kim, a slave doctor who knew the house. 'Right, Princess.' He moved off at a run along the passage. Modesty wiped sweat from her eyes, moved to the dead men, picked up both BARs, then settled herself in a prone position in the doorway and put her two grenades con-

239

veniently to hand. The stairhead lay obliquely along the passage, ten paces away, and the muzzle of one automatic rifle was trained steadily upon it.

She was only distantly aware of the wound beginning to hurt. Part of her being was totally engaged with the stair-head, the rest was with Willie Garvin. Ninety seconds later she heard the roar of his second grenade from below.

*   *   *

Marker said, 'Christ, you hear that? Paxero and his boys are as busy as they're ever going to be now!'

He was hunched in the back of the Land Rover, carbine in his hands. Beside him, Bissau carried another. Danny was at the wheel, Stavros in the passenger seat with the remaining carbine. The slaves Schultz had brought from below were watching and listening, showing every emotion from be-wildered fear to sombre hope. Teresa started to clamber into the back, one of the .45's in her hand. Marker said, 'Stop acting, you silly bitch. This is for real.'

She glared at him. 'You go screw, Marker! I *know* this-a for real, and I want in! Three years I pick coffee, get humped by overseers—' Her English failed her and she lapsed into a torrent of Italian.

Kim Crozier appeared behind her, breathless from running. He plucked her out of the truck, took the gun away and slapped her bottom gently. 'Doctor's orders, Teresa, honey. Schultz, Chard, get hold of her.'

He jammed himself into the truck. Danny said, 'Kim, you're a doctor.'

'Save it. I've stayed cool for six years now.' Kim's voice was hard, angry. He lifted the gun. 'Anyway, I'm thinking of my patients. A little preventative medicine. Now get going.'

Marker laughed harshly. The engine roared and the truck swooped out from behind the laundry, heading for the big house.

240

*   *   *

The Chinook pilot cut the engines, waited for the dust outside to settle, then moved to open the door, letting down the lower section with the integral steps. The Special in the bush hat who stood outside was a new man, but that did not particularly surprise the pilot. He knew there had been losses of recent weeks. He was mildly surprised when the man climbed the steps, but had no time to think about it before a hard fist wrapped round a heavy object hit him in the face, knocking him backwards. Next minute the man in the bush hat was inside the helicopter, looking down the length of it at eighteen armed men, a revolver held in a none too steady right hand.

They were mostly Guatemalans, Valdez decided, Paxero's own people. He lifted his left hand, holding the grenade, and said in Spanish, 'Listen carefully, you scum. This is a grenade, and the pin is drawn.' He held it out towards the nearest man for inspection. 'Now, if anything happens to me, causing me to release my hold, the grenade will explode, yes?'

Frozen faces stared back as his eyes ranged down the helicopter. Confidence surged within him, and his nerves grew quiet. 'Furthermore,' he said, 'a colleague of mine is flooding the ground beneath this helicopter with gasoline, ready to fry any who survive the grenade. Do you comprehend, you evil-smelling pigs?'

Nobody spoke, but the aura of fear was almost tangible.

'You will now lay down your weapons and leave this aircraft one by one,' said Valdez. He moved back a little from the doorway. 'Another colleague outside will be covering you with an automatic rifle, and will shoot to kill at the first hint of disobedience. As soon as each man has disembarked, he will move straight forward, twenty paces away from the aircraft, and lie flat on his face. Now let us begin.'

241

Nobody spoke, nobody moved. Valdez smiled, and his eyes gleamed.

'I sense an atmosphere of passive resistance,' he said. 'Let us dispel it at once.' He lifted the revolver and put a bullet through the foot of a man three paces away. The man screamed and fell out of his seat. The whole mass stirred with shock. Valdez lifted the grenade and thumbed back the trigger of the revolver. 'If you please,' he said.

Ten seconds later, lying with the Stoner aimed, Maude saw the first man exit from the helicopter.

* * *

Modesty Blaise got to her feet. After two minutes of listening to sporadic outbursts of shooting she had decided that nobody was going to come up the stairs now. They were too busy below. She put the grenades in her pouch, and moved to the stairhead with the automatic rifles and her Colt.

The air was still full of fine dust. Willie's first grenade had gouged chips from floor and walls. Sinclair and the Welshman lay dead at the foot of the stairs, another Special in the hall. She moved halfway down, seated herself, checked that she could cover the three doors in her view, and began to add up. Three dead men here. Paxero and the other two upstairs. One or more in the room the truck had demolished. And Willie was not likely to have wasted his second grenade. The opposition must have been halved by now. More important, it no longer had a head. The rifle twitched in her hands as a man came tottering through a doorway. It was one of the overseers. As he fell, she saw the knife-hilt jutting from his neck.

There came a sudden burst of firing from outside the rear of the house, and a moment later the crash of a grenade within, at the western end. She sat trying to interpret the sounds.

A white-clad figure moved into her view from the back of the house, carbine poised. She said, 'Marker.'

He spun round, staring, then gave an exultant grin. 'They broke, Modesty, they bloody broke! Two of 'em were running from the back as we came in, and we all blasted the hell out of 'em!'

'Where are Danny and the others now?'

'I posted Stavros and Bissau outside, to clobber any more runaways.' He jerked a thumb over his shoulder. 'Danny and Kim are watching my back.' He moved to the foot of the stairs, and saw the great red stain that soaked her pants, the long drying trickles on her legs. His jaw dropped in shock. 'Oh Jesus, is it bad, girl?'

'No. Now listen, Willie's that way somewhere.' She nodded her head. 'I think he must have done the job, but go and help him do any winkling out.'

'Right.' He turned and shouted, 'Kim! Upstairs, man! Fast!' Then moved through the doorway where the man with the knife in his neck lay.

Kim Crozier appeared and came running up the stairs, revolver in hand. His eyes flickered from her blood-soaked loins to her face, then back again. 'You don't look as bad as you ought to with a stomach wound.' There was query in his voice, and a rare sharpness.

'It's not a stomach wound, just a big sort of in-and-out bodkin hole through the flesh.'

He relaxed a little. 'Let's take a look.'

She glared at him. 'Take a look? And then what? You haven't got your bag with you, so what do you do about it?' Her voice rose. 'What the hell are you doing with that gun, anyway? You're supposed to be a goddam doctor!'

He grinned, moved down the stairs, rummaged in a dead man's pockets, and returned with cigarettes and a lighter. Sitting down beside her he said, 'It's a relief to know you've got nerves, just like anyone else. I sent Danny back for my bag as soon as Marker yelled.'

He passed her a lit cigarette. The house had fallen completely silent now. Outside, a Land Rover started up.

Marker re-appeared in the hall, looking oddly subdued. 'There's no-one left,' he said with a touch of awe. 'Man, you should see what that truck did.' He shook his head. 'You should see what your boy Garvin did.'

She said, 'Where is he now?'

'Took off with Stavros for the landing pad, to give Valdez and this Maude girl a hand. She told him on the radio they've got eighteen prisoners up there. Eighteen! Bloody hell, we'd have been finished if they got going.'

'Did we lose anybody?'

'Only casualty I know of is Danny got a finger slammed in a door somewhere.'

She let out a long breath. 'We've been lucky.'

Kim said, 'Maybe somebody around here earned us a little luck.' He crushed out his cigarette. 'Well . . . I guess we must be the first ex-slaves since the Civil War. It feels pretty strange.' He stood up. 'Let's get you in a truck and down to the surgery.'

Danny Chavasse met them as they came out of the house, Modesty walking gingerly, a hand on Kim's arm, the other pressed to her stomach. Danny was carrying Kim's medical bag, and his face in the gathering dusk seemed haggard. He said, 'I'm sorry, there's bad news. Teresa's dead.'

Modesty's fingers gripped hard, and her voice was ragged. 'Dead? For God's sake, *how?*'

'A bullet. It must have been a stray, fired from the house just as we were going in. She was standing by the laundry, right beside Thurston, watching. Suddenly she went down. It got her in the heart.' He wiped his grimed face with the sleeve of his shirt. 'Thurston keeps asking why it couldn't have been him. He's dying anyway.'

She rubbed an eye with the heel of her hand, leaving a red smear across her brow, and said flatly, 'I suppose it comes out the way it's written. See that Berry and the church group

244

look after her, Danny. We'll take her out with us.'

Five minutes later she lay on the table in Kim Crozier's surgery, waiting while he washed his hands. He had wanted to give her a sedative, but she had snapped at him angrily. 'Hasn't it dawned on you that there's an airlift to get organised? Just plug me so I stop bleeding, then forget it.'

She was immediately sorry for her manner. At that moment she would have given anything to be alone with Willie Garvin for a few minutes, to put her head on his shoulder and weep away the doubts, anxieties and fears she had sealed off in a corner of her being these past weeks. They would all dissolve in a little while; but tears were an immediate catharsis she would have welcomed, for she had been lonely in Limbo under her heavy burden, very lonely, and felt almost sick with weariness now.

Kim moved to stand looking down at her, drying his hands. His face suddenly hostile, he said, 'Well, I guess you're pretty sore at Teresa for getting herself killed, huh? You wanted a clean score. No casualties to spoil it for you.'

She stared, then shock hit her and she struggled to sit up, wincing. 'Kim. No. You don't think . . . ? Oh, of course I wanted a clean score, but not for *me*—'

'You telling me you give a damn about Teresa?'

She looked at him from cavernous eyes for long seconds, then croaked, 'You can believe just what the hell you like, doctor . . .' Her voice faltered, she chewed at her lower lip desperately for a moment, then the tears came and she twisted to look away from him.

His arm held her firmly round the shoulders, and gently he drew her head round to rest on his chest. 'That's better.' His voice was soft now. 'You were wound up so tight, I had to get those strings loose anyway I could.'

She relaxed against him and let the tears come easily, making scarcely a sound as she wept. After a minute she drew in a long, wavering breath, pulled away a little, wiped her face on his shirt-sleeve, and said shakily, 'Sneaky bastard.

I *never* do that. Well, hardly ever . . . and only with Willie.'

'Your secret's safe with me, honey. Come on now, lie down again and let's have a look at that wound. How about a local while I'm fooling around with it?'

'There's no need, Kim. I'm fine now, and I'm just going to have a little sleep for ten minutes. You go ahead.'

He laughed, moving away to assemble what he would need. When he returned to the table he said, 'You're going to do what?' But she was deeply asleep, with a breathing rate of no more than five to the minute, and she did not wake when he peeled off the dressing and began to clean the wound.

*　　*　　*

The eighteen prisoners were moving down from the landing pad in two files of nine. Each man had his left-hand thumb tied with a few inches of twine to the right-hand thumb of the man in front. It was an effective and economical system.

Willie Garvin and Maude Tiller walked behind the two files. She was saying, 'And that big helicopter will take everyone out to Benque Viejo in one go?'

'Sure. A CH-47 is rated to carry about forty-five troops, but they've carried over a hundred in emergency. It'll only take 'alf-an-hour.'

'My God. It seemed a lot longer when we were coming in.'

'You were in bad company then.'

She laughed, a little sleepily. Now that tension was gone, everything seemed unreal. 'What happens next, Willie?'

'We leave this bunch 'ere, with any Limbo people still alive, and we bung all the slaves on the Chinook, stick a gun in the pilot's ear, and tell 'im to fly us to Benque Viejo.'

'Let Valdez do the ear bit. He's got a way with him.'

'I noticed the pilot looked a bit subdued.'

'And when we land at Benque Viejo?'

246

'Ah, that's when we disappear.'

'We what?'

'Vanish. You, me, and the Princess. We were never 'ere, Maude.'

'You mean we're not heroes? We don't win a medal?'

'Not even a cigar.'

'Ah, well. There's always St. Thomas.'

'Who?'

'The Virgin Isle of St Thomas. That orgy we're going to have.'

Willie rubbed an ear. 'Ah . . . yes. There's always that.'

By the landing-pad, Valdez and Stavros stood guarding the helicopter. The pilot sat on the ground a little way off with his feet bound, looking pale and worried.

Valdez said, 'So it ends, and we return from Limbo. How will it be for you, my friend?'

Stavros lifted his shoulders. He was a short, powerful man in his forties, who had inherited a small shipping fortune and built it into a vast one. 'God knows. Three years and a half I have been here. I had a wife, children growing up. Many relatives. But who will be happy to see me return from the dead after so long? Truly, I do not know.'

Valdez said thoughtfully, 'I was not married, thank God. But there will be problems enough.' He gave a little shrug. 'For everybody.'

'What will you do when you return Outside?'

'Who can say? I am another man now, Stavros. We are all different now.'

'Yes. Except Kim, perhaps. We must not forget Kim. We must learn what he wishes to do, and make provision for him to do it.'

Valdez smiled. 'Yes, Kim will not lack support, I think.'

'And Modesty. How do we repay what she has done?'

'Who?'

'Modesty.' Stavros peered at his friend, puzzled. 'Modesty Blaise.'

247

'No such person was ever here, Stavros. You must help me to impress that on our fellow slaves.'

'No such—?' Stavros broke off, his bewilderment giving way to a look of appraisal. 'Ah, is this what she wishes? Is this what Willie Garvin told you, when he was speaking with you a little time ago?'

'Who?'

'Willie! The English—' Stavros stopped, grinning suddenly. 'But no such person was ever here, of course?'

'Of course.'

Sixteen

'It's a very effective conspiracy of silence,' said Tarrant. 'The Press are going mad with frustration, especially in the States. They're up against sixty-odd people who simply say they were kidnapped, used as slaves, and finally revolted. No further comment.'

Maude Tiller sat across the desk from him. Her eyes were clear, and the strained look she had worn after the Paxero assignment in Switzerland had been wiped away. She was looking very attractive and full of life, Tarrant thought.

She said, 'Danny Chavasse told me it would be like that, sir. The only one of the slaves who might have wanted to tell a detailed story of life in Limbo was Teresa. The others don't want publicity, don't need money, and have more than enough problems of adjustment. Especially husbands whose wives married again.'

'Sad about the Italian girl.' Tarrant took out a cigar. 'But I suppose she'd be pleased to know she's now the heroine of Limbo, who organised and led the rebellion.'

'Danny said she'd be furious. She wasn't that kind of scene-stealer.'

'Well . . . it's an academic point. But the girl certainly made a very convenient focus of attention.' He pierced the cigar carefully. 'It was also convenient that John Dall had moved up to Benque Viejo when they came flying in. He improvised some very far-sighted emergency arrangements.'

'Yes. After he'd cooled down. He started off by storming at Modesty. Willie was only just quick enough to stop Marker hitting him with a rifle-butt.'

249

'Oh well, one must expect a little temperament on these occasions.'

'Yes. I expect some of the truth about Limbo will leak out in time, sir.'

'It won't be headlines by then, so it won't matter. And according to Modesty there are certain reliables, like Dr Crozier, Valdez, Marker, Schultz and a few others, who'll flatly deny any wild stories which happen to be true.' He put a match to his cigar, and sat back in his chair. 'You've done a very satisfactory job, Maude. I want you to put in some time as an Instructor when you return from leave.'

She looked surprised. 'In what subject, sir?'

'General. Did you learn anything from your trip with Willie? I mean, apart from practical points of jungle survival.'

'Well . . . yes. I learned a great deal.'

'How would you describe what you learned, as a subject?'

She shook her head slowly. 'It's not something you can classify, sir. It's more of an attitude, a mental posture. But you couldn't set it down in words.'

'How did you learn it from Willie?'

Without thinking, she made one of her demented grimaces, hastily converted it into a look of profound concentration, and said at last, 'I suppose the same way he got it from Modesty. At least, I think he did. You absorb it. Like osmosis?' she added, hoping the word meant what she imagined.

'Good. Let me have suggestions for a training scheme which will enable you to impart this indefinable mental posture. I rate it as the most valuable contribution you can make to this department. Think about it, Maude. Good morning.'

'Good morning, sir.' She rose.

'And enjoy yourself on St Thomas.'

*　　*　　*

'I was born,' said Collier, 'on the stroke of midnight, twixt a Monday and Tuesday, which explains why I'm not only fair of face but full of grace, being both a Monday child and a Tuesday child. It's amazing how accurate some of these old sayings are.'

'I always figured you'd fallen between two stools,' said Dinah. 'What's the relevance, anyway?'

'None, my sweet. I was simply making an interesting remark. I shall now make another. As long as the spirit of England lives, there will always be village cricket. Which gives village cricket about another six weeks.'

He glanced across the field, shading his eyes. It was a Sunday afternoon, and the village of Wixford was playing the visiting eleven from Tunbury. Rooks dozed in the elms. Two wood-pigeons were courting on the roof of the small pavilion. On the field, the Wixford leg-spinner began his run-up. The fielders crouched. There came the clack of willow on leather, and a patter of sleepy applause from the few score spectators spread in little groups round the boundary. It was a scene which had changed little in half a century. Dinah sat on a car-rug, her back against an elm. Modesty lay on her back on the warm grass, hands behind her head, eyes closed. Collier sat cross-legged beside the picnic basket. It was late afternoon, and they had lunched at *The Treadmill*, a mile away on the Thames.

Collier wished dreamily that he could cause time to stand still, so that he might hold this perfect moment, if not for ever then for a long time. His gaze rested on Modesty, her bare brown legs vanishing into the yellow skirt, a thin band of flesh showing between the waistband and the brown shirt top. It was still hard for him to believe she was safely home. Even now, a month later, he sometimes woke in the morning to the twisting wrench of fear before memory brought relief. Dinah had told him that it was the same for her.

Strange, he thought idly, that Modesty always looked a

little smaller than he remembered her. No doubt his recollection of what he had seen her do added inches to her stature in his mental picture of her. She looked very good now, relaxed in sleep. A warm, soft, serene girl with little crow's-feet of laughter at the corners of her eyes. Beautiful, yes. Not exceptional. You'd look twice, of course, and then perhaps you'd look again. You might even keep looking. Especially if you saw her move. Or smile.

He sighed, took his wife's hand, and sat contentedly watching the cricket for two or three overs, then turned to open the picnic basket and took a can of beer from the coldbox. He poured it into a glass, sipped, and gave an appreciative murmur.

Dinah said, 'I'm no beer drinker, but have you offered one to Modesty?'

'Well, actually, no. I was afraid she might get a taste for it, my darling, and anyway she's asleep.'

'I'm not asleep,' said Modesty. 'I'm listening to cricket, like Dinah. It's a beautiful collection of sounds. Try it, Steve.'

'Ugh. Bring on the violins.'

Modesty said lazily, 'You're always too busy talking to listen to anything, that's your trouble.'

Dinah giggled. 'Sock it to him, honey.'

Collier said coldly, 'Your duty is to spring to the defence of your spouse, not to encourage his abuse by some wretched female with three belly-buttons.'

Modesty said, 'I haven't got three belly-buttons now. They've healed up. Well, two of them have.'

Collier sniffed. 'A likely story.'

'Look for yourself.' Eyes still closed, she hooked a thumb in her skirt and pushed it down an inch or two. Collier leaned towards her. Next moment Dinah heard a startled gasp, a cry of indignation, then a sudden scuffle and the quick thud of running feet fading into the distance. She sat up, head cocked, waiting. Two minutes later she heard quiet

252

feet approaching and caught the brandy-tasting smell that was Modesty.

'What was that all about?'

'He put an ice-cold beer-can on my belly, the brute.' Modesty gave a snuffle of laughter, and sat down beside Dinah.

'Did you catch him?'

'No, I was gaining, but then he circled the soft-drinks stall and button-holed Mr Peake, the vicar. Oh, there was something else, but I'll leave it for Steve to tell. He'll revel in it.'

'You spoil him. What's happening with the cricket?'

'Let's see what the scoreboard says. Oh, Tunbury need nine to win, and there's only one wicket to fall, so it's anybody's game. Man bowling from the pavilion end now is sending down leg-breaks . . .'

Collier returned three minutes later looking woebegone. 'I'm suitably punished. Under threat of hell-fire from the Reverend Henry Peake, I've undertaken that we'll provide and run a home-made jam stall at his fête on Sunday week.'

Modesty said, 'You haven't!'

Dinah said, '*Jam?*'

'I have. And jam was the only thing I could think of. I get confused in the presence of the clergy. Keep wondering how they get their heads through those collars.'

'But where are you going to get a hundred or so pounds of home-made jam?' his wife demanded.

'Where?' Collier said indignantly, and threw out his arms. 'Well, surely that's up to you! God knows, I've done my bit. Now do let's forget all this trivia and watch the cricket. After all, that's why we're here.'

Even as he spoke there came a very solid sound of bat meeting ball. The batsmen began to run. The ball, travelling fast and very low, hit the ground once. The fielder thirty yards away at square leg, who wore a shirt and white trousers considerably too small for him, leaned sideways, plucked the ball from the air, and flicked it with what

253

seemed a casual manner at the single stump he could see from his position.

The wicket went down with both batsmen in mid-pitch. Applause pattered round the ground. Dinah said, 'What's happened?' Modesty began to tell her. Batsmen, fielders and umpires were walking to the pavilion, all except the fielder at square leg, who made for the leg boundary.

'Enter William Garvin Esquire wearing the new mid-calf trousers,' said Collier as he approached. 'I can see the story now. Local Publican Makes Good. Today Wixford presented Mr Garvin with the Freedom of the Village after his triumph in the match against the old enemy, Tunbury. Conscripted by the Reverend Peake when the vice captain retired hurt, and wearing trousers borrowed from the curate, Mr Garvin, who is shortly taking Holy Orders, fielded substitute throughout the Tunbury innings and achieved an amazing run-out in the closing over. Asked to comment, Mr Garvin said, "The curate and I are just good friends. I owe it all to my Tip-Top Truss".'

Willie eased the fold under his groin and said, 'It's tight all right. I could put in for danger-money. Got a beer?'

'Two, my little match winner. The girls wanted to sink both, but I fought them off.' Collier patted him sympathetically on the shoulder. 'Poor old Willie, I said to them. Poor old Willie. How can you be so rotten to him when he's all to pieces? I said. Weeks of celibacy in the jungle with the delectable Maude, I said to them, and never a nibble. Then, as soon as it's all over, she flies off to the Virgin Islands with that all-time woo-champion, Danny Chavasse. Oh, I said to them, have you no feeling? Have you no pity for this poor lonely boy?'

Dinah said, 'One more gloat from you, buster, and I'll make it up to Willie myself. It's a real shame.'

Willie drained his glass and shrugged. 'Can't win 'em all, love. I'll just go an' change. See you by the car in five minutes.'

Modesty said, 'I'll come along. I want to talk to you about jam.'

'Jam?' Willie looked baffled.

'Yes. Home-made jam.' She slipped an arm through his. 'What we need is to find a fête being held next week-end, about ten miles away, where we can buy up a whole stall of home-made jam . . .' They moved away.

Collier began to pack up the picnic basket. After a while he said, 'It's funny about that girl Maude. Don't you think so, darling? I mean, I know Danny Chavasse has got this magic thing, but you wouldn't think she'd fall for that, would you? Not after all she went through with Willie.'

Dinah said, 'You're beautiful when you're stupid, tiger.'

'Eh? Why am I stupid?'

'Because I have to explain things to you. But stay that way, because I love you just the way you are.'

'Nice and dopey?'

She laughed. 'Sort of. It's just that Willie *asked* Danny Chavasse to carry Maude away for a spell of island romance.'

'Asked him? But why?'

'Because Willie had sort of promised Maude, but he didn't want to be away from Modesty until she was all healed and well again.'

'Oh. Down to one belly-button?'

'Right.'

'Did Willie tell you this himself?'

'Of course not, dopey.'

'Then how do you know?'

'I know because I'm a girl, that's how.'

'Wait a minute . . . Modesty's a girl, too. And so is Maude.'

'Good thinking, Professor. You can bet they also know. We just don't voice our knowledge.'

'Good God. And Maude went along with it?'

'Why not? Number one, the idea of sampling the woo-champion's magic is going to intrigue *any* girl. Number two, she's got too much sense to get upset about Willie putting

Modesty first—what else? And number three, if she wants to pick up Willie's rain-cheque there's always another day.'

Collier ran a hand through his hair. 'And even the vastly experienced Willie has no idea that you all know about his cunning subterfuge?'

'Of course he hasn't. And if you tell him I'll kill you.'

'In that case I won't. In fact I wouldn't anyway. It needs a man of rare calibre to remain unshattered by these revelations of gross feminine duplicity, and there aren't many of us left.'

Collier closed the picnic basket, picked it up, took his wife's arm, and began to stroll with her towards the green where Willie had parked the car. What Dinah had just told him had given him great delight, for he liked women enormously and found them a constant source of wonder. Tonight, at dinner, he would give a vivid description of the hilarious moment by the soft-drinks stall, when Modesty, pursuing him, had been called to order by a policeman and stood meekly contrite as he reprimanded her for what he called romping on the cricket ground.

At peace with the world, Collier gave a large happy sigh. One way and another it had been a very good day.